LEBANON

BOOKS BY
CAROLINE MILLER

Lebanon
Lamb in His Bosom

Lebanon

CAROLINE MILLER

THE BLAKISTON COMPANY

Philadelphia

This book is dedicated to
whosoever shall take Lebanon to his heart,
and make her his own,
and shall below inscribe his name,
making this book his own:

LEBANON

Chapter 1

HIGH IN THE REACHES OF WET SKY a buzzard lazed, still-winged—an amazing queer thing for him to do in this cold drizzle. All his kin were drooped high in a dead cypress crown, oiling their feathers drowsily, watching for any little death on earth below.

The tall, bleached cypress was a landmark—from miles in the swamp you could see it, like a milepost set on a sapling at a certain windy crossroad in the sky.

The birds were hushed in wet thickets, the squirrels were home in dry tree hollows, the bears were off in warm, dark places of their own choosing and keeping.

It was a rainy February to be out in.

Lebanon stilled the dugout, easing it quiet in an open space of black water, steadying the pole in mud three feet down. Overhead, water oaks and tupelos met, and now and again a drop of cold rain fell on her head. The air was that still you could hear the raindrop fall. You could hear and feel the still of the swamp.

Lebanon stood motionless, her hand on the sleek pole, her feet planted apart in the dugout's bottom, her head listening. The still of the swamp was somewhat like that of a sleeping body; it was somewhat like that most careless, soft sound of a deep fog rolling; it was somewhat like the sound of mists descending, or deep water in low country flowing the way it knows the sea lies. Above the sound of the sleeping swamp, all you could hear was a sudden, soft flight of wet wings, hidden from you in a near bush, or the falling of clustered rain from a twig tired of holding the burden of it.

All you could see was that one witless buzzard away yonder, and surging rain clouds.

Close in about the waters were bay trees that would sweeten the swamp air in June, maples that would burn like woods fires in March, and tupelos and oaks, and high above the other growth, everywhere the cypresses stood, naked and lean-bodied and tall-growing.

Since the wind was against Lebanon, she saw the deer herd before they scented her. Here they lay in a dimmed high noon. Not yet had the old buck led them out. If they were thirsty, here was black water to guzzle and here was in open places a tough water growth of grass. They lay in the canebrake, not thirty yards from the stilled dugout on a brown, hidden bank of Crooked Arm, free to arrange their hours as best pleased them—to go or stay, rest or find food, and make a holyday of any time it rained. The buck tossed his head and flared his nostrils, sieving the air and finding no danger. An old doe lay with her head outstretched on extended, fawnish forelegs.

The little rain came down, keeping them home till noon. Lebanon moved no more than an eyelid muscle: not often could you find deer at home. Now you could hear even the stillish water flowing against the prow of the weathered boat. You could hear a young doe lick her fawn as a cow licks her calf in a man's cowpen. The old buck tossed his head, and his nostrils flickered again, sifting the wind for peril. His tawny eyes surveyed the world, and went about the herd, as a man will study the wind beyond his walls, and bring his eyes back to his fire again, and those it warms. A fawn scratched his neck on his mother's haunch, to ease some little itching. The little gray rain hooded them in the covert, where they lay bedded down on dry, dun-colored cane, with winter growth for roof.

It is a pity you cannot come near to one of them without killing him with a musket, Lebanon was thinking. What wouldn't you give to go with them one long day, and eat their delicate victuals, and drink their strange, sweet water, and with them see the sun come up, and with them see it go down again in a far place!

Lebanon sighed.

Though she had held her head still in the quiet, though her hands were hard and quiet on the water pole, the deer herd stumbled up and went suddenly in desperate haste away from there. The sound of Lebanon's sigh was scarce more than when you brush your hands free of ashes when you have knelt and built a fire on a dead hearth, but now the deer were gone. The undergrowth settled into stillness again after their going.

Lebanon spat on the slow, black water, in disgust of her careless sighing. The spittle drifted south, a white coin of foam on gloomy water. The only way to learn a swamp is to hold your mouth still, and listen, hold your feet quiet in going. Lebanon learned that long ago, but the sigh had somehow got past her lips.

She had cast off the hood of knit worsted. It lay in the prow of the dugout along with Lady, the little old dog that knew when to stay quiet, too. When you start out to see things, you never know how long you will be. She had loosed the hair knobs and her hair hung free; the rain had spangled it and was like a bright fall of dew on a dark veil. Against the cold, she had put on a bearskin tippet, but she had poled far down into the swamp till the fur was too hot about her throat. It is time to go home when you have seen a lone buzzard flying high in a rainy day, and a herd of deer scatter at a sigh from your lips. She ate a biscuit with ham inside it, and threw the crumbs into the water, and saw the speckled fish come, fins hovering, and saw them go flashing down, her white bread in their mouths.

Suddenly Lebanon whooped at the buzzards, and Lady began to bark, tired of holding still to hear the swamp run away south forever. "Whoooo-eeee!" Lebanon called to the rain-dulled buzzards roosting away yonder in gray drizzle, and you could hear Lady's barking everywhere in the trees' faces. The sounds leveled out across the low, huddling wilderness of river and slough and bog and grassy knoll. High in the cypress crown the buzzards hulked: one or two crooked their snaky necks and ogled toward the calling from earth; they stirred their claws about, shook their wings cumbrously, and dozed again, hiding a head under a folded wing.

Lebanon poled back north. She threw the last of the meat and bread to the fish, and saw the water bubbling the least bit where they thanked her.

Papa and Joel were in Birdtown and would not be home till this night. She would not have to excuse her idling in the swamp while she should be busy at soapmaking or sowing more greens. If she should be forced to excuse herself, she would say she was looking for the lost heifer again. Sleek and yellow as yesterday's cream, the heifer did not come up with the other cows, four days ago. They searched that night, with pine knots for light, till the moon came up, and next morning till the dew was gone. But that early afternoon buzzards were wheeling in over the inlet south of Sour John Creek, lowering in a wavering funnel to where some dead thing lay, Lebanon's little cream heifer, doubtless. A rattler was perhaps fooled by the sunny still of the morning and thought it was time to out and shed his skin; if so the little heifer stepped a blind hoof too near him.

Lebanon poled toward home, ducking her head under the low boughs when they cluttered her way. Now and then, for the bother of it, she touched the pole to a low bough to watch it suddenly rain gathered wet onto the dark water.

It was not much of a house, Crease Fairgale would tell you—but the Fairgale house was a good house. Crease had built it when it was the only house south of Birdtown. Lebanon was born here. Now she was eighteen.

Toward the swamp the earth was hidden in growth, but north toward Birdtown the land was open and bright. Pines and gallberry bushes and wire grass lived on the land, too. The cabin was set on a rise, at the end of a cart path that wound among palmetto clumps. There was a narrow, slant-floored porch across the front, sleeping sheds at each end of the big room; the cookshed was a few steps apart, past a covered walk from the back door, and the smokehouse was beside the cookshed. The well was convenient to the kitchen, and its big sweep went up like a gray arm akimbo, over the roof. Out to the right were the corncrib and cow lot and wagon shelter, the horse stall for old Buckingham, and the pigpen used in the fall for fattening the shoats. Behind the kitchen shed there was the garden patch. Out in the clean-swept backyard the washpot stood, not too far from the well. The wash shelter was built to hold one trough and one woman at it; there were a thousand burnt-out fires there under the old iron washpot, and before Lebanon, her mother had stood at the wash trough, hollowed from a cypress block, battling the clothes clean, boiling and wringing and rinsing again, to guard against dinginess. The little cocked-roof privy sat downhill to the left of the garden patch.

There was a front yard, fenced in saplings, and a walk went up to the front door block. Along the walk Lebanon or her mother had laid in flower beds, and pinks were readying for spring blooming. Here and yonder were lily clumps, dead under winter frost, and along the fence there were Cape Jessamine bushes and crape-myrtle trees. Every root had been a burden in a woman's hands—men will not trifle with such things. Every leafing, flowering thing had a history: the parent of this quince was planted in a tub in China and came to this shore; this bush's father's father lived in Massachusetts once; this evergreen came from Virginia—Grandma dug the root after the waggons were all loaded; these lilies are from England and were brought over dried in a chest.

There was a tulip tree over the well house; casually seeded, it had no family history. But behind the house, showing over the shallow roof, were two mulberry trees. They were thick with birds in summertime. Lebanon's mother, Lollie, had some thought of growing silk, and Crease had brought her these two trees from Savannah when they were little switches.

Never did Lollie Fairgale wear silk from her own worms, or any other silk, after she left Virginia and came South with Crease. It had all come to little more than bird chatter in summertime, and the trees showing above the roof.

Lebanon went in the back way, scuffing her boots on the shuck mat. A sleeping fire smoked on the kitchen hearth. She swung out the pothook to be certain the dried pease did not lack water. She had left old Caesar in the house to guard matters. Caesar walked toward Lebanon and Lady to welcome them home again. Caesar was all manners, but Lady, being much younger, hasseled her little red tongue, and laughed and whimpered. Now on two feet, now on four, she danced on the clean-scrubbed flooring, pointed ears tilted and eyes bright in worship. Papa always gave away her litters, and Lady would grieve a week, unforgiving, and having no explanation of so monstrous a loss. Then she would see grief as a dull, unreasonable attitude—or maybe she would forget a little. She would come out to Lebanon and would lick her hand as though she pleaded apology for all manner of things gone wrong.

The kitchen shed was still, but for Lady flurrying about and

Caesar licking his flews and yawning cavernously. It made Caesar solemn and proud to see his little bitch joyful over any matter.

Lebanon looked in again on the pease cooking. In among them was a little slab of salt meat, sliced to its rind in white petals. A scum of grease and salt whitened the seething water. Through the cabin you could catch a scent of fresh pease, from these old ones, like summer weather left over from last year.

Papa and Joel had carried in a load of salted gator skins and a few mink and beaver.

Lebanon had carefully told Papa:

"Trade my bolt of skins for a length of thin red goods. I want a skirt that will swing as I walk and switch about my ankles."

"Red, damnation," Crease said, "with red beads about your throat, doubtless."

Crease's graying hair stuck out about his head like a child's, for it had curls hidden in it. His face wore a sober, kind look. His eyes were brown and gentle as a deer's. Lebanon had her mother's fiery blue eyes; Joel had Crease's sober brown ones. Crease had a gored house cap made of lambskin that he scarcely ever took off, except to put on an outdoors hat of wool, or a skin cap. There was a place on his head where the hair would not grow, from an old scalp wound he got in the last war. The wound burned like fire, now and then, if there was rain in the air, or if he got overheated.

For the longest while Lebanon had fevered for a necklace of gold beads, without any great hope of ever possessing them. Past the wish for the gold beads was the yearning for a heart locket, betwixt her breasts, with flat holes for likenesses of faces held too dear for kissing.

"If I did not forbid it, doubtless you'd be rouging your mouth and face, like a Frenchwoman," Crease said roughly.

"I sometimes wish I might," said Lebanon, her hands going secretly and lovingly about her waist where she wished a bright bodice to be, and about her throat where she could all but feel the dragging gold of a gift from some man from some big town, Philadelphia or Boston, Richmond or Charles Town.

Lebanon was much like her mother in looks—she had the same

prettiness of feature you cannot place, much as you hear a thrush singing in a thicket and never expect a sight of it. Crease had married Lollie up there in Virginia on a bright street of a coast town. Trees grew along the streets of that town, and the sun was always shining through the branches. Lollie could remember the wooden walks and greased cobbles speckled in sunshine.

There was in Lebanon's face a hunger: the swamp still fed it. So did a bear cub glimpsed deep in the swamp, a young bird huddled on its home limb.

Lebanon could not have told you why she liked her hair swinging free more than done up in a crown on her head and buckled down with polished walnut pins. Papa said it was high time she put on a woman's slow walk and still face. "Smile when you will—and not so much laughter," Papa counseled her. "Why?" she asked him. "Good women are quiet," he said.

Sometimes Crease thought: What will become of her? A pain gnawed in his stomach if he ate more than a little buttermilk and a crust, but he said nothing of it. Joel would stand on his feet—a man can. But what will become of Lebanon if anything should happen to me? Crease wished he understood women better. Lollie used to tell him he knew nothing of women. "You pay no attention to me, and you do not care for hurting me over little things; you never tried to learn the inside ways of my heart," she used to tell him passionately, her voice hard and compressed, her hands gripped in a sock she was knitting, or frantically winding a hank of worsted. "You do not care, Crease," she would say, her face set against him. He would lay his hand on her shoulder, and she would pull away. "I do care," he would say, humbly. But I do not know what to do, he told himself. Only keep your own tongue still, when a woman goes tearing against things. Only be there ready when she is ready to weep when the hard words are all safely out.

Mostly Lollie wanted to go home. "I'll take you home in the fall," he would tell her—"I will take you home in the spring." She was homesick for the white house in the sorry lane, and her brother's tavern down the street. Grandmamma was always by the hearth, her face tilted toward the door, her hair untamed, her tongue making little jokes. Lollie thought Lebanon was much like Grand-mamma. Lebanon was named for Grandmamma—and she was named for the cedars of Lebanon in the Bible.

Lebanon wished to go into Birdtown every time Crease and Joel went, but Crease would not allow it: too many bright lamps there, too much idle talk, too much going and coming, too many careless-eyed men. If ever you allow a woman to stay too long in a place like Birdtown's Tavern, she will always be remembering it and will scarcely stay in her still house again. It is a strange circumstance, but a true one. "Keep a woman innocent," Crease said, "and she may be longing for bright lamps with roses on them, in place of tallow dips—and for lacy garters and sattin-lined stays—but she will not know the name of the thing she is longing for."

Lebanon wanted gold beads and a locket.

When I am married, I shall have earrings dangling to my shoul-ders, fleured in red and green glass, swinging like ice boggles! And he will touch the ear bangles, and then he cannot contain his love, and he will take my hand and he will say: "If I may be so bold, Miss Lebanon, this earth was midnight till I saw your face. . . ."

The time she had spent in fashioning a man to suit her taste, this one man! As she lay shut-eyed, before the first of sleep, he would tread across her mind, full-bodied yet immaculate, searching for her as she had sought for him. "At last we meet," he would tell her. Then she would go away with him.

He had blue eyes, dark hair, cloak of fine twilled cloth with a crimson lining. He did not wear a coonskin cap or deerskin mocca-sins—nor ever had. He came from the Coast on serious business of land or law. He saw her and knew her instantly as the woman his house had craved to keep it and its children. They would know one another when they met.

He would call her name, without love nicknames. "Lebanon?" he would ask. "Yes?" she would reply, wishing to know his least wish for living. And he would give her the red-and-green eardrops, and a skirt of flowered silk cloth—and her best frock would have sixty ruffled gores in its skirt, not one less. No matter how dull or bitter a day might be, he would be there, somewhere near, so that she could find him and see his unspeaking smile. It would not be needful for her to explain the matter—he would know of it: "Yes," he would interrupt her. "I know. . . ."

If she had told Crease, or any other sensible soul, how she felt toward this man, he would have told her: "But, my dear child, that is how a mortal feels toward God!"

And maybe she would have replied: "Yes . . . yes . . . that is how . . ."

But she did not tell Crease.

Growing to be a woman is a simple matter, and each woman has her own method of changing herself from childhood to height and stable judgment. Many little hours go toward forming her for those times when she shall be tried and shall show what manner of woman she may be.

Lebanon had made her own company—for Joel, two years older, never cared to play much more than hopscotch.

Many a morning, when she was little, she had sat in the mulberry boughs and sewed leaves for her children's garments. Many long evenings she had counted slow-coming stars, and made a same old wish on each new star: "I wish I shall be happy. . . . I wish I shall be happy. . . . Not now . . . not soon . . . but someday. . . . I wish I shall be happy."

She never told the wish, for then it would not have come true. Through the long, moping days, when time must be laboriously spent, and your mother is dead, and you must somehow grow to be a woman without her, you remember a bird's blue flight in morning air, like a sharp blade cutting through time. Some mornings you see a fussy old hen with a new brood of chickens following her faithful clucking over mighty hill and low plain of sand. And you wish you could for one day be a chicken two inches high, and eat what he eats, and be child to a hen with great warm wings, and walk through that world that extends all the way across earth under grass blades and seeding weeds and flowers in a woman's yard yonder. Then the devil would be a chicken snake or a hawk—and heaven an early dark and mother's wings.

Then suddenly you are thinking of a man, and his hands on your hot cheeks, his mouth heavy on yours, his steps to match yours somehow, his days on earth to coincide with yours, down to the last one, if you be lucky—so that you two may die together under a thunder-strike, or a falling wall, as some old people do die together.

The man—and the tight bodice and the swinging skirt . . . There should be gold leathern braiding on the deep yoke of the bodice, and gold buttons no bigger than mice's eyes down the front closing. A boned-lace collar should go up around her throat—then the gold beads, or the locket—and the eardrops at her ears—and his face would be pleased when he saw her so beautiful for him.

When Papa and Joel came in home from Birdtown, three men came with them. They wished to look over Crease's land; they wished logging rights to his cypress, or outright purchase of the land.

"How would you like to sell out and move to Birdtown?" Crease asked Lebanon.

Something told him he must make his plans for these children. He had eaten a piece of spiced meat at the tavern, and his stomach was a torment. You can't leave an untried son and a pretty daughter and a fine piece of land loose in the world together.

She had heard Joel pop the whip at the bend as they came in home. She paid it little mind. Joel always popped the whip at the bend, so she would know to set the biscuits on the trivet to bake and set on the milk and butter. She did not know the three men were coming home with Crease—so she did not know to brace her heart.

When he stood in the door, all she could say was howd'ye, and shrink away to the hearth again. They had come on horseback. Joel took the horses on to the crib, to rub them down and feed and water them.

"This is my daughter, Lebanon, gentlemen," said Papa. "Lebanon, these are the Ratcliffs."

She learned his first name from listening from the hearth. The men sat at the eating table. In a hurry at the cook table near the hearth, she rolled out dough for a berry dumpling and stirred up a johnnycake and set it on the hearth. There were dried pease aplenty, but she went to the smokehouse for ham to fry and a helping of pear preserves from the crock.

They lounged about the table, while she cooked. Crease offered them a drink. "Lebanon," he ordered, "get out the loaf sugar and we'll have a toddy around." She brought out the loaf sugar and the nutmeg and its grater—and Papa brought the black bottle of rum from his room. The water was ready hot.

The men had their mugs in their hands, and the oldest man, Raphael Ratcliff, said a toast to her:

"To as sweet a face as ever I did see!" he said.

Lebanon's heart foundered. Her face was sobered and still. The youngest of the three men was watching her, too, and his eyes were full of pleasurable discovery. Lebanon dropped her eyes away from his face, but thence on, her heart struggled within her like a fish on a bloody hook.

Raphael Ratcliff was big-bodied, and his face was all but hidden in a bristling, graying beard. He spoke slowly, and you found yourself listening for anything he said. He wore elegant garments; you could part your hair in the shine of his top hat, but the creases were gone from the fine cloth of his pantaloons, and the tails of his big double-breasted coat were bedraggled. You could see he was rough and ready and kind—or you would think so, from looking him over. His manners were a little roughened, too, or maybe it was that his beard caused him to seem groomless and wild. His eyes shone friendly as a house dog's; he had a manner that would lead you to trust him.

His brother, Luke Ratcliff, was oldish, too, yet lean and lank-limbed. He spoke in a high, thin voice, speaking more yet saying less, as the old saying goes, than his brother Raphael.

Then there was their nephew whose name was Sebastian Ratcliff.

From the beginning Lebanon loved him, even to the sounding of his name the first time she heard it called. It was like the sound an ear of green corn makes when you shuck it in your hands and find the naked, sweet body ripe for eating. His name was like the sudden, ragged spilling of cool water when you tilt the well bucket too far and find your feet in a little puddle of fresh well water you have spilled. His name was like the soft rustling of rushes when your fingers are weaving flaskets to hold sliced fresh fruits to dry for winter use. The first thing she loved about him was the sounding of his name.

Of course, she loved also the least lifting of his left eyebrow, and the little crooked quirk his lips took on, to the left side of his face, when he commenced to smile. His beard was none too heavy, and it seemed as though it would be silky to the touch of your hand. His brows were laid straight across the light of his eyes, which were blue, with midges of brown in their blue. His brow was tall, showing his fine brains, and his hair went up in a shining comb and fell carelessly down the left side of his head. Always his left hand was caressing that fallen lock back into place. His hands were long-fingered, with blue veins across their backs; the palms of them seemed as though they might be soft as China silk to the touch. His boots were foreign-made, and their toes twinkled in the changeful firelight. Papa said you could judge a man's whole history by looking at his boots— where he has been today, where he will go tomorrow. Lebanon could make Joel's boots and Papa's boots, from tanning the hide on up. She could not have made these boots for this man: they were seamed so that the awl marks never showed, their leather was finished soft as a feather, the toes were crimped and ornamented in an overlapping design of loops and whorls, the soles were new. From that first moment, down to the very soles of his boots, she loved him.

He was that manner of man who can fill a room when he comes in and leave it empty when he goes out again. He went to the well for a drink, and it was as though you had blown out all the dips, though the other Ratcliffs and Joel and Papa were talking loudly. He came in again from the dark and the room was suddenly bright and merry again.

She ate the little remainders of sugar in the mugs, when the men had their drinks—all but one mug: she set that mug up till tomorrow. Like a fool she set her lips on its cool edge where his lips had been and shuddered.

When they had eaten supper, they stayed on in the kitchen shed, and when the things were washed and set in place Lebanon sat awhile on the stool, in beside the wood box, and kept quiet over the sock she was doing for Joel.

"That is a fancy blue coloring you have given the wool," Raphael Ratcliff said, showing her courtesy. Where he came from, ladies were not ignored.

"Thank you, sir," Lebanon said, bending her head a little lower over the pretty blue wool. "I used indigo," she said.

Sebastian Ratcliff was lighting a cheroot, and his face was gathered close in on the little flame of a fine flinder, but his eyes came to her face, too, past the flame. Her heart stumbled and fell down, but she went on knitting. She was thinking how she would think up and try out most marvelous dyes for wool for his ankles—Sebastian's. She set the knitting down one moment and lifted a fresh pine knot to lay it on the low fire. Though he sat away across the hearth, he was suddenly tall in the dusk beside her. "Give me leave," he said, and he took the fat pine knot and gave it to the flames. Now she could scarcely knit, so bothered her heart was. She sat in the dark and laid her face against the cool wall, and her cheek was hot against the wood. In the fire gloom she could see the soft shine of his dun waistcoat across the hearth. The light of the fire was on his head, and his hair ringleting about his tall collar. Her fingers smoothed a fold of her black skirt, over and over again. She wished she were wearing a swirling red skirt and a velvet bodice with gold buttons, and a locket in the shape of a heart, an ungrown heart, with a vacant space for a likeness. She laid aside the knitting for good. The men's talk went on. She knew every growth of cypress Crease told of. She laid her left hand over her right hand to keep it still on her skirt. She watched the growing flame under the water kittle hung out over the fire. Steam was sighing from the black lips of the kittle's spout.

Suddenly Sebastian Ratcliff sneezed—no snorting, thunderous sneeze such as Papa's or Joel's. This was a kitten sound, but louder. He brought out a flutter of nose rag from his waistcoat pocket. Her eyes did not leave the growing flame, but she saw the flutter of linnen in his hand. "Your pardon," he said softly, excusing his noise in the midst of the talk. Lady lay at Lebanon's feet, her throat across the arch of Lebanon's foot.

Lebanon stayed only so long as to make a show of politeness. When she caught a lull, she said her little say:

"I shall be saying good night," she said, bringing out the words painfully.

Suddenly the Ratcliff men were all on foot and bowing her out. Sebastian opened the door to the passage. "Is there anything I can do for you, madam?" he asked, bowing his head a little.

She knew no reply to make but a brusque, "No, I thank you, sir."
She stood with the lighted candle in her hand.

"See that the beds are readied, Lebanon," Papa said.

And old Raphael said:

"Do, Miss Lebanon, for neither love nor conscience could keep
me wakeful this night. I'll wager even Sebastian is tired till he'll
scarce dream of his Lucie."

She had seen Sebastian's teeth in a smile white as new hominy in
his dark face.

The door closed, and wind blew across the passage to the big
room. She shielded the candle flame with her hand. The big room
was dark and still, holding her and Lady and the candle flame—
and the men's talk in the kitchen shed a long way off now.

Joel had a torn boot sole, and Papa's greatcoat had a tear in it,
but her fingers were itchy and hated the thought of a needle. She
made up the wall cot in the big room. One of the men could sleep
there, and there would be beds aplenty.

There was a reach of black water that would lead through sloughs
and inland islands out through Loon Lake and so to St. Therese
River, and from there to the Gulf of Mechiko. But still, there with
the candle flame and the dog looking up into her face, the room
seemed closed and still indeed—and no way out.

She went about readying the beds, thinking of the woman named
Lucie. Lucie had a pale, cold face, probably, with burnished hair
under a feathered bonnet. Lebanon could see her, even here in the
gloom of this low house. Was he married to her, then? Did she have
blue eyes or brown, did she wear lace-trimmed stays and white
tippets? No doubt. Lebanon's feet heavied in her homemade boots.
He was already tied to a woman's heart, then, tethered and penned?
It was like playing at spilikins and handy-dandy—guess which hand,
fool! That's what her heart had been doing this last hour, hanging
after a strange man's face there beyond the width of room. And
nothing to do but grow old and quinsied and wear russet shoes and
worsted stockings till you die. Be warmed and fed by remembering
—and nothing to remember but an hour and a half with his face in
the firelight, and his hand lifting the heavy pine knot. Some women

have everything, and nothing is left for the others! So her name was
Lucie, then. . . .

There will be a lot of nights in which to remember this night,
when I fell in love and out again, she was thinking; nights of
nothing but the sound of the wheel or the needles, or rain hissing
and dying in flame down the chimney.

She set the candle down on the cask head by her bed. On the
cask head was the old Scot Bible and a little jug with broken pear
twigs set in water in it, to bud, if they would, in air warmer than
the air outside in cold February. In the Bible's pages was first one
thing and then another—such as a browned violet bloom, pressed
flat as flooring. Even when you wished to open The Word hap-
hazardly for guidance, The Book would still open to a dead violet or
a lost and gathered egret feather, its flat-plumed frond so fine you
could scarce trace its form on the yellowed printing. The egret frond
stayed in a certain place. Lebanon could not read, but Crease could,
and here under the egret feather were those sad words of wailing:
"O Jerusalem, Jerusalem, thou that killest the prophets . . . how
often would I have gathered thy children together, even as a hen
gathereth her chickens under her wings, and ye would not! . . ."

Crease had always intended that Lebanon should learn her letters when she was old enough, but there never came a time. There
was always corn to be planted or shocked or ground. And when
Lollie had tried to teach Lebanon the mingled markings at the
beginning of The Book, Lebanon would not set herself hard to the
study of them. It was a meaningless jumble, with senseless spac-
ings in between: inthebeginninggodcreatedthe heavenandthe earth
andthe earthwas withoutformandvoid. Lebanon could not set her
heart on learning this hard first part about "without form and
void." Always she would run off to set the traps or snare quail for
supper. So now that she was eighteen all she could do was hold The
Book and open it to a place where violets were like stains, and
where it said: "I charge you, O ye daughters of Jerusalem, by the
roes and by the hinds of the field, that ye stir not up, nor awake my
love, till he please. . . ." Lebanon could speak pieces from the
Bible, having learned them word by word from Papa's reading.

Lebanon reached off her dark frock, loosing the bone buttons from their holdings down the front of the waist. She crept in under the cold covers. She told herself on and on: This man is not the one intended for me. This man was for another woman.

She folded her hands into a little steeple, tight-shut against her breast. She held her fingers still. Her fingers knew niceties Lucie's fingers did not know—that much she would wager: she knew how to fox a shoe tongue, and to basket-stitch a seam in a fearnaught cloak. Her hands were not as clever as her mother's, though: in the pig-hide chest in the loft there was a robe of feathers her mother had made. Crease had been offered two double eagles for the thing if he would trade it, but he would not. Lollie had made it with waxed thread and a needle made of a heron's leg bone: one could hardly find the stitches in it; small and carefully the stitching was set about the barbs of glassy-green feathers, around each fiery mote of breast down, each small, sheened quill of purplish coloring. It was a shoulder robe made of all manner of feathers. About the throat of it there was a ruff of feathers, a mingled rainbow of colored down. There was every color in that robe—heart's-ease gold and moonwort's gaudy green, and ruby coloring from hummingbirds' throats. Twice a year Lebanon took the robe from the pigskin chest and laid it out in the sun to air away its mustiness. With no wind stirring, and the light still as night on it, the colors would shimmer and would wake and die again.

Lebanon could remember days when her mother would stoop and find a lost bird feather: even a sparrow's wing quill has a light in it that is rich as a storm cloud's. Lollie had died of a pulmonary complaint. Sometimes she was in bed for a week or so, after a blood purge. Most times she was up and out and doing. Lebanon learned how to cook and sew and make a feather bed smooth when she was barely tall enough to reach halfway across a bed to make it.

Sometimes they would be out walking, and Lollie would have a coughing fit. Lebanon would watch her mother leaning there holding to a tree for support, while the cough racked her, and when the coughing was over, leaning her head wearily on the tree's body as she might lean on an old friend's heart. Lebanon could remember those times when she had seen her mother spit blood on fallen leaves riffling along the earth, and the sight of it was ugly and sickening and frightening.

Crease had treated Lollie's lung fever with butterfly weed and moonseed roots flavored pleasantly with curcumin and cumin. He had even taken her in the cart to Birdtown, and the physician had bled her half a dozen times. But the slow croupiness in her chest had worsened with time. If she could have gone to the Springs, or up into the hills, out of the heat and summer fevers, maybe she could have lived. But she could not leave home. Her eyes were sunken, though still blue and bright, and she walked wearily everywhere she went.

At the last Lebanon could remember the flenses of salt pork infused in honeywort, and the little doses of mulberry juice thickened down in honey and fermented till it made your head swim. Lebanon was given a spoonful of the sweet, to keep her quiet. She was seven years old, and Joel was nine, and Joel cried.

Raphael Ratcliff could not keep his mind from the Fairgale girl gone off to bed. Never had Rafe liked Sebastian's fast troth with Lucie Birdsong. That was Julia Birdsong's doing, for she liked the Ratcliff name and the Ratcliff money. Lucie, with her little cleft chin and mild blue eyes, could never have snagged Sebastian alone. When Sebastian had asked him as to the wisdom of taking the little Birdsong to wife, Rafe said little except to tell Sebastian that he would have a long time to stay married, all the rest of his time on earth.

Well, no need to worry over it now, for the Birdsong-Ratcliff troth was fast-set now and known to all of Baltimore. Mistress Birdsong had brought Lucie South to see the world and catch a change of air. And Mistress Birdsong cared to see Birdtown where her daughter was to live, once married, before she gave her last and full consent. That was why the Birdsongs were in Birdtown. A dull, depraved, benighted place they found it to be. What Raphael Ratcliff could mean, burying Sebastian in any such hidden hole of the world, Mistress Birdsong could not see, and frankly told him so. If South it must be, why not Charles Town—or, at the very least, Beaufort? Rafe could be one of the great merchants of the world in Charles

Town. And Sebastian could meet with his equals at the Carolina Coffee House in Tradd Street. There was no reason on earth why Lucie and Sebastian could not shine at the St. Cecilia Ball, given the chance.

With all this severe industrial crisis since 'nineteen, and no man knowing what might come, here Rafe Ratcliff wanted to reach out into lumbering, and in this dismal country where only the crows knew how to get home in the wilderness.

"A man can give his wife a gracious marriage or a rough one," Julia Birdsong said. "There is a point to dancing schools and grace cups and Supreme Chicken with truffles, and lettuces to decorate a roasted duck."

Rafe said:

"Phut, Julia! Did it ever occur to you that Lucie might have been born in Wales instead of Baltimore, and if her pappy had certain convictions and any insides to him, she would have been forced to feel persecution and come to this country? Any time you look around in the world, you can see a political refugee come to these shores, or a man that left Old England because of a crime he had to do or a debt he couldn't pay. Lambs' Shanks, Julia, if you were not a lady I'd say you were foolish indeed, and nearsighted to the point of a weak wit. If you keep on at Sebastian and Lucie, they'll never make a go of living together, and this is where Sebastian's future lies, for he will go where I say and do as I say."

Julia crimped her lips then and upped her chin a trifle.

"Of course, indeed, now, Raphael, you know best. But you can never blame me for thinking of my daughter."

"Let their young 'uns grow up tough and uncouth—then they'll know all sides and not one little flowered aisle. The world's a big place—you'll see. Not in my time, maybe—but it is a big place. There's more to it than Baltimore, Julia."

Julia was shut up then, for she considered mention of Lucie's children-to-be in rough order, indeed.

That was why Raphael could not forget Lebanon's face. Here down in the backwoods was a wife that could make a fortune for Sebastian. Julia Birdsong was a fool to hold up the wedding for the sake of a full year's proper troth. With Sebastian on one side of the

fire and Lebanon Fairgale on a stool at the other side, you could see
Sebastian look toward her face, and it was like water going downhill, their natural taking to one another. Rafe was no fool; he could
feel it, this liking of a man for a girl. It was like strong, sweet scent.
If Julia Birdsong could catch one glimpse of Sebastian's face when
he looked at this little backwoods chit, she would haste the wedding.
No wile so sure as innocence, Rafe was thinking.

When the others were asleep, and his head was laid down on one
of Lebanon Fairgale's feather pillows, he remembered Amalia
again, not for the first or last time. It would be a pity for Sebastian
to marry Lucie and miss this Lebanon. Yet it was none of his business. There was one thing he had said a thousand times to Sebastian:
"Stand on your own judgment, son. Don't ask anybody what to do.
Ask *yourself!*"

Sebastian showed little more liking for being buried in Birdtown
and its swamps than did Lucie. . . . And even a fool could see
Lucie's distaste. There was but one stage a week, and the swamp
seeped nigh into the very streets in wet weather. Not even the
houses were set in ordered rows, but every which way. Sebastian
and Lucie would like better the life of a bigger town—but all in
good time, when they had earned it. Rafe wondered how Sebastian
and Lucie would make out married and buried in Birdtown. They
would take board at Madame Lateuse's when these three remaining
months of troth were out and the marriage done in Baltimore.
Madame Lateuse's was as good a place as any to live, if you like
taverns. Rafe could not fancy a man and his bride kissing under
any roof but their own, those first nights. Better a shabby roof with
your own flour barrel and your own fire and your own wife. He had
wished to build a house for Sebastian and Lucie, but Julia Birdsong
went into a temper. "Not while I live," she said. "Do *call* it tem-
porary, Raphael. I'll not have my child buried forever in a frontier."
So Madame Lateuse's it would be.

There was a hedge of oleanders half as high as the roof, all about
the deep courtyard of the tavern. The trees girdled the grounds and
leaned inside the floor-deep windows of the ordinary where the
tables were set in white cloths and shining pewter. The leathery
fronds of the oleanders flowered in heavy spikes, bowing their heads

to the weight of a singing bird. Hitched horses whinnied along the rack, and heavenly odors drifted out from Madame Lateuse's kitchens.

Lebanon made Rafe think of an oleander's blooming on its tough, leathery stem. No delicate flower that! How she could be like a copper coin and an oleander blossom was a quirky thing, yet so she seemed, strong-rooted and slow-growing and sweet to the eyes, and charactered as a coin that does not alter its face or value through any changing from palm to palm. Sebastian would need a smart-wit wife to hold him, and Rafe wondered if Lucie were smart-wit enough. He liked the busy clatting of feet on boardwalks of cities, the cantering of horses and the rolling of carriages. He liked bright-washed cobbles of squared streets, and the rushing around of the fire brigade with a red-painted cart and white horses, the clanging of dispatch bells and the horns of post riders, the to-do about the posthouse at all hours. Always a coming and going was what Sebastian craved about him—yarning of a tapster in Chaco's, the fine buffooning on the boards at the Lyric. Truth to tell, Sebastian liked, too, sleek tights and painted faces of women capering—to watch them, that is.

Lucie would like town life better, too. Bodiced in stammel and fashionably bonneted, she would like it better if she could ride amarketing and lean, ladylike, from the carriage, to point out this fish or that saddle of mutton. She would like calling o' mornings, till three, and calling again till late supper, with maybe a dainty of nog or cherry mulse and a teacake as refreshment here and yonder. Where would there be to call, in Birdtown?

The more he thought of it, the less Rafe liked Sebastian's being anchored to Julia Birdsong's daughter. Yet it was none of his business. Sebastian would have to choose his own wife and chart his own course. He could begin at keeping a close ledger on the lumber in Birdtown. It was Rafe's notion to have Sebastian move here and there and learn all angles to the trade. He must learn to cast anchor in any sounding, and let it drag if it must.

When morning came, the men stirred and Crease built up the fire. Lebanon was already in the kitchen shed, and breakfast was ready by light. Dawn came glimmering through the cracks. The little cool of morning seeped through the floor cracks where bear throws were laid to keep out the cold.

Crease politely asked if the strangers slept well, and they all said yes, and a hospitable shelter, too. Then Crease said: "In the early night I did very well, but the last half, the dead walked across my feet, back and forth, most of the time."

Lebanon had biscuits, and fried ham, and hominy, and flenses of bacon, floured and browned, and hoecake, and mush and milk, and preserves and blackberry jelly, and cups of hot water to drink. They had no coffee to offer the Ratcliffs. For the last longest Lebanon had begged Papa to bring some home, so now all she could offer was hot water flavored with molasses. The Ratcliffs had fine manners; they said it made a delicious drink. It was a good breakfast, they said. Her hands trembled faintly, as did her heart, as she set the mugs around the places and waited on the men and passed the plates of food.

"Your girl here would make a fine wife for some man," Rafe said, passing her a smile.

"It is the truth," Crease said, "and we thank you for kind words. She has not had many chances back here in the sticks."

Then Sebastian said a bold thing.

"You say she has not, now?" he laughed. "That is a wonder to me." He smiled straight at Lebanon. "You could see her eyes all the way from here to Baltimore."

Rafe took a breath. Lordamercy! he thought, and him fast-trothed to Julia's girl!

Luke sighed. As well one as another, he thought.

Joel giggled.

Lebanon all but swooned. That was a wild thing for a married man to be saying to her. Then Rafe said another thing: "When Sebastian has a wife, wonder will he go about saying such things to pretty girls?"

"No," Luke said.

Lebanon looked hard into Sebastian's face, and he was looking at her, and he knew as well as did she what were her thoughts:

then you are *not* married to some other woman, and I thought you were.

Lebanon's face was sober till Sebastian's laughter caused her face to break into smiling, too, and her eyes into fiery blue light. But Crease eased off the gored house cap and stroked his head slowly, as though his thoughts pained him.

Chapter 2

THE MEN STAYED IN THE HOUSE some days; it was never said loud how long they would stay. One day they went southeast, one day south, another day southwest, searching through the reaches of best cypress to see how much Rafe would pay for it and how much Crease would take.

And every night they came back to Lebanon's house, and she had new sweets and browned meat or broiled partridges and white biscuits and butter-and-flour gravy.

It was, these days, a marvel to be alive, to have two feet and a hot head, a heart beating, and a mouth to tell things with. But what to tell? And who to listen? She could not say the things that crowded her heart, and there was none to tell them to. Sebastian? There was no need to tell him: his eyes knew. It was the strangest thing. When the men came in from their surveying, at sundown, or later, or earlier, his eyes would seek her face and she would smile— a common welcome smile; it was he who made the difference.

If she had greens for him to eat, the gathering of them and the tedious washing of each leaf at the well was a delight to her hands. She put in a drop of molasses as they cooked, to bring out their goodness. All her cooking took on a delicate finish now. Crease said so. She braised a haunch of venison in wheaten flour and butter, then added herbs—thyme and a little dried parsley to make it French— and thick cream to make it good. She would seal the flavor in quick heat, then watch and turn the spit, thinking. Rafe Ratcliff said never had he tasted such meat in his born days! Unless it were the partridges broiled in nothing but butter and salt and Indies pepper. Luke liked best the turkey breasts roasted and sliced cold. But Sebastian liked best the young squirrels steamed with rice and butter and herbs.

Sebastian put a gloss on every hour of every day for Lebanon. She would not let herself think, When will he go? She could not bear to ask, or to think, when he would not be here under the roof. Still, she would say to herself: "He could never leave me quite. I should remember the brown mug he drank ginger tea from. I should remember the pillow sham his sleek head slept on." When the men were gone from the house, and she was setting the house right, she would lift a discarded jacket of Sebastian's, or a waistcoat he wore day before yesterday; she would hold it lightly, scarcely caressing it with the warmth of her cheek. He was too high up and far off for her. He would never know that he sweetened her days like fine music always running, like sunlight falling steadily all day down a lane of pine boles. She fell asleep thinking of him. She waked and still he was there, the thought of him heavy, sweeter than comb honey, dearer than any telling. If she had been asked if she loved that man, she would have given a startled smile, scarce knowing the meaning of the words. If anyone had asked her: "Should you like to be near him all the remainder of your years on earth?" she would have given a soft and uncomplaining and complete reply: "That could never be."

Even his limitations were sweet in her thoughts. He and Luke had gone for squirrels long before day one morning. They came home with none. Luke claimed his failing eyesight. Sebastian had no excuse and said so. "The whiffety little fellows wouldn't hold still, is all I know," he said, smiling at himself. "Time I aimed, they went flickety-whack out of sight!"

It was a weakness, Lebanon knew, for any sort of a man ought to be able to kill some sort of meat, any hour of day or night. But this weakness in him endeared him the more to her. Since she could hold the weight of a musket, she could knock a squirrel out of a tree. Now she made excuses for Sebastian to her heart; just as well he did not kill a squirrel. Town people know no more than to kill the old ones and leave the young to starve in a high tree.

She could not know that Sebastian was as deeply moiled as she. His fingers fumbled on a cup as though he were a big baby, though he was careful that none should see. This girl out of the swamp was a pretty thing, and there was some strong current that went from her to him and back again any time the same room held them, and even when they were apart. Never had this happened to Sebastian before. He had seen women—gad, yes. He had seen little dandiprats, little tempered tarts, young fireballs that could warm up old Uncle Rafe if he would give them the chance. And he was fast-trothed to Lucie.

But this little swamp sparrow was another bird and of a different color. He was big and clumsy in her presence. He could give no name to it. If he walked across the floor to get him a coal for the Indian pipe he affected down here in the sticks, his big feet sounded too loud on the planking. If he picked up a knot for the fire, his big hands fumbled. If he laughed, it was too loud. If he closed the door, he slammed it; Lebanon would be sitting there, her head drooped over a wool stocking for her father or Joel, or breaking and hatcheling flax her father got in town, or shredding and carding old cotton for a new quilt—and she would never seem to note his clumsiness.

And still the current—call it current—ran from her to him, or from him to her, and back again, and neither of them could prevent it. If one left the big room, it was as though the other felt a cold blow in the face, and the room was comfortless and empty. A face would lose its light, the lips their laughter; it was like a lamp blown out; it was like cold fog shrouding the swamp. Neither of the two young fools thought that any other eyes saw their state.

For the worst time of all, Lebanon now wished her mother were living. I would tell her about this, Lebanon thought. Death had disbodied Lollie complete, death and distance—now Lebanon could call her mother's figure to only a most careless accounting. She could remember a warmth of cheek and hand, and a voice, and the bright blood on dead leaves a long time ago.

"Your mother was a good woman, a kind-tongued woman," Crease would say, and Lebanon envied him his complete remembrance of her. Yet if anyone asked Crease a question concerning that loving wraith, he would change the subject straightway, would spit into the fire, and a hardness would come on his face, and a dull light in his eyes. He would speak of some other matter—fish to fertilize an acre of corn, a trace-chain broken, and how to mend it. A mile toward Birdtown lay Lollie's grave, a cedar at its head and one at its foot, and that was all. When spring began to show in all the warm hollows, Lebanon would walk the track to Birdtown, taking a little jug of well water, and she would pick some flowers to go with those from home. Lollie liked the wild ones better than the tame, Crease said.

From her father and her mother Lebanon had her tough-muscled heart. When they were small, if Joel whimpered over a fester's being opened, Lebanon would call him a dandilly, curling her lips; if she had a splinter dug, tears might show in her eyes, but no crying would come from her mouth. Once in a long time her face might show a secret scorn her heart might be knowing, but it would be much as pines quiver and blow about in the face of a tormenting wind, their roots steadied many a year in the earth.

It was a time of moonless nights. It was blowy outside, and now and then there would come a light rush of rain across the roof, as though a ragged pine bough, loosed from somewhere, were dipped into the wet, blowing sky and brushed on this lonely roof.

This was eight nights the Ratcliffs were here, bargaining over the land.

Joel had given up his front shed room to the older Ratcliffs, and Sebastian slept on the wall cot in the big room. Joel slept with Crease, and neither one of them liked the arrangement.

The wall cot was a pleasant, give-y sleeping place: Lebanon had woven a new hammock bottom for it only last year, from slubbed hemp.

With the men in from wet places, there was a soft, heavy odor of foot leather rising from the boots laid to dry. Each night Lebanon greased the men's boots with neat's oil and laid them to season in the warmth. Soles laid toward the flame, stranger's boots spell good luck, the Indians say. But to Lebanon's hands Sebastian's boots seemed not strange. She left them last for greasing each night, while the talk of the men ran on, and now one, now another went off to sleep.

If we could talk together, she thought.

But there was never a time for that. There were only her hands on his boots and he away across the fireplace with his eyes sometimes on the fire, sometimes busy with talk, and sometimes looking toward her. Shadows from the fire quivered over the time-dark walls; the ceiling was lost in dark. The fire was never dead, so shadows haunted the room all through the night, calling ghosts of light that footed lightly in uncertain rhythm, measures beaten out into the quiet by the flames.

And now Sebastian one night, seeing her eyes on the walls, said: "They are like the shadows of dancers, are they not?"

And her lips fell apart and she said nothing—for everything had been said.

Lebanon mended Joel's boot, where the tongue had slipped its stitching; one could hear the tick-tack of the little hammer, one could hear the waxed thread pulled through the leather, and the awl doing its duty.

Sebastian lay down before the others, saying he was wearied. He lay along the wall, his face muffled in shadows. His tall length was bosomed on the hammock Lebanon had woven and swung taut between walnut posts with carven knobs. He could not smooth his mind down to sleep. The torment a man's flesh can feel in one little day, he was thinking. I am no cad, yet I do crave to make love to that girl. And now I no more know whether I can marry Lucie or not.

Crease would never leave them be in the room alone, and Sebastian, being a gentleman, would not be left alone with her. And she, being a lady, would never allow such impertinence. Try her and see what she will do! the fork-tailed devil whispered, but Sebastian knew it was the devil, so no harm done. He would be glad when his uncles came to a settlement and finished tramping the swamp. Or would he? If she were a hallion, he would know what to do and quickly. If she had a contemptuous tongue, and a black, licking flame in her eyes, he would know how to heal them both. Lebanon ruffled his mind past believing. She was no hallion, nor ever could be. There was no viperish curl to her lips. The whole while she drooped her head over a task in her hands, you could see naught but firelight in her hair and the design of her shoulders against the wall. Why should his hands so wish to set themselves on her shoulders and draw her to himself? Never had he felt so toward Lucie. Lucie would be a good wife and a good mother to his children. That much was settled. Never had Lebanon said a secret word to him. But always her eyes besought him: Love me—love me forever; if not present with me, then absent from me. Never forget me. Keep me safe in your heart, so I shall never be hurt.

And his eyes—what did his eyes say? They said: You are lovely in my sight; your hands are beautiful on a piece of worn cloth, sewing a bone button home, patching a ragged hole in a piece of worsted.

And each of them said to the other one: We need never say things loudly.

The backlog was wasting in flame, its oak heart broken into nacre and fire-opal coloring; beyond a sheaf of throbbing flame you could see the waste. And the changeful pattern of firelight came and went all along the log walls. She was there by the fire, and her presence overcrowded the room for him. He watched her go and stack little horn cups by candlelight, hushing their clinking in her hands. He shut his eyes manfully and turned on his side away from the room and the fire. No need to lie and look at her. But in the red dark, with his face to the wall, she came and tormented him. He could hear her ladling hot water from the jug on the hearth; he could hear the small hissing sound of the spilled water on the stones of the fireplace, as though the water kissed suddenly the hot stones and was lost. He could hear her lay the small burden of the washbasin on the washstand under the window blind. It seemed to him, clenching his fists in the gloom, that he must go to her, though ten thousand might be watching. Though here far from the fire the air was cold, he could sleep no more easily than if the wall cot were lined with rocks. He must kiss her, and he knew he could not: that is a hard judgment to lay on a strong-minded man. He turned his face back to the room and opened his eyes a little, and through his half-shut lids came a dust of candlelight, strained through the mesh of the lashes and the rosy glow of the fire. He watched covertly Lebanon's movements near the fire.

One by one the men went to bed, Crease and Joel to the back shed room, the two older Ratcliffs to the front room. Now the girl was spinning, her foot going steadily, her hands solemn in the air, building comfort for the men of this house. The girl's body was only a little less still than the fire. The whirring of the wheel sounded. Now and then Lady would sleepily scratch a flea and lie down again, her back to the fire, her shut eyes toward Lebanon's face.

The low light touched Lebanon's face, and shadows came and went on it. She had blown out the single dip—no use to waste tallow, firelight is enough for simple spinning. Sebastian studied her face when she thought he was asleep, and he thought: Her face is as clean as though carved.

But suddenly in her face there came a change. He saw her brush away tears on the backs of her hands. The wheel was stopped. He had seen other women cry, his mother and Lucie, and Aunt Maria. But their weeping was mingled with a lot of words, soft threats, strident justification or recrimination. But this girl was weeping quietly as rain falls.

The wheel was whirring again in the firelight, and still her cheeks were wet, and still with one hand she dried the tears as they came. Then of a sudden she lifted her shoulders and quit weeping; he knew she was finished with it. She left the wheel and caught up the old fur tippet from a wall peg, lifted the dry water piggin and went out into the whipping cold.

Sebastian eased from the wall cot. He took up his greatcoat where it hung spread-armed over a chair. He went out into the dark. The well sweep was creaking—the weight of it should be heavy even for a man. It was a black blowing night. The well sweep hushed its lumbering. The firelight fondled the split-log walls of the cabin and the bear throws lay patient, warming hopelessly cracks where wind was forever coming in.

It was later that she brought the newest bearskin throw and laid it softly across him where he lay on the wall cot. He lay with his eyes fast-shut in false sleep. She laid the warm skin on his feet. The coarse, wild scent of it struck his nostrils, and he could feel its warmth. She went noiselessly across the flooring, quiet in her deer-skin shoes, and out into the cold shed room away from the fire and his warm breathing.

It was a hard thing to do—for when he had set his arms about her shoulders, it seemed that there she was meant to be. Yet there was nothing to do but say: "You are a fool. Do go back."

Her mother was dead and had never told her the way of a man's love, yet she knew this to be a treachersome, deadly device in the heart of a man, and a hard danger to a soft woman.

"We should be together. Fate intended it," he said.

All she could say was: "Then why did not Fate set us together, if such were her intentions?"

But he was no way angered at her.

"You will not love me, then?" he asked.

"I will love you till I die," she promised.

The warmth of the bearskin throw warmed his feet and spread through all his body till he was too hot. Here was a strange and unsuspected summer hidden in his veins. And here was a new love, and a faithful one, and one he would wish to keep forever—and here he was faithfully trothed to Lucie Birdsong. He resolutely set his mind on Lucie, with little thanks to Lebanon for holding his feet on a narrow path.

He must trust Lucie to keep his thoughts straight in future. He busied himself recalling her languid, white hands, the polished blue light of her eyes. She wore a piled crown of bronze hair tucked in high on her head, and gold circlets swung in the sattiny lobes of her ears. When they were wed fast, he would kiss the lobes of her ears and the stretch of her throat. Many times he had longed to, though of course he never spoke of it. Once married, he would love her, and no mistake. He went on thinking of Lucie, yet he could not bring her home to his heart. It was as though Lucie were a figurine with a painted porcelain face.

Suppose he should tell her father, as he had told Lucie's father:

"I have been turning over in my mind a question. To put it briefly, would you honor me with the hand of your daughter in marriage?"

What would Crease do and say? Swoon and laugh perhaps?

If he should tell his uncles: "I have changed my mind and no longer care for Miss Birdsong in a romantic way which leads to marriage," what then?

Why, the troth was already spoken, and Mistress Birdsong had people to tea and cake in Lucie's honor. Later when the men came a toast was drunk all about, first to Lucie, then to her mother, then to Aunt Maria, and then, in order, to everyone—in ruby glasses with gold etching. He could no more change this matter than he could move a mountain or change a river's course. His life was ordered.

Ah, he could run away to the Floridas, or West somewhere, with thieves and culprits and mad adventurers—and he could take Lebanon with him. That was a temptation, come to think of it. He would buy her a bright wedding bodice, and her eyes would flash softly. She would see no danger in strange territories west of the Mississippi. She was not afraid of wildcats or pards. She was only afraid of his hurting her.

Such thoughts put sleep from him as though a bucket of cold water were dashed upon him. He had kissed her hard under the tulip tree at the well in the middle of a black night, and she had drawn herself away and said: "You are a fool. Do go back." But further she had said: "I will love you till I die."

For a time he lay on his back thinking of the Birdsongs and the girl he was bound by honor to marry.

"Think of it," Mistress Birdsong had said, with a little air of distasteful generosity, unfurling her jet fan, tapping quietly the ends of her fingers as though they had petulantly objected to her words.

"Dear me," Lucie murmured, turning her left cheek toward the soft touch of her bonnet plume.

Sebastian had said a little jest to tease their pomposity; he had said these women in the swamp country looked bumptious and good armfuls!

"Sebastian!" Lucie cried, her lower lip quivering appealingly. Yet Sebastian's bold pleasantries pleased them where no one saw, and they laughed a little, in spite of themselves. He abased himself for his boorish manners, and they forgave him. Lucie had a loving, quiet way about her; always you thought of her in a still room, with a scent of flowers somewhere on a table and candles burning steadily in curtained quiet. Sebastian thought of her so, because of the many times he had seen her so, sitting meekly beside her mother, handing claret or the sugar mallet or a drop of hot water, doing her mother's bidding in a most well-bred fashion.

He would make a naughty joke, only to see Lucie laugh; he would stretch his long legs and pull down his waistcoat. He knew that Lucie adored him, and he turned in the sight of her eyes as you might turn before a mirror.

What would Lucie be doing now? thought Sebastian, resolutely putting his mind on his future wife who would in three more little months be Mistress Sebastian Ratcliff and inside his arms for the rest of eternity. She would be muffled down in sleep now, maybe. Or often, she said, when Mama was fast-snoring, she would get up and light a candle and shade it and write her thoughts to him, her head low over the blue leather portfolio he had given her. Now he could see her through the miles, her head sedate and sweet among clustered candles, writing to him a letter which he would read after he saw her—for she kept the letters, fearing to trust them to the post. Her letters were innocent enough, words set in small, careful script.

"My dear Sebastian," she would begin. Only at the end she would write: "I love you madly," and Mama would have been shocked past swooning at that. "My dear Sebastian . . . Mama is in the attic whilst I pen these few poor lines to you, searching manfully for last summer's foulard she has mislaid. You would smile to see her so cockbrained over a trifle she beyond doubt gave to the chambermaid a long while since. Or maybe the slave stole the thing. They are not what they once were. Now you can pay any price for a body servant and find them careless of your desires and thoughtless of anything farther than the next frolic in the quarters. I do not know what is to become of us. Papa charges me with my pale cheeks, saying it is the sweet grief of love ailing me. Yet I hold myself firm, it seems to me. Mama and I have re-set the last of the asters from the hotbed, and you should see my poor, grubby hands. You know what I wish you would do to my hands. Samson has

grubbed out the bed of vervain. He does not pay mind to his work as
he once did. Papa swears he will have him beaten if he does not
improve his attitude toward his work, though I should hate to hear
of that, and have begged him off from Papa's anger. You know I
cannot bear unkindness. Mama has found the foulard. You see it
was just as I told you. She and I baked a Cheshire pudding yesterday and the sauce curdled past belief. Rather to say, Emmeline
baked it with our knowledge. She is a trial to poor Mama and I
cannot say why poor Mama should be called upon to bear so heavy
a burden of petty harassments at the hands of those who should
give thanks to us instead of small aggravations. . . ."

And so on and on.

Lucie's missives were always no more than bright tittle-tattle of
her little days: a slave lashed once, a bonnet ruined in rain, a glove
lost, a new house visited, overseeing the honey clarified, a flower
sampler nearing completion by one leaf. Sometimes there would be
some harmless clish-clash concerning some of their friends: one had
invested overheavily in sea trade and lost his best money, or another
one had bought a bonnet in a certain shop and found later that the
shop was kept by a strumpet, and the flowered toque set there in
the window as enticement to snag the patronage of nice people.
Nothing harmful to any good name—ah, no. Lucie abhorred un-
kind talk of anyone, even in jest. Sebastian knew what the letters
would say before he broke the small waxed seal of two twined lilies.
Sometimes he thrust the letters into an inner pocket of his greatcoat,
and the laundry maid returned them to him days later, still unread.
Naturally, he did not tell Lucie of those days when he did not read
her letters, but laid them in the fire, if he were hurried, watching
the flame curl over the wild, passionate assertion set there bold as
a strumpet at the ending: "I love you madly." But there would
have been no great to-do if he had told her, for she thought anything he did was perfection. "Sebastian!" she would have said to
him, cloaking any rebuke in tenderness in a little way she had of
making him feel under the mark. Now in the dark night between
them he could feel her face more clear—her face was placid and
small-featured, a dust of freckles showed across her nose and cheeks
if she dared the sun and did not carefully preserve her fairness with

buttermilk and strawberry juice and cucumber cream. She was a dutiful daughter, any dull man could judge, and she would be a dutiful wife. His heart chilled when he thought of marrying any woman, to tell the truth.

Oh, Lucie would be a dutiful wife. And he was as well as wed to her now. A gentleman does not alter his word; nor does a lady go back on her word to a gentleman. Anyway, Lucie loved him most exquisitely and sensibly. She was all those things the word "wife" brings to a man's mind when he is wishing. Sebastian's best friend, Tom Batterwaite, had jilted Phillida Tuttle on their wedding eve, but it was so shameful a thing to do that he left town in a hired gig under cover of darkness, and poor Phillida went gently mad in a month and no one but the servants ever saw her face again.

Tom had come by Sebastian's quarters with cold terror in his eyes, and his face pale, and his hands jerking. He seemed drunken, or mad, yet his breath was not brandied, nor was his speech any but sensible.

"Tell her for me," Tom told Sebastian, "that it is better for me to go now than for both of us to be miserable all the rest of our lives. I cannot marry her, 'Bas. You do not understand. I cannot go through with it. I have lain sleepless, night on night, wishing that somehow I might blot the whole matter into oblivion and change things to what they once were—but now all I can do is run away. You do not understand, 'Bas . . . you do not understand." He said that over and over like a broken music box harping on a phrase of an unfinished song.

But now Sebastian understood.

Never did he have so hard a task as to go and tell Phillida Tuttle's father that Tom Batterwaite was gone.

Next morning it all came out that he had gone with the pale-haired lambkin of the fine Grossett family, and that made things far worse. Often Sebastian had wondered where Tom and the little cosseted daughter of the Grossetts were. She was gentle and sang at musicals. She used to sing that little song that begins: "The mists lay low in the valley that day I told you good-by." She sang it so prettily that people asked for it, and each time it seemed sadder on her pretty lips. After the Batterwaite incident, one couldn't hear the song and not remember her, stealing out from home and leaving a life behind—never telling her mother good-by. Not a word did any soul ever hear from them—none but the little note Sebastian had saying:

"Thank you, and forgive us. We have had enough complete happiness this while, so that if we must forever afterward suffer, we are sworn never to complain. Good-by, and God keep you all." And he signed his name with a flourish: "Thomas Masters Batterwaite," as though he were not yet ashamed of what he had done.

And there was an end to that.

Now Sebastian understood what ailed Tom that night, for he never intended to hurt Phillida Tuttle—that Sebastian knew.

There is another way, Sebastian thought; when a young man sours in his marriage resolve he can goad his promised wife into breaking her troth with him by this means or that. Open drinking will do the trick, or consorting with a low woman, even briefly, though only to have it mulled abroad. Sebastian wondered if even such drastic tactics would cause Lucie to flinch.

For good or ill, she would stiffen her pale features, she would bow and smile in the face of evil innuendo, as though the earth did not quake under her heart. Woe to any talebearer who might bring her word of Sebastian's defaulting in faith with her! When he had broached the subject of marriage, Sebastian had told her openly: "You know that I drink upon occasion, as who does not? And I have had a fling with the fellows, yet not so wide or high a fling as most men."

He wondered did not all prospective husbands say the same words. Lucie listened to his words, holding her hands still and her mouth quiet. Then she told him this, and it was worthier of an older woman's wisdom:

"I should never allow the forked tongue of another person, even my own mother, to come betwixt you and me. Our life will belong to us equally; the two halves are yours and mine together. When there is something I should know, you will tell me of it and we will settle the matter, as becomes you and me—no other one. When there is something I should tell you, I will tell you."

Because of such words, and more like them, Sebastian felt all the more fast to his troth.

Now through the dark he could see her face and hear her voice. She was prettier than a picture. Mistress Birdsong had her portrait done for the wedding, by an Englishman all the rage in this country, yet Lucie was prettier far than the portrait.

She wore a buff brocade traveling suit that last morning when he saw her at early breakfast in Birdtown. Her forelocks were crimped across her brow; it gave her a baby look. Even now he could recall the warmth of her hands through their brown chamois garments as he told her good-by for a little while. Though she was to marry him in three months, she was still decorously shy of him. He had never kissed Lucie, more than the back of her hand. From behind her mother she smiled him farewell, and where her mother could not see, her lips formed soundlessly the words she always put in the silly letters:

I—love—you—madly, her lips said, and he doffed his hat once more and bowed away from the door.

Ah, but now he had kissed Lebanon Fairgale.

He could not say which last thought formed in his mind before he slept at last, belly-flat in the curving rope bunk, warm under the bearskin throw Lebanon had laid upon him. One thing he could say: in troubled dreaming she came to him and offered him cold water in a long-handled gourd dipper. The gourd was splotched in dark mottles that had come upon it in its sun-drying. Its inner cup, where the bright water lay quivering, smelled of dry leaves and tree bark and sunny reaches of sedge. He drank the water, and in the far dream he took her again within the holding of his arms, and in the far dream he kissed her again; and in the far dream a strange glory bound them and her mouth was like a flower for his devouring. Never had he so clear a dream! He lay, steeped in delight, shut-eyed, long after the dream was gone. This was no cheap and bawdy desiring; this was a clean body need. He could see the gourd still, he could nigh hold it in his hands! Some connection there was in his mind between Lebanon and water—that was clear!

He lay wakeful in the deepened dark, in the thickened cold. The fire had smoldered into coals. Through the thin walls of the shed room he could hear hoarse snoring—that would be Uncle Rafe. He could hear a heavy breathing—that would be Crease Fairgale. He could hear nothing from Lebanon's hushed shed room to the right. There was stillness there.

So thin a wall, so low a door, stood betwixt him and Lebanon. Yet Sebastian did not break the thin confine that stood betwixt them, and she did not ask him to. If one of them had broken that light bar, then the lives of all about might have been changed. This life might run leftwise instead of right, another would have gone east instead of west; one would have died, perhaps, instead of living, and one would have lived, and not died—all because of a little door.

Suddenly Sebastian noted a strange thing. Here close-curled under his cot he heard the quick, even breathing of the little dog that belonged to Lebanon Fairgale. Sebastian could not find the outline of his mental quandary in the murk of his thoughts; he could not think for thinking. He thrust back the covers and went to lay a new log length on the fire. No wonder he could not sleep; this business of sleeping in your clothes was new and bothersome; but you can do no better in strange country.

The planking of the floor, where the skins did not cover it, was icy. He went and laid his palm on the cold wood of Lebanon's door as though to quiet a quaking in his life.

The little dog, roused by his walking, came with him and lifted her head and watched him, to be sure he took no harm to Lebanon's threshold. He stood, listening at her door, but he could hear no signal of her woman's breathing.

Till he died he would remember this small, cold minute in the dark when his hand lay on the black face of her door, and she beyond, a long way off.

He remembered he was a fool to stand barefoot beyond Lebanon's door. He stole with a shamed face back to the bunk and laid himself down. He put his mind doggedly on Lucie Birdsong and her child-pure face, her peach-pink cheeks, and her chin with the kiss dimple in it, and the hood of her bronze hair. In sweet pretense he kissed her eyelids shut now as though her face were there beside his face as it would be in three short months more, and then for all the remain-

der of his nights on earth. He tried to sleep, trying to enclose her
hands, naked and white, within his hands.

Lebanon lay a long while watching the shadow of dark swerve
across the low, slanting ceiling. The heavy wooden shutter, barred
against the cold, shuddered a little in the blowing of the wind. Now
and then from an unseen crevice there would blow a sudden icy
gust of new cold, tempering to the still of the room. There was no
warmth, no comfort, here on the goose-down bed. There was terror,
and hard grief, and mad and hopeless desire, here all together in a
small room, to hound her out of sleep.

Till she died, she would recall this night as that time when she
was no more a child.

I shall not even so much as give him leave to come into my mind,
Lebanon resolved savagely.

Yet he came.

You with your shining boots I have held and oiled these nights;
you with your fleece-lined cloak hung just so on the coat rack beside
the front door . . . you with your stem-winder watch with twined
serpent heads you got when you were twenty-one . . . you are too
fine for me and I cannot be suddenly born again in Philadelphia so
that you can marry me. You with your pale, restless hands on a black
colorado cigar from Spain, a frown of displeasure or bewilderment
betwixt your brows, and your teeth dragging at your lower lip . . .
I know the wrinkles and sewed designs on your imported boots, because I have greased them for you, night on night. Just so I know the
features of your heart, the breaking of your smile, having learned
them a lifetime. You cannot marry me, and I know it, yet I must
learn it over and over, minute by long minute. . . .

So went Lebanon's thoughts.

After a long stretch of time the wind died, shortening its gusts like
a wild breathing slowing. Daylight was near. Lebanon rose to make
breakfast. She put a new log to the flame and stood to hear the bright
crackle of flame on dry, rich wood. The long night was over.

She wore a butternut wool sack with bone buttons, and her hands
did not trouble the buttons as yesterday. Rafe studied her face as
an old bee studies a new rose, to judge its opening. Her face was

still, Indian-y, dark, quiet as a slough of swamp water when the wind is gone.

It was about time the deal was closed. They would go to Birdtown and have a lawyer draw papers to be signed, to cover intricacies. They had quills and writing racks and ink in their valises, and they figured this way and that, before Lebanon's fire. They agreed, and disagreed, and agreed again. Lebanon was always praised for her cooking.

"Happy to serve, gentlemen," Lebanon said softly, passing a new load of hot biscuits fresh from the kitchen hearth. She was red-faced under praise.

"She can kill a rattler with a rawhide at twenty feet, too," Crease bragged. "I have seen her do it."

Lebanon blushed like a rose.

"Could I go into Birdtown when you go, Papa?" she asked over the busy table.

Rafe Ratcliff wondered how he could manage that some other man could see to matters here in the swamp; the farther apart these two should be the better for all concerned, including themselves.

But Lebanon was thinking: I shall see her, this chitmouse he is to marry. I shall look hard, believe me. She washes in Marseilles soap, no doubt, and I grind lilywort for mine. She whitens her throat with sweet powders and flakes her cheeks with French rouge, and Sebastian never recognizes the fraud; she reads a book with girandoles set just so to light her page. There are always slaves to lackey her, one to rub her feet when she has walked, one to wash her hair when the wind has blown in it, one to shade her eyes from firelight, and one to stir the air so that she shall breathe fresh all day long. They play harps for her and she laughs. They hold gold silk rags for her and she weeps. . . . Lackadaisy! Lebanon told herself, the problem solved. And still the problem heavied her heart more and more.

Chapter 3

THE VARIED ROOFS of Birdtown were a sight to Lebanon's eyes. Never could she accustom her eyes to the sight of so many varied roofs, if she lived in town all her days. She would not choose to live in a place so smoky and dusty and loud, cluttered by a hundred houses—that is, not unless there were some big cause for it. She liked better one little roof for the sunshine to hover, and the wild woods south to the Gulf of Mechiko, and New Spain past that, and nothing between her face, when she stood in her back door, and that wild unknown territory but the black, soft-breathing swamp, and the cypress crowns with the eagles' nests on them.

The men tethered their horses at the hitching rack out in the back of Lateuse's Tavern. Then they swung off down the street or into Lateuse's Bar and left Lebanon to amuse herself. Crease gave her some money—not much, but some. She scarce knew where to spend the money, or whether to keep it. She walked along the street and looked into the shops, and felt free-footed and lighthearted, as good people feel on happy holydays.

There was a harness shop, a strong male odor of leather coming out into the street from it. There was a toggery; on forms set near the opened shutters there were superfine colored clothes, a gentleman's greatcoat lined in scarlet silk stuff, a lady's frock frilled in pale yellow gossamer. There was on a stand a cloak bag of polished leather for far traveling, and even a silk-lined portmanteau with a handle of margarite to hold a lady's face powders and kerchiefs and small garments.

Lebanon stood awhile mooning over the little portmanteau. She had not enough money to buy it, nor anywhere to go with it, but she had a merry morning looking at such things made for the gentility. There were glove boxes and silver stoppered camphire bottles and Bokhara head shawls; there were stiff-boned underbodices and hair fringes—vain things, for fools like the Birdsong women. Lebanon envied the foolishness, yet she would never say so. She put up her hands and dared herself to be ashamed for her hair sleeked down from its parting and pinned up at the back of her head and covered in a black wool bonnet with a ruffled tail. Let the other butter-mouthed women wear their gold buttons and silk pelisses and dress their hair in sweet pomades, and let the rich, pottle-bellied old gentlemen enjoy their surcoats of sattin. She must be content with stitched mittens of lamb-skin and a cloak from skins she had trapped and cured. When she tired of wearing her black wool bonnet, she could knit a hood, any color she pleased.

Down the street the roofs made a fanciful pattern of tops—some pointed as steeples, some tall-boxed, some flat and sturdy of English brick. A delighting marvel the rooftops were to her, less lovely than the green-pointed pine tops and stubby cypress crowns to which her eyes were accustomed, but pretty in their way.

Lateuse's Tavern stood in the midst of a cobbled courtyard; around the courtyard was a low wall of whited bricks, and the oleander trees. All day long, and deep into the night, there was apt to be always an ever so pleasant clish-clash of noise; the posts and stages made the tavern headquarters, and all manner of travelers came in time. One could find near it a shop to meet any need—saddlers, wool staplers, farriers, and even a steam bathhouse whence hot, sweet odors issued at all hours. There were greengrocers, fusty seed shops, clothiers, hatters, linnen mercers with hanks of flax in the windows, and even an oil painting with faces framed in brass and gold and ivory and bone looking into the cobbled road.

Through the gate of the tavern, always a-sag on its big iron hinges, she could see the drinking trough and pump in the front court; the round drinking basin was grayed by time and greened by water lichens. Water lapped over its rim; the basin was built up waist-high about the spring and hedged in rough stones. The spring was the beginning of Birdtown in the old days when the Spaniards came through on their cream-colored barbs. The Indians drank at this spring, going east and west and north and south. Englishmen boxed the spring and cobbled the courtyard and made a stage stop around which the town grew, and a man named Bird bought the tavern and the town took his name.

Lebanon never watched a horse drink at the watering basin that she did not remember Crease telling of how the Indians once tortured their captives there, tethering them a little way from the water, so they should die in sight and sound of redemption.

The door of the tavern was swung wide, too; there were heavy iron grills that opened outward before a wooden door into a large vestibule. Through the glassed windows the oleanders leaned in. They crowded the window spaces and brushed the iron bars of the windows, shading the room to a delicate, watery green. The barkeep was named Fernald d'Aussy. He was shy and dark-faced. His duties were to tend the backlogs in the big fireplaces in the vestibule and ordinary. He kept a little fire in the hearth at the end of the little cubbyhole behind the counter for his own warmth and for the wines. When the sanded floor was darking and odorous from tobaca spittle, he swept the floor clean and scattered more coarse river sand for new feet and other spittle. He had eyes that were clever as a mouse's, and a careful mouth. His hands were forever smoothing and polishing the squat tumblers and tall glasses and gold-lipped beakers, as though they were dear familiars. He was a Frencher but not from Paris.

The first time Lebanon laid eyes on him was the day her mother was buried.

Crease had taken the children into town. He had set Lebanon on the counter—she was seven—and Joel sat in a leather chair, and Crease took one hearty drink after another. "He buried his wife today," the other men said, and one by one the other men went away and left the one man, the little girl on the counter, and the boy in the leather chair. Lebanon could remember the green bottle with the big body and the small throat. And finally Crease was swaying and cursing and weeping. He laid his face in his arms on the counter, and his shoulders heaved. Joel, sitting straight in the leather chair, began to cry. Then Fernald led Crease somewhere and laid him to sleep that night. That was eleven years ago, and Lebanon could remember the little Frencher holding her on his knee and making funny faces behind a false face of red-painted cloth, to make her and Joel laugh. They slept in his bed that night, at the end of a dark corridor in a second story, and Fernald stroked

Lebanon's head and they went to sleep, she and Joel, under the spell of a story about a French queen and a white pony. He had stayed beside the narrow bed till they fell asleep so they would not be afeared. Now Lebanon could remember it.

Lebanon had not been to town many times in her life. About twice a year was as much as she could hope for. But when she went, she always paid a call to the tavern. Always she would go and lean on the counter of the little bar and talk with Fernald d'Aussy when no one else was there. He would bring out a special jug of sweet stuff from a dark corner under the counter and pour for her a little thimbleful. It would have a sting sharp as the bite of a fer-de-lance, but it was heavily sweet and lifted the crown of her head.

This morning she went into the tavern, when she was done with going up and down the streets and window-trading. She walked up to the time-darkened counter, and he did not at first see her. He was polishing a crystal glass, blowing upon it and shining it with a linnen cloth. The counter shone where he had polished it, too.

The bearskin tippet was muffled high against her wind-blown cheeks, and the black woolen bonnet hooded her face most becomingly.

He smiled. "Well, draw and quarter the devil if here is not Lebanon Fairgale come to see me."

He bowed most elaborately, to tease her, took her hand and set a courtly kiss on the back of it. "You cancel all your months of absence. You banish the loneliness of my heart. You are a miracle," he said.

Then, as he looked closer on her, he hushed his bright chiding, for here was a woman before him suddenly in place of the child he had known.

She was looking down the long, dim room. A slave boy was scrubbing brass andirons at the big hearth, holding them away from the heat. He had a bucket of sand and a suds of lye soap.

Fernald's eyes stayed on her face.

"The Birdsongs are staying here, I hear," she said.

"So they are," he said, his eyes taking in the manner in which her hair grew like bright wings close about her head.

"Where is she?" asked Lebanon. ". . . Where are they?"

Then she blushed.

"Most mornings they walk," he said, studying still the blue light in her eyes.

"With a veil across her face and tom-walker heels and feathers in her bonnet?" Lebanon asked carelessly.

"Why, so she does," he said, in slow amazement.

The matter was suddenly clear to him. He saw her hands trembling ever so slightly on the counter. Her finger took itself away from smoothing a circle deep in the dark, polished mahogany of the counter. Fernald's eyes closed a very little, as though his eyelids wearied suddenly.

Lucie's eyes fell dully on the carved lions that were mounted on the high headboard of the bedstead. Mama was hidden beyond the tall footboard, beyond another crouched wooden lion that watched Lucie vacantly. Mama sat at the spindle-legged writing table at the foot of the bed, writing. When Mama was not talking, she was writing, or asleep.

Lucie could be writing Sebastian, too. But there was no post route to that swamp. She worried, day and night, after Sebastian's welfare. The swamp gave her horrors, and there was no need to pretend not—the snakes, the wildcats, the bears, the creeping quicksands. Every hour of her life she prayed for Sebastian. If she were at home, she would run out through the bare orchard, or whip Dexter to a better gallop, or better still, she would have Moze row her across the river to Aunt Sully's and tell her all about this strange Sebastian she was finding out about.

But here in this horrible tavern there was nothing to do but listen to Mama complain delicately of the universe—of the brass spittoons astride the crimson roses of the carpet, the shade of dust about the fat body of the ewer, the ghost of scum along the inner rim of the basin.

"If put to it, I shall scour the basin myself," Mama said each morning.

Lucie wished she would, for as it was, she was forever taking the chambermaid to task, till the poor thing shivered in her skin when she must set their room to rights. Each day Mama grew worse. The more frightened the slave girl became, the more peevish Mama was. Often Madame Lateuse came blowing up the staircase to see after cleaning the room herself, and not even that appeased Mama.

Everything was going wrong. With the wedding only three months off, here she had to be South, in a billikin crossroad tavern, and not able to see to her fittings. Cousin Alice had not her old eyesight, anyway, and Heaven only knew how the wedding petticoat would hang. She was not so skillful with the shears any more, either; once she basted a left sleeve into a right armhole, right before Mama's eyes!

"You *will* be happier with the best cloak in brown, won't you, my own?" asked Mama, in a command like a trooper's sergeant.

"Yes, Mama," said Lucie.

She had wept secretly for longer than half an hour because the cloak could not by any dispensation of Mighty Providence be fashioned of black, with a ruff of ivory sattin about the throat. It must be brown with a ruff of cream sattin. It was nearly a certainty that Sebastian would give her as a marriage-day gift the fleur-de-luce of diamonds and pearls and rubies that had been his mother's—and how fairly it would shine against midnight black and pearl-colored sattin! Lucie had seen Sebastian's sister Margrette wear the jewel at the ball the Drurys gave for their last daughter. It swung in cold, torpid beauty on its gold fastening on Margrette Ratcliff's shoulder. It stood to reason it would be Sebastian's gift to his bride—unless Margrette kept it.

When Sebastian first asked her if he might pay court to her, she pruned and prismed her lips in careful maidenly decorum and said that if her parents found no fault in him neither should she. Thereupon he took her hand and kissed it politely, and she was as good as married. In the dark of night she would hold her right hand lovingly, as though the kiss were still there, cool and tender upon her flesh. She would try to forget the kiss, but never quite succeed. It troubled her when she was lonely for him.

Mama spent all her waking hours, and some when she should have been sleeping, in making Lucie's clothes—that is, in imagination. A thousand times she had rearranged a certain number of rows of baby ruching across the bosom of a bodice, or added one more tucked flounce to the wraith of a garment heavy in her still hands. For nine months Cousin Alice had all but gone mad over Lucie's wedding clothes. If she put five ruffles on the bustle of a ball gown, Mama decided there should be six.

Mama preferred yellow ribands for all trimmings of undergarments. She liked the color.

"But, Mama," Lucie protested feebly, "yellow is unlucky to a bride. I shall be jealous of my husband——"

"Sebastian would be the last man to give you cause for jealousy," Mama decided firmly. "You might live out your days in a frock of clear-starched gold cloth, and you would be happy or unhappy, depending on yourself. Anyhow, a wife is due to be jealous, yellow or no yellow—I can tell you that, Miss—when the man is one like Sebastian."

In the night Lucie remembered her mother's words. Needless to say, she did not press, nor even begin, arguments with Mama. Yet with herself she carried on an interminable argument. This marriage seemed not half so simple as Mama put it. And must she be jealous of Sebastian? What agony! She knew that never had Sebastian spent all his days watching his mother and sister design and knot counterpanes! If she should make of herself the most capable of wives, and Sebastian proved restive—then what! Mama was luckily married, as a blind man could see, yet with Papa it was he who was always saying: "Just as you will, my love," or "As you say, Julia." If she fuss-budgeted all of a day over a lazy firewood slave, he soothed her instead of pointing out to her the fact that she demanded more than a just service from her slaves. Moreover, so far as Lucie could see, Mama made no least effort toward being a good wife—that is, no more than allowing people to address her as Mistress Bradley Birdsong. In wifehood, as in all things, she followed her own fancies, with little thought to any other soul.

On the other hand there was Mama's sister, Sully, who had married that wild Jeb Christy! Aunt Sully was far sweeter, gentle-tongued and loving-hearted and lovable. No outsider would ever dream that Aunt Sully was so miserably married. Many days there was not a copper penny in her petticoat pocket, and nothing to cook. Many days her children were taunted at the academy because of their father's drunken brawling and wenching. Aunt Sully's oldest boy had run away to sea when he was two months past thirteen years old. Until you saw Aunt Sully's head bowed, you could not say her heart was broken, though; you could only say that Jeb Christy had tried to break it. Mama would not help Aunt Sully. None of her family would help her, because she was warned when she married Christy that he was worthless and a cad. But Lucie had seen him take Aunt Sully's face between his palms and kiss her brow, and the tip of her nose, and her chin, and last her lips, and he would storm: "Why did you not get yourself a better man?" and she would tell him, "Because I wanted you, Jeb Christy!" Then he would see her smile, and she would keep the smile till he came home drunk again.

It all troubled Lucie, for there was more than a small resemblance to Uncle Jeb in Sebastian's ready curse and his overly handsome eyes.

Drat his never writing her! She sent her thoughts toward him, hoping they would, like white doves, light about him and bring him peace.

Any other morning she could go walking, but not in this damp weather; the ground was not yet dry enough, Mama said. Now there was naught to do but call her body keep and have a poultice of milkweed wash and sour cream and powdered almonds to whiten her skin—or have the girl wash her hair and tie it up in rags. Yet when she tried it, Aretha had one of her sullen days and Lucie was ill from the trial of her hair being done before the water was cool. She would not take Aretha with her when she married Sebastian. Papa must give her another body maid for a wedding gift. If he could find one. . . .

Mama's writing quill went on, scratching its small complaining to Papa, or Aunt Irina in Italy. If only Mama would take her meals downstairs in the ordinary, this place would take on more excitement. But no, Mama said the ordinary was no place for ladies. So all their meals came up in covered trenchers, the china clinking all the way up the corridor. Mama would scold Aretha, and her own woman, Hurlburt, if a fat fly followed the sugar about. The food was long-cooked and deftly seasoned, Lucie thought. Madame

Lateuse had a reputation all up and down the seaboard. But Mama would complain of this or that or the other.

Lucie liked Madame Lateuse ever so much. Sometimes she came up with the meals, to see that a pudding was not overcreamed or a sauce too hot or too mild. There was a faint scent of asafetida and vinegar hanging about her, but she was jovial and friendly, and Lucie craved to talk with her. Delicately but carefully Lucie held her breath when Madame came too near. She wore a full-skirted, high-yoked frock of indigo-dyed cotton, and about her big middle was swung a thong from which a handful of keys jangled and jounced as she walked heavily about. Her manners gave her the appearance of a jovial monk. Mama said Madame *could* wear stays since she was so much in the company of men. Her hips *were* a trifle forthright; her jolly eyes were near to buried in her good, frank face. On the left side of her chin was a brown mole which grew three hairs; never had Lucie desired any small thing in life so much as she wished to extract those three hairs from that mole.

When they were new at the tavern, Madame had taken Lucie's chin in her hands and had said:

"So you're to be married to young Ratcliff. I know him well. Ah, he's a good man to catch. So you're to be married in three months— well, well. He will love you, if I know him. He will love you," and she went laughing down the corridor. Mama did not dare call down Madame. She was famous all the way to New York and back for telling people what she pleased. Mama was puffed up like a lioness disturbed, but she said nothing. "Madame!" was all Mama said, and you could hear Madame laughing going down the stairs, her keys jangling and dancing at her waist, as though they were laughing, too.

Lucie thought Madame's words over carefully. There was a tinge of French accent through them, but not much more than garlic will season a saddle of mutton. Madame had been long in this country. Lucie thought the words over. She saw no cause for laughter. True, Sebastian would love her, she hoped in all faith, for all the years till she died.

Suddenly Lucie began to sob as she thought about Sebastian and what Madame had replied.

"God's mercy!" cried Mama, and she dropped the quill hurriedly and ink sprawled across the letter form, ruining the carefully set words. So suddenly did Mama rise from the writing table that she near burst a seam in her left sleeve.

"God's grace!" Mama said.

Just at that awful moment there came a thudding at the door. Mama was so fuddled that she opened the door before Lucie could properly dry her eyes.

There at the door was standing a girl in a black country bonnet and a black fur shoulder throw. The girl was straight-backed and high-chinned, though she was not so tall as Lucie. She had somewhere about her the air of an Indian runner you see halting, heavy with his message, eyes heedful, face awaiting a new command.

"Come, girl, what can the matter be?" Mama asked peevishly.

Lebanon's face lost its listening look.

"I am Lebanon Fairgale," she said. "I live south of here, by twenty miles. The Ratcliff gentlemen have been staying at our house." She unfolded her hands and folded them fast again. (What in God's loving-kindness *had* she come to say? Why had she come at all?)

"Well?" the old woman said, waiting. Beyond her Lebanon could see the fair-haired girl he was to marry.

Lebanon would have given a lot then to run away, suddenly as a child.

"Fernald d'Aussy is a friend of mine. . . . He said . . ."

"Who!" the woman asked, rearing her shoulders the least bit impatiently.

"He keeps the bar for Madame," Lebanon amended lamely.

"The *bar!*" Mistress Birdsong was really nettled now.

Lebanon saw the fair-haired girl Sebastian was going to marry. She noted each little newness about that one who held his affections fast. Lucie stood properly, waiting to see what came of this matter. Lebanon decided that Lucie was newly grown and lovely in her way, a way of softness and delicacy. Lebanon could have hated her the more heartily if it were not for that air of tenderness, as though she could be bitterly hurt with but little effort. Lebanon's eyes had long been accustomed to taking in much in the very small fraction of a long moment—a deer's leap, a bird's startled flight. Now she saw Lucie's white hands quivering faintly on the lion's mane along the foot of the bed. They were white and silk-skinned as a baby's; they would be gloved against wind and sun. Lucie was gloved against hurts herself, Lebanon thought, and so must she always be.

Lebanon had thought she would say: I have an hour or two to spend and no way to spend it, and I thought I would spend it here, sitting and talking with you.

That was Fernald's bright thought.

Now she knew she could not say that. There was no welcome here, and she had in any case seen what she had come to see: the build of Lucie's face and the trend of her heart.

Lebanon's face shone a little. "I thought I would tell you your men are in town and will soon be along, if they have not already come," she said.

"Mama!" cried Lucie.

"Lucie! Don't burst my ears," Mama rebuked her.

Lebanon had not been asked in, to touch her deerskin shoes to the red roses of the carpet. Mistress Birdsong minced her mouth and got out a polite word:

"Our thanks to you," she said. "Good day."

There was nothing to do but go. Lebanon went away hating them and all the world. Lucie would have asked her in for teacake and blackberry wine if one could judge her face. But not that old she-beef! The old lady's eyes had snapped: What trash is this come to my door!

Lebanon fumbled her way back to Fernald's counter. "It was a mistake to go," she said.

"I knew it would be," he said. "But you would never have been contented till you did."

Suddenly behind her she heard a step.

"Why, here you are," Sebastian said. "I have looked everywhere for you. I wished you to eat a little snack with me, if you will pardon me while I go and speak a moment with friends who are staying here. I'll be down directly."

She was like putty under the sound of his voice.

Never was there such a dinner as that one! The oleanders leaned

in, leafed in their leathery fronds. Rain came suddenly again and
beat on the glass panes till the gold curtains swerved in against the
room. And there was a little table, so narrow betwixt their faces
and their hands. There was a white cloth and they two alone.

They spoke little. Now they could talk together—and found there
was nothing to say, nothing that would not be too much or too
little.

They were alone, in a monstrous world beset all about by conceal-
ing walls of circumstance and mighty reaches of time. Yet they were
bound together here in this little place by a thing that would never
loose them. They might forget it now and then, but when they remembered, this time would be strong and complete again, no way
moldered or time-eaten, perfect to keep.

Fernald watched the play, thinking: He is a cad; he has no good
intention. Fernald did not like the way of things. He would speak
to Crease Fairgale of this, yet that would only make a bad matter
worse.

Chapter 4

IT WAS SPRING NOW, true spring, with leaves feathered out and the
world new again, water singing white in the rivers, and the black
land yearning for seed. Little fruit trees stood fuming in flowers on
the horizons, and the plum trees looked as though a thousand nuns
had stitched and starched a long time for this.

On their gaunt, blackened boughs the trees wore leaf buds and
flowers in dim garlands, and full-feathered leaves. When one looked
up through the trees it was as though green dusk lay high on all the
black twigs. After this there could come only full summer. The sky
was far and blue, but busy with making spring. New winds were
scudding about; little clouds were restless and wild, scattering before the wind.

Now when she looked on Sebastian, Lebanon felt a sudden failing
of her heart. Sebastian told her that the world is more round than
a bird's egg, that this dark star is one of a company of motley stars

and small suns and burnt worlds that walk lonesome, carefully marked paths in heaven.

With a quiet face Lebanon considered his words.

"No," she said. "That is past any sane man's belief."

"I would not give *you* a lie," he assured her.

"Who told you any such thing?" she asked.

"You can find it in any number of books," he said.

"But no fool could ever prove any such fool thing," she argued. "Who ever walked up there in all that business?"

"It is in books," he said.

He did not know she could not read a book.

She leaned her head against the rough body of a pine; her eyes were on the white sky. A slow wind from the south seethed in the pine tops over their heads. Although her reason told her that Sebastian would never impugn his honor, her imagination could not but dwell on the bliss that their marriage would be. She went on thinking how she might learn knowledge so that she could be a credit to this man, and his house in Baltimore, and his sister Margrette, and his mother, whose name was Silena. Would his mother love her, or try to? Would his sister make room in the Ratcliff family for her?

I will slave to please them all, Lebanon was thinking.

Crease could teach her letters, but where was she to find the knowledge a lady knows? One thing certain: she must learn to write, else how could she ever speak to him when he was absent from her? And she must learn to read so that she could make out his words to her from afar.

If she had money, she could buy a schooled slave to read and write for her. She would love the slave and pity him. All the slaves she had seen in town were a piteous lot, meek-mouthed and grief-eyed. Or maybe she could find a quick-witted white the judge would have bound to Crease, to help with the house and field, to paint and polish the floor, and set in glass windows and weave woolen carpets.

She decided to tell Sebastian that she had no schooling and did not know where to look for any.

"I never had schooling," she said, her body proudly taut against the rough-barked pine. Then to defend her father from ridicule, she went on: "We lived a ways from town, and maybe there was no money for a tutor, and Lollie was dead."

Sebastian was scornful in short, hot words:

"And a good thing, too. I hate seminary women." (Lucie Birdsong had gone to Forth's Seminary for Young Women, for Lebanon had heard Sebastian say so!) "I have never believed schooling a good thing for a woman; all they learn to do is mou and mince."

Never did she know, till the day she died, whether he held any such opinion, or only said such words to comfort her ignorance.

In his fingers he was crumbling dried seed panicles of grass from last autumn. He had plucked them idly from a low cluster of bush heads. There was his mouth, free to her kissing if she willed it. And there were her hands free for his holding, if he desired to hold them. Yet her hands clung to the rough-barked pine and his mouth stayed where it was. This was no common love affair, they both knew, so best handle it carefully. He had kissed her once in a black, blowy midnight, and that was sufficient for now. They needed no long words of explanation, and they required no warm hand-holding.

Lebanon was moon-eyed these days. Her heart went about and about in the manner of a gay-painted carrousel she saw once at an autumn fair in town. Children were riding around and around on it, and she had wished to ride, too, but Crease had a slim purse at the time. The little painted horses went forever, following the pull of two living horses that went round and round in a tramped-earth ring inside the carrousel. They moved on fixed, stamping forefeet and woodenly flexed haunches, bearing the laughing children forever nowhere.

Now near to a month Rafe and Sebastian had idled in the swamp, with Luke gone back North.

They rode into Birdtown, and were soon back, pleading a pretext of the Ratcliff Lumber Company. But they did not fool themselves, nor anyone else. It was a pleasant time, and as the days passed they knew to hold these days, for they would not be back soon—they or the days.

By nights they would sit beside the fire and talk. Crease would tell a tale of his father's time, when this country was new. No man would wager a copper penny on the Colonies then. One had better talk two ways and stay in with the Tories. But there were men back there who did not talk two ways, and hung on. Sure enough, the matter wore itself out, and they had a capital in Philadelphia and the whole thing going.

It all seemed a long time ago, as they talked of it. Why, not twenty-five years gone one could have bivouacked with old Daniel Boone, with a saddle for a pillow and stars for candles, guessing the way from a chart drawn in sand by a green twig in the hands of a friendly stranger, sleeping with a pistol half-cocked and loaded rifle at hand.

"If I were young again, I'd go West," Crease said. And Uncle Rafe grunted assent.

Once when a good tale was ended Sebastian looked toward Lebanon and wished to call her name and say, "Let's go." But that was as far as his courage went.

"Why are we buried here in these low bogs of content," Crease would ask himself and Rafe, "with the world burning down in good chances?"

But Rafe said, "You pay much the same price for a fortune wherever you seek and find it: fear of death and the beginning of all evil."

Sebastian dreamed of taking Lebanon with him, out of all this, and going West. They would never be heard of again, except maybe a letter once a year. He and Lebanon would go into oblivion together. The more he thought of it, the stronger grew his desire.

There was but one thing wrong with it: he would be running away from things, turning his back on his own problems. It would trouble him, the things people said two thousand miles away. He could never be with Lebanon here. He must go away to be with her; he must be no more than a runagate thief losing himself to westward. Or would he find himself? Was this courage or cowardice which counseled him against dropping this life and finding another? Sometimes it seemed cowardice, for how rich and full life would be in a far settlement, with Lebanon in a door to meet him, all cares behind—or at least, all old cares behind! He would work like a common laborer. He would take a new name, if necessary, for a Ratcliff does not undertake a life and then drop it. He would make a new settlement that would stand a hundred years from now. "Lebanon" they would call it, Lebanon in the Californias, Lebanon somewhere in Northwest Territory, Lebanon down in a little gold desert high up in New Mechiko Province. All he must do was build a house and lay in a few stores and make rooms enough to sleep and feed travelers—have hams cured, and fresh water, horses to lend and sell, a smithy, some whisky laid in—and he would have established a town. Sebastian fancied such a new beginning. In Crease Fairgale's fire flames he could see store fronts rising, cobbled streets lengthening, and a new rooftree always going up here and there. He and Lebanon would keep the tavern as a beginning, somewhat like Madame Lateuse's—only it would be called "Lebanon's." Lebanon would have slaves to help her run the tavern. With a stage-route contract he could make a money business of it.

Once he came near to speaking of such a venture to Crease:

"You never seriously considered going West, did you?" asked Sebastian.

Joel, listening, his eyes full of brazen adventure, turned his face full toward the fire and saw in the fire much the same things Sebastian had seen.

"Lawksamercy, no," Crease said, soberly. "I was only talking of what might be if a man were young and venturesome."

"I am young," Sebastian said, and bit his lower lip.

Lebanon was gone to bed, and a good thing, too. Uncle Rafe was already snoring.

"I knew these things here would pan out for me, and they have," Crease said to Sebastian. "The other thing was gold away off in a wild mountain, and maybe I'd find it and maybe I wouldn't."

Later Sebastian lay on the wall cot and thought, with all his thoughts gone West, to find bright country where gold lies in common earth to dig out. All a man can think of when he thinks West is gold. But Lebanon was the gold Sebastian wished to hoard, West or East.

Uncle Rafe said they would have to go back now.

Sebastian had secretly hoped that Mistress Birdsong would take her daughter North again and stumble on a man she liked better, and would so break the betrothal. Or perhaps the Birdsongs would come to consider him a trifling whiffet of a man idling so long at hunting and fishing and would herd Lucie back home and give her wedding-word to a better man, more sensible in his ways. There was no means by which he could effect this, without seeming to have a heavy hand in the matter. He was promised; his word was hers, and she must hand it back to him. He could not demand it; his name would be anathema up and down the seaboard.

He even went so far as to pen a withdrawal note to Lucie, knowing he would never let her eyes see it.

Honored Miss Birdsong:

Your name remains high in my personal esteem. I lie ill of swamp fever and it would be as well that you await my return no longer in Birdtown but return with your worthy mother North again to Baltimore. I doubt that I shall be in such state even by autumn as to be able to carry out our wedding agreement as planned. I have considered your sentiments in this matter, and hereby express the hope that if for any reason you feel desirous of breaking our betrothal you shall do so, knowing I shall lay no least blame at the door of your heart.

> *Your loving and obedient servant,*
> Sebastian Cheswick Ratcliff, Esq.

It was a pretty letter.

All that ailed it was that it was a lie. Ratcliff men do not lie. When they say yes or no, or state a fact, one can depend on the words of their mouths. Their mothers, the Ratcliff women, brought them up to speak the truth.

Sebastian came as near as he dared to telling Uncle Rafe how things lay. Would Uncle Rafe take any such letter into Birdtown and give it to Lucie? One could never tell. And then he found again that there was never any need to tell Uncle Rafe anything any time. Uncle Rafe always knew it before it happened.

"Sebastian, my boy," he said, "you're twenty-one and so as much a man as me, but don't you consider we'd better be going?"

They were sitting by the fire, alone, their stockinged feet to the last of the bright flames. Then Sebastian blurted out:

"I am all but in love with this girl . . ."

Then he hid his brow in his hands.

Uncle Rafe set his fingers together, and his eyes narrowed on the fire.

"Well . . ." he said. And he sighed. "There are some matters one man will not advise another man in, and one of them is loving a woman. I made a big mistake a long time ago, I thought. I do not know. All I know is that a man must do what he must do, and the honorable way is the easiest way. At this moment I do not know what you could do about Miss Lucie Birdsong and not prove yourself a lout. It would all boil down to how much and what manner of love you bear toward Lebanon Fairgale. I'll say no more than that, for you have brains and heart aplenty to solve your own problems, if you do not get too close in up against them. Stand off, boy, and look at it forty years from now. . . ."

It was solved, then—for Uncle Rafe had unthinkingly pronounced his opinion, for all his sympathy. "Miss Lucie Birdsong," he had said. "Lebanon Fairgale," he had said. Sebastian thought sadly: A woman is poor without a "Miss" to her name. It angered him secretly and shamed him yet more secretly.

He stood slowly, making a mock yawn. "Not much to do and not prove myself the lout, sir," he said slowly.

"Did I say the wrong thing now?" asked Uncle Rafe.

"Indeed, no, sir!" Sebastian replied formally, fondly. "You did not *say*, did you?"

But Rafe went to bed wondering why he could not keep his mouth tight shut. Trouble was he loved the boy. Lebanon Fairgale was pretty as any thousand other women, and had more common sense. All the trouble, as Sebastian might see it, was that she was not good enough to marry a Ratcliff. Maybe he would fear to take her home to Baltimore. But then again if Sebastian could endure the breach, it would heal. Lebanon's tongue had no silken way with words—in truth, there was a slight savage roughness to it. Even so, Rafe thought more highly of Lebanon than he thought of the pretty doll Lucie, whom her mother had hung up as bright bait for Sebastian. He had gulped her down, Heaven knew why, and now was snagged pretty as any. Rafe would not be one to break up Sebastian's handfast with Lucie Birdsong; he never believed in meddling in another man's life. But he would not move a muscle if Lebanon broke the handfast. Rafe wished Sebastian would tear loose and leave out for parts unknown and take the girl Lebanon for luggage. He would not tell of this mad, sultry wish, but it was there. Just once he would like to see a man cut free and ride wild and see where he would camp when day was done. Lebanon did not know— or care—sattinette from russet cloth, or a double rose-cut diamond fleur-de-luce from a throat lacet of red glass. But she had other knowledge: she could hamstring a deer and bake his haunch in sweetened vinegar and pepper root. Rafe had seen her do both, so he knew. She knew how to cut and sew a boot to bear a certain foot. He had seen her do it. She knew the uses of moonseed root for urinary complaint. She had all but cured him of his old night trouble. She had a whole medicinal garden on a kitchen shelf, and a green one at the side of her garden—velvetleaf and comfrey and borage and homewort. She knew that wild parsnips and sassy bark are poison, that aloes have a cathartic virtue, that butterfly weed will cool a chest cold, that pinkroot is a prime vermifuge. She was an apothecary a long way from a university of learning. Maybe her fingers would be helpless on the strings of a viola da braccio if one were set inside her arms, yet she would know what to do with a brawl-lunged infant of her own; how to feed him when he cried for more ninny; how to trounce him if he needed it; how to wash him; how to name him and make him hold to pride in his name; how to teach him to sit still in meetinghouse; how to be a man! Further, she would know how to content his father the while!

Lebanon would have plenty for her man and children to eat; Rafe could swear to that. There was always a hotchpotch of meat and dumplings on her hearth, potatoes cooling in the ashes, or new meat roasting so you could smell it a cotton field away. Always Lebanon's washing was white, riding the line, whipping in clean wind.

Rafe's eyelids were netted up in mischief wrinkles. Sebastian was no tamehearted witling to heave up the dragging of Lucie Birdsong's dress tail all the rest of his life! Her children would be spindling and flower-faced. Laid out on lace and silk pillows Sebastian's children would be, on a slave's lap that did nothing but hold that one spoiled young 'un. "Don't run," their dear grandmamma would call, "or you'll overflush your face. . . . Don't jump about so, or you'll overturn your little liver!" Just so had Lucie been brought up till her fingers were afraid to touch the earth, she was that dainty-minded. It was all she could do to press hard on the keys of a pianoforte.

But Sebastian . . .

Rafe wanted to say: Up anchor, son! Tear out! Go from here! Take Lebanon all the way to the Californias, and kiss her in a dark night for your old uncle Rafe. Love her the way a frontiersman loves his woman, knowing they may die in an Indian fire tonight. There should be desperation to a man's days on earth. Brother Jardine had dared a man to cross a line drawn on the floor by a burnt-out coal. The man stepped over, and Jardine killed him. Sebastian would have a softness from his mother, but some of his father's iron will, too. Jardine was his father, and he went down on a ship, they supposed, for the ship never came back to port.

That next night Lebanon had a jar of spring flowers on the eating table in the kitchen. Always when he rose from eating, Sebastian would take a flower from the pot and bring it on up to the big room, and there would be the flower in his hands, and he toying with it. Lebanon these nights would sometimes have in her hands a music pipe that she had fashioned from reeds, bracing and binding them with a red-stained slender tie of parfleche. She would begin to blow on the pipes, making a soft tune. Sebastian would set his locked hands behind his head, and the flower would lie withering on his knee. There was great contentment by this fire. Sometimes Joel would be cleaning his gun. And Crease would watch the fire, and now and then lay his hand over his stomach where the hard fire burned, no matter what he ate. Every mouth would be hushed, except the cool brown mouths of Lebanon's fluting reeds making music in the firelight. There was peace here, and no house can falsify peace for so long a time.

On this night Lebanon sang a song:

> *"Build for me a bed of clay, lay me down to sleep;*
> *Rough and stony is the way, now the night is deep.*

"I will take you there with me, in my heart to keep;
Lonely you will never be, oh, sweeting, do not weep!"

Sebastian's face was stony and sad, hearing the song, and even Lebanon's face had a gray look to it. They were saying one of many small and final good-bys, and one could feel it. Sebastian sat with his hands locked behind his head, his face like iron toward the fire.

Lebanon was desperate in her thinking. Her heart most urgently besought him to stay with her, knowing he could not. Her fingers went on playing softly on the reeds of the Panpipe. (My heart is a book for your reading. There are no long and hard words in it. Read it and tell me what it says, back to me again: I-love-you—for I have never learned my letters.)

He took his eyes from the fire and looked in her face, love bold in his eyes. It was as though he had leaped across the hard flooring and had caught her shoulders in his big hands; he could feel her shoulders fragile in the gripping of his hands, and she could feel his kiss of love. She could feel her face close against his face, though they were yards apart across the warm hearth and the talk of Crease was going on. You are sweet, he told her, with the hard caress of his eyes. How sweet?—she smiled in one corner of her lips, saying nothing at all.

The trial of his eyes in hers caused Lebanon to hold the little pipe of reeds too closely. She had cut and dried them. Now the longest reed broke against her bodice with a slight crackle of dead reed. "Oh, now," Lebanon said, glooming over the little musicmaker. "I broke it with my clumsiness."

They were words which Sebastian would remember forever after; this matter betwixt them would never be broken by any clumsiness.

"I'll have to find another reed of the same size and mend it," she said, smoothing the broken reed under the soft thick of her thumb.

Before she slept she set pannikins of warm mush for Lady and Caesar beyond the kitchen door. She swept the hearth clean again of dust that would gather as fresh pine knots were thrown to the fire. From her workbox she took some scarlet glass beads to be strung on strong fioselle for a waistband. She had found the beads in her mother's things in the loft. The chest was covered in pigskin and had brass bands, and in nailheads there was set a small design of her mother's name: L.J.F.—Lollie Justice Fairgale.

Lebanon had a mind to make a long frock of black goods, silk if she could get it, and it would be fastened at the throat with a brooch of pearls. She could wear this bead belt with the black dress, if she liked.

Rafe mumbled his apologies and went off yawning to the upper shed room.

"And what might you be doing now with all that?" Crease asked.

"Oh . . . nothing much, I reckon," she said. "A belt, or something."

Then Sebastian said:

"My mother has a trinket made in the form of a fleur-de-luce. My father gave it to her when they were married. It is of pearls and diamonds and rubies. I wish you could see it."

"I like the fleur-de-luce as well as any flowering thing," Lebanon said, bending assiduously to the red beads and the strong fioselle. (So his mother has a fleur-de-luce of gold and diamonds and pearls and rubies. . . .) Then it all came back to her, the manner in which she envisioned him: a polished table, and swapping talk with laced and ribanded peppercorns like Miss Lucie Birdsong, sitting too long with bottles of wine, fingering cruets of spice, downing, one after another, caudle-cups of negus. She could see Sebastian's hands soft on silver forks. She could see him squeeze a woman's fingers under crimson damask.

Then she said openly, for Crease and Joel to hear, too:

"My mother had a fan of egret plumes. It's wrapped in lining silk in the loft. I saw it today when I was getting out these beads. You should see it. Papa gave it to her when they were married."

For a workbox she had a flat-bottomed gourd which she had chosen when it was green. She had notched the two halves and carefully dried it in not-too-hot sun. It was mottled and sweet-smelling, and its notches fitted exactly in one another, in light latchets.

Sebastian took the work gourd into his hands, after Crease and Joel had said a quiet good night.

"The first night here, or one of the nights, I dreamed that you gave me a drink of water from a gourd," he said.

She nodded her head. "I have prayed to dream of you, but I cannot make it come true in my own head." Then suddenly she exclaimed: "Your boots are wet!"

She knelt and unlaced his boots, even against his soft denial, and eased them from his feet. She brought the foot basin and a load of warm water in it, and dusted alum powder into it. He set his feet into the water, as though they were fast-married. She went back to beading while his feet took ease from the hot water. He did not look anyway strange to her, sitting there with his boots and stockings off and his feet bared to his knees. She took down her hair and began to brush it with the colt's-tail brush, as she did each night, there before the fire. Suddenly his feet stumbled in the foot bath and he reached and took her hands. She called his name just once, her lips scarce moving, and the cry was low and lonely in the room. She clenched her hands within his hands and lifted her face toward the dark roof and beyond it toward the cold stars. "I cannot bear your absence," she told him hotly. "Any fool knows you will never come back."

Her face was hidden against his breast; her tears went quickly and quietly into the washed linnen over his heart. He kissed her wet face as though it were the sweet countenance of an angel.

"We'll go and gather egret plumes first thing in the morning. Leaving after dinner instead of at daybreak cannot greatly upset matters," she said.

Yet, even so, it did.

Chapter 5

IT WAS DARK STILL as they stepped from the door block and went down the narrow kitchen walk that was bordered by two old bay trees and new-growing lily bulbs. These were Lebanon's fleur-de-luces, the tips of their leaves sharp-drawn as poniards. Lebanon reached low and plucked a little branch of coronation blooming white in darkness and gave it to Sebastian's hand. There were on the spike five pale blossoms, bunched carelessly and smelling like a lady's powder closet.

There was no gate here toward the swamp. At night the cows and sheep were penned in the barn lot, running wild in daytime. The pigs ran wild always. The chickens still roosted in the crab-apple trees in preference to the fowl house Joel had mended.

A clatter of geese went up before Lebanon's and Sebastian's feet, and the ducks stirred softly. Crease kept them for feathers, and to eat, though Lebanon could catch a brace of wild fowl any time in the shallows of the swamp ponds with a little corn scattered on a rabbit trap two feet under water. Lebanon had saved goose down till there were feather beds enough to dower ten brides away from this house.

Old Caesar wanted to go, too. He curveted lazily about them, whimpering in complaint that Lady could go when he was left home. "Go back, Caesar!" Lebanon stormed, and the old fellow turned away. Lady frisked ahead, her tail quick as a rabbit's in the dark.

They must be at the egret rookery before sunup if they were to catch the flocking egrets. Nesting spoils the white tail plumes, and it was nigh to time for nesting. Lebanon craved for Sebastian to see the egrets falling and rising, like guided smoke.

In the thick muck where the water began, two miles from home, Crease's old dugout was bogged down. All about its bow were deer sign, small heart-shaped stampings where the deer had come to drink—fresh sign, the impressions clear in the mud. Lady whimpered, wishing to know if Lebanon would give her leave to go in the dugout, too. The little dog lay down in the bottom, her nose scenting toward newness over the rounded side.

Deep through the overhanging trees Lebanon poled the boat, out through sleeping bayous where now and then a loon cried sharply, wary of their coming. Night things were still out, and they could hear the night stir of the swamp. Later, in the east, the sky would be clear carnelian, but now there was no sign. Sebastian wrapped his camlet cloak closer about him.

Little by little the sky came to that time before earliest morning.

"I never saw a day born before this," he said, his lips hard to manage in the cold.

"That is a strange thing to say," she said.

She was not cold; she was hot from pulling the pole. She wore a woolen vest and the deerskin jacket. Sebastian protested her poling whilst he sat, but he would jam the boat on a mudbank, first thing, and she knew it.

In the east there was a flow of soft, sunrise light. Of a sudden the birds were loud in the thickets and swift in the boughs of the trees.

"It was a jay, this time," Lebanon said.

There was a blue going of wings across their sight. And then, sure enough, the jay called derisively, reproaching the swamp for laziness.

Sebastian was taking in a new manner of life through his eyes and ears; even to his nostrils came a new scent—the thick, ancient, rotten-sweet odor of the swamp, clean carrion of leaf and bough and bone.

The mists began to stir and rise, eddying and drifting as the air stirred. In the bottom of the dugout, where Lady lay decorously, there was a flat box of sand for the building of a fire if they should be foundered somewhere in the swamp. Lebanon's musket lay ready-loaded beside the sandbox. She never knew when she might sight a choice kill, or when a gator might prove dangerous. Lebanon had brought along a few flinders of resinous wood for the building of a fire, if they should need one, and the gator hook and the hunting knife. In a flasket of peeled honeysuckle vines she had brought biscuits, too, and fried ham.

In the strain and warmth of poling she threw aside her hood. She thrust the dugout forward by hard leaning on the sapling pole. Her hair was pale in the dark.

Sebastian balanced the stern end, sitting on the scarred bottom of the dugout. His broad, everyday wool hat was pulled low on his brow. White about his throat a scarflet of carmelite part way hid his beard. He watched the swamp, but more he watched Lebanon. For all the lightness of her bones and the smallness of her waist, the pulling seemed little labor to her.

"I could span your waist with my two hands, if I tried," he said, to tease her. "Yet the poling seems an easy task for you."

"I was born to it," she said, blushing pink.

"So you were," he said, studying her, to her discomfiture.

"Habit makes us weak or strong," she said, to say something.

"Those words are wise enough to go in a book," he said. "Someday I will write a book about you."

"Oh, never do!" she said desperately.

"If a man were tilted in these trees watching us, he would think me a carlot, for fair," Sebastian said, "allowing a woman to pole, whilst I sit."

"It pleases me to serve you," she said, but looked away from him when she said it.

Sebastian's eyes were on her face, modeled clearly there above her shoulder against a slow screen of dark swamp growth. She had for this morning's jaunt braided her hair, and it was bound to her head in a sleek coronet, with shining walnut pins, rubbed to a shine with oil of olives and a woolen cloth. Sebastian had watched her shine them by the fire at night. High on her cheeks a dust of color had gathered. Her breathing came fast and regular and full. Her lips were parted, and there was on them a shining of the wet of her mouth. There was silvered sweat on her upper lip and in the half-moon cleft of her chin. Never had he studied any face so closely as he was studying Lebanon's. Clear and fresh and living, unchanged and never lost, he would keep this face and this hour and this place.

They came upon the shore of a crowded cypress knoll set low in black coiling water. They had come a long way south, and now the day was full and the sun near to showing its face on earth. Suddenly she lifted her hand, and he turned his eyes from her face, and there, a little distance beyond, were the egrets rising in spirals like blown snow. They circled high over the trees, crying low to one another. The dugout was stilled now, and nothing moved but the leaves and those white birds.

Lebanon shoved home the dugout on a low mudbank. They softly footed it through the undergrowth. Her cowhide boots bogged in wet ooze, and he spoiled the shine of his second-best boots. He slipped on a lichened log and would have cursed but for the quiet. The air was sweet in bitter jessamine scent.

Lebanon sighted the musket across the flintlock and saw the wavering white bird there. There was a powder flash, and the stock thudded against her shoulder. The bird fell, its wings frantically fighting a long fall. The long shafts of snow circled toward black ooze.

When Lebanon lifted the bird in her hand, its small, sleek head was gone, yet its body struggled a little still, headless and hopeless. Luckily it had fallen on dead brush and leaves from last year. No mud or blood stained its tail plumes, long and silken and drooping. So delicately were the feathers fashioned that even the quills were nigh as small as hairs. With a fine, quick hand, Lebanon lifted the bird. With her barlow knife she clipped out the four tail plumes. She laid the four plumes on his palm.

Mad from the sound of the gun's firing, the flocking egrets circled and circled beyond their rookery. Higher than the others, a lone bird circled, crying. Far off in the swamp a fox barked, loped a little way, and barked again, farther still.

"In some places they are precious as water pearls," Lebanon said, her eyes on his hand and the little weight of feathers. Her eyes had fathomed Sebastian's face. He had not much liked the killing of this bird. He felt a quiet distaste. He was a gentle man, squeamish as to blood and murder.

"Four is enough for a lady's evening cap," she went on talking. "Thrust in the front of a pearl hood, they would be pretty, indeed. I saw such a cap in a shop in Birdtown."

She was watching his face. He knew she was giving him these feathers to be a pretty trifle on Lucie Birdsong's head in Baltimore —to discipline herself more than to please him or Lucie Birdsong.

For all the delicacy and lightness of the feathers, they were a clumsy burden to be carried back to the dugout. Sebastian felt them heavy on his fingers.

When they went back to the dugout the tidewaters were silvered and black. They could see lagoons columned in cypress trunks, paved in marble water and roofed in greening boughs. There were meadows of young grass on the islands that went softly by the dugout, and seas of sedge of a deep ivory color from last autumn.

The old dugout followed the bend of Lebanon's will as a called hound or an old horse. Years and years gone, Crease had laid a fire against a felled tree to make this dugout. Crease was proud of the little boat. It was of light cypress, slender-waisted and deep-bodied. This dugout that was weeks in making was easy to handle, light of weight, yet able to hold its balance in a strong current. Water is not wearing to a cypress that lives out its long life in water. The dugout had long since lost its burn scars. Now it was weathered, pale and grayed. Long since it was smooth-polished, first by a stone scraper in Crease's hands, further by the wearing of time.

Lebanon handled the dugout lightly as a cypress ball riding the water. By going westward past three stocky little islands deep in sedge, there was a sight Lebanon wished Sebastian to see. The sight lay past a larger horned island set deep in water, a little south by west. Here was all green wall and coiling water. Lebanon pointed out landmarks, a broken stump, three trees growing embraced, but it was all water and sky and growth to Sebastian. Loons took to the air at their quiet passing. They could hear gators waking and shuffling down into the water before they came to view, unless they surprised one sleeping, and then he hasted to get from there—leaving slow foam on the water.

Lebanon watched the marish shores—for that is the first lesson one learns. Through the tree-hooded, moss-hung wilderness they passed, on black slough and slow, concealed rivers winding among reeded islands. Some of the little islands were clear, sedged and bright under the hard morning sun. Some were matted and thickety. Now deeper in the swamp, they caught gators sleeping sullenly at the water's edge, and deer sucking daintily at the mirrored black water.

Now the sky was bright as white brass. Sunlight burned on the water in tremulous, blinding glare. Here and yonder, like guideposts in lost waters, stood the old eagles' nests in the tops of the oldest cypresses, safe from all things but wind and rain and lightning. Lebanon knew every eagle nest. They were markers of distance and place. Each had some small peculiarity of design or position—a forked underbrace, or some such thing. Now and then they could hear the lusty, sharp screaming of an eagle that eyed the little dugout.

Past an eddying junction of currents the dugout moved softly as a seasoned log might float on its own will. Suddenly Lebanon thrust the pole hard down, brought the boat to rest against the current's pull, and headed the prow into a little shore.

"Shut your eyelids down," she told him softly. Now the boat moved no more, but rested in the ebb of a shore. She moved it six yards farther.

He had closed his eyes, imagining she wished to kiss him here in the deep of the swamp. His breath began to hurry to meet that kiss.

When she had the dugout exactly to please her, she stilled it again finally.

"Open your eyes," she told him.

And he opened his eyes.

She stood and smiled into his eyes, and she did not kiss him, and he was a little disappointed, thinking that she did not love him as he loved her.

Heaped in sudden, wild splendor, he saw a bank of flowers—a low hill of flowers—no more than that. Morning-glories he would call them, yet they were large as coffee mugs in the tavern. Lebanon called them sunflowers, a merry mistaking, he thought.

"They're closed by high sun," she said. "They'll have none but morning light on their faces."

It was a sight to fill his eyes to fullness. These flowers were massed lightly and piled deep, yet never crushing one another. This might be the flower foundry of all earth, this blowing bank of bloom with morning wind soft upon it. Here, deep in swamp quiet, was a founderous maze of beauty, naked and unashamed under a naked sky.

Few eyes had seen this sight. Crease had found it and taken Lollie there, years gone. Crease had taken Lebanon there when she was little more than walking, and she had held her hands toward the pretties and cried for them. Lollie had clucked her tongue softly and smoothed her cheek on Lebanon's baby hair. Lebanon could remember that first time. None others than Crease and Lollie and Joel and Lebanon had seen this hill of flowers in spring.

Nearer to the bright bank Lebanon poled till Sebastian could see a black beetle crawling into a white flower mouth. He closed his eyes as though the flowers had crowded his face too nearly, scenting above the drowsing water the poppied sweetness of banked flowers.

Then he opened his eyes again.

"It is a sight a body would never believe in, never having seen it," he said. "I wonder will it not seem impossible to myself, when I go home and tell of it."

He saw her face set betwixt him and the flowers. They blew a little on their short stems. She stood still as the water and air and flowers. I will remember her so, he thought, her face carved against bright sky and clouds and the whole underpinned by water with its multitudinous dark shadings.

"I never before saw any such sight," he said, thinking of her face now as well as of the flowers.

"They'll soon be shutting fast," she said. "Let's not wait to see their closing. It will make you disbelieve this." She turned her head toward the bank of mingled color.

"Like love," he said suddenly. "Let's go up on the bank and rest awhile."

"You'd step on a dozen blooms with your big feet," she laughed. "If you will come back next spring and the flowers are still here, I will walk all across the island with you," she said. "The flowers will be here still, I know," she said. "I will go with you now if you tell me to," she said.

He did not lift his hand.

He turned his face away from the flowers and from her.

She lifted the pole and turned the prow of the dugout north again. After a time she spoke:

"Tell you what I'll do. I'll get you a clothesbag for traveling. I know where a big bull gator lives that will be just a right size."

He was a little afeared of that but would not tell her so. They turned away from the flowering hill and faced into the sun again, east by north.

Lebanon beached the dugout and got out on a bare, sun-dried mud bar. She drove down her gator hook and rubbed a length of fallen tree limb across its top, back and forth, swinging all her weight on the vibrating hook till all the earth about jarred a little.

"That angers them past endurance," she said. "They'll out of their dens so you can make your choice."

He was squeamish. Was she making a fool of him because she would not kiss him?

Would the things board their dugout? He could see no call in going out of one's way to rouse a wild alligator, yet he could not very well say so. It would seem all too flimsy-hearted before a woman like Lebanon.

When she was done with rubbing wood on the gator hook, she got back in the dugout and poled it to deeper water. Sure enough, just as she said, now here, now yonder, a gnarled gator face showed itself above water, hissing like meat frying. Black and rough as rotted stumps their heads were, the nostrils showing and a little flat surface of head. To Sebastian their anger was like the whispering of death hot on his neck.

"They'll not hurt you," she said. "They're harmless as chickens in a pen."

She spotted a gator whose looks pleased her. She poled toward him, tampering with his head, prodding him a little till he spread wide his deep jaws. Suddenly she rammed the musket down his gullet and fired off. The gator floundered mightily, bloodying the water.

She speared him neatly with the gator hook, chopped a gash in his spine at the back of his head, and when his floundering was near ceased, she hauled him into the bow of the dugout.

Then she poled homeward again, his head hanging over the black water, drooling red blood. She kept a watch out for any other gator that might try to eat him.

Sebastian was asweat from fear of the rough-hided creature, too near.

There was a new dent in Lebanon's musket barrel. Bite down they will—but they soon loose their hold. Lebanon laughed. Sebastian said:

"I don't know that I can hide any longer the fact that I hate the things."

On a dried mudbank toward home, Lebanon dragged the gator from the boat and rid the hide of its bleeding hulk. She did it as easily as Sebastian might gut a partridge. "We'll take the steak home and fry it, if you wish," she said. But he said, "No, thanks the same."

She wielded the long knife as though it were a picktooth. The gator hide seemed no heavier in her hands than a square of flimsy. The hem of his cloak dropped near to the blood of the gator. He lifted his cloak up and away. He was the least mite ill in the pit of his stomach.

"No wild thing will attack you, unless it be a moccasin or a famished panther," she was saying. "Nothing has ever bothered me. A fear of wild things has always seemed a trifle foolish to my mind."

She swung the hide free of blood in the water and hung it on the bow. Off a little way, alligators shuffled in the water, smelling new blood. She had loaded the musket afresh and kept it readied near to her.

They were poling homeward, saying this and that small thing. There were not many more hours in which to say anything, and they knew it. The gator blood had foiled his desire somewhat, and he sat calm, to get his inward parts settled properly again. This was a new Lebanon he had seen.

Here was a Lebanon soft yet fierce. She was a wild thing caged, he decided, panther-wise, moccasin-soft. A pard favors her mate with as fast-set a passion as Lebanon's. Wild creatures live dangerously and without hope of security. So would she live for a man she loved. The deeps of the swamp had given to her more than a lack of fear of a black gator's hissing.

Now his qualms were quieted, and he loved her more. This morning was somewhat like those nights when they had sat on the door block saying nothing.

They had sat quietly and watched dusk come over the cabin. They had watched the first stars come, many a night. They had heard the whippoorwills, as now they heard eagles lonesome in the morning sky. Now they were quietened, going home. The musket was ready-loaded near to Lebanon's hand.

Steadily Lebanon poled north toward home on the last morning.

Never till the last of her memories was gone would Lebanon forget these last moments.

One moment they were gliding past a bank of ferns, newly green and tender. The ferns grew to the water's edge.

"The roots of the male fern are good for worms," she said as one says anything, to be saying something. Her thoughts were on a pleasant fancy remembered from childhood.

She told Sebastian of the fancy now.

"If you'll gather a handful of fern seeds on the first night of the first moon of summer and eat them, you can forever afterward decide yourself to be invisible and it will happen just so," she told him, laughing a little. Her eyes followed the wavering fern shadows that were troubled by the dugout's passing.

"They told me that when I was a child," she said, "and I believed it."

She smiled at what a fool she was then, long ago.

"Well, then," Sebastian spoke, "with things as they are with you and me, let's by all means gather a handful, come summer!" He laughed, too, to make her see how happy a circumstance invisibility could prove to be. He tilted his head backward in a little habit he used when he laughed.

He shoved his long legs down the length of the dugout to stretch them and ease his leg muscles. . . .

Lebanon screamed when she saw it. His boot toe touched the musket barrel while her hands were still helpless on the pole. His weight turned the barrel of the musket toward him. She heard the musket explode.

Sebastian crumpled his hand against his knee, against his breast.

Wherever he crumpled it, his clothes seethed in blood.

Where his long fingers had been, blood jetted from a mangled stump.

She leaned down and gathered his arm against her, but he groaned at her touch, and his eyes were dull in horror.

She ripped a long tear from the footing of her skirt and bound a broken flinder of wood on the inner curve of his handless wrist. She stretched him on the floor of the dugout, laid his wool hat over his face to shade him from the sun. She dipped his neck kerchief in swamp water and laid it on his throat, for his face was green and he was near to fainting. "Lie still," she told him. "No matter how it pains you, lie still. I will have you home in no time."

She held her hands a moment against her jaws to stop their chattering; then she picked up the pole, gathered her fists on it, and leaned with all her might, with all her love, on the pole.

Tendrils of her hair leaned in on her cheeks, and her eyes seemed as though smoke had got into them, dulling them somewhat. Her jaws were braced upon one another, her feet faithfully held her weight.

He groaned softly now and then. A dull and pounding and growing pain came to his ragged wrist, gathered there, and grew, pain on pain, layered and alive.

She could not forget the sight of his wrist. Even he had looked away from it. There was no help for it in Birdtown, nor in Baltimore. His hand was gone, clean as the head of the falling egret. Why had she brought him to the swamp to kill an egret, to kill a gator to be a hand satchel for him to take to Baltimore? It was a child's fancy. He could never carry any satchel in that hand now. Why had she brought him to see a hill of flowers to remember?

They had not come to the end of their small talk of fern seeds, and never would they come to the end of it.

"Ferns have no seeds," she had intended to tell him, "under the first moon of summer, or any moon whatever. Ferns have only roots, and they are a task to grub out." That was the point of the jest over two lovers who might be so foolish as to try to gather fern seeds on the first night of the first moon of summer.

Crease Fairgale poured clear turpentine over the stump of Sebastian's hand. The pine's boiled sap is as fine for a flesh wound as terebinth oil. The fiery turpentine whitened the ragged flesh, and Sebastian quivered under the burning drench as though his lost hand were in white-hot flame. Lebanon brought the gallipot of treated goose grease and then the green ointment, and the burning was soothed a little.

Crease poured laudanum for Sebastian to drink, and followed the drink with a dram of rum. He caught the ragged artery and tied it close-mouthed. The blood stopped dripping. Crease tied up the loose places with horse hairs, cut away a little fringe, and seamed the edges with a waxed thread slipped through the eye of a needle cleansed in flame.

They piled pillows in the road cart. Over Sebastian Lebanon laid her silk quilt pieced in stars and every seam feather-stitched or crow-stitched in silk threads of many colors. Desperately she was thinking how glad she would be if she might set the ax head to her wrist and give to him her own hand in payment for the loss of his.

His head was pressed deep into a square goose-down pillow. He did not open his eyes. He was weak and sleepy.

Lebanon longed to go, too, to soothe the hard jolting of the cart, to brush troublesome flies from circling too near, to swing the air into a little coolness above his face. Already his eyes seemed sunken and blue-lidded, his brow was pasty pale and wet in sweat, his voice said no weak thank-you-for-your-trouble. His sound left hand lay gentled on his breast.

Toward the very last, when no one saw, Lebanon bent her head and laid her face on his hand, and her cheek was warm a moment against him.

Crease lashed the cracker whip softly over old Buckingham's rump. "Go it," he called to the old horse.

It was so quickly done, this break in a slow current of days. Till now time had moved slowly, sleekly as water flowing, so drowned in pleasant habit as speckled garlands of frog chapelets in old water. True, there had been her heart aching after Miss Lucie Birdsong, but now that seemed so small an imperfection. Only this morning, in the last hour of night, they had walked down the back walk, she following his long striding, to gather egret plumes and an alligator hide for him to take to Baltimore, to show what he had found in wild southern swamps—and to remember her by, if they should never meet again. This very last morning she had surprised his eyes with the hill of flowers she had seen every spring, the gaudy fragile sunflowers of coquelicot color and fuchsia and margarite.

Never again would she lift that egret fan her father had given to her mother, its small quills built up by riband bands so that its body would swing substantially in a lady's hand. Many a time she had lifted the fan from its wrapping of lining silk and had swung it softly in her left hand. But she would not do it again. It would mind her too passionately of the falling dead bird.

She could not take her mind from his hand, larger and stronger than her hand, but soft-skinned, for it had dealt in book leaves and writing quills, money paper and silk kerchiefs.

Chapter 6

JULIA BIRDSONG ALL BUT SWOONED when they bore Sebastian up the narrow staircase. Lucie held herself more calm, though her heart felt much as a wearied bird lost in strange country. Madame Lateuse was all adoing, her woolen house slippers slap-slapping along the corridor, shuffling down the stairs and back again, the keys chattering metallically on their silver ring at her waist.

Soon a physician was there, a scent of medicaments in his greatcoat. He drugged Sebastian into deep sleep and closely examined the seamed stub of hand.

"Neat work as an English cobbler's," he jeered, angered because a bastard surgeon had preceded him.

"I only stopped the blood. I did the best I knew," Crease said, in apology.

"Well enough," the physician said, but opened the place anyhow, and did a little sewing to justify his presence.

Afterward, when he saw Lucie's flour-white face, he tapped her cheek and waggled his head jocularly, to comfort her. She was the type of woman a man pets.

"He'll be up and about presently," the physician said; "there's no need for tears. When danger of blood poisoning is over, he'll be fit and dandy. The old country fellow did a good job on his hand. Put a smile on when you see your Mr. Ratcliff now. That has hap-

pened to many a good man, and you must be thankful it was no
worse. Don't let him think you love him any the less."

Love him less! Lucie wept heartily alone in the hallway. A thousand times more she loved him now, for the look on his face when
he looked drunkenly into her eyes and said: "I have lost my hand,
Lucie."

She would be his lost hand, his two hands. How could he pine
for one hand gone, when he would have her whole body now to
serve him?

As far as the wound went, it gave him less trouble than one
would have thought. He had nothing to do but regain lost blood
and to adjust himself. The loss was inevitable and clean, and the
more easily overed.

When Lucie came to his side, bringing a comfit from Madame
Lateuse's cellar, or a jar of new roses for his bed cupboard, Sebastian would turn his face away a little. Once she brought him a bottle
of sweet wine which was sent up as a sick gift from Fernald d'Aussy,
the barkeep. Lucie poured a goblet of the gold-colored wine and she
called it a loving cup. She drank of it and then he drank the remainder. Sebastian flinched a little, and Lucie thought that his
flinching came from his sudden thought that their love was over
now that he was maimed. She thought she knew all he must feel of
mistrust and shyness. Certainly nothing could change her love for
him, and she would let him know it.

He turned his face to the wall and thought: If I had not been
witless from pain, I should have elected to stay there with Lebanon.
Her hands would hold more healing for me than all these pellets
and flasks. I did not even tell her thank you or fare you well.

Now he felt so guilty and unforgiven, as he had felt as a child
when he had killed a singing bird his mother loved to hear. When
he was chided, there was naught to do but hide in the dark of the
kitchen pantry till called. There was more scolding for hiding away
like this where nobody could find him. All the while he had fallen
asleep while half the town searched the streets and alleys for him.
Now he had much the same feeling; there was a misunderstanding
all about him, and he could not alter it.

Some hours alone he would think of Lebanon till he was drugged anew and pleasantly fevered. The very remembrance of her was a soft pain in his heart. She was the woman for him, and now he knew it. No other one—not even a woman as sweet as Lucie—would do. All well if he had never known Lebanon. But having known her, all things were set askelter in his heart, till she was safe in it, named by his name, home in his house. He would plead this loss as excuse to cancel betrothal with Lucie; he would ask Uncle Rafe to send him to England, if need be, and then he would come home again and go back to the swamp. When they met again there would indeed be no words to say. Lebanon would murmur against his mouth as he kissed her, and he would wrap her deep in his arms, and he would tell Crease and Mother and the world: "She is mine. We were made for one another. I never wooed her nor she me. We chanced upon one another. So spring chances on earth; so mornings break out of night."

While he was in England, Lucie would marry. Or he would stay in England till she did, and then send for Lebanon. Uncle Rafe had said it would all depend on the quality of his feeling for Lebanon. Now he knew the quality of that feeling.

On Wednesday morning, while Sebastian was eating his brioche and jellied plums and cream curds, Madame Lateuse bustled in at the door, her arms full-laden.

"You are to have a fancy caller this morning, and I am not to tell you his name," she said, her face merry. "It's to be a surprise. He ordered me most minutely not to tell you he was in town, but I don't wish him to see one of my rooms in this poor state."

"Damnation!" Sebastian said, wishing no caller to sit and ask him did he greatly miss his hand, to tell him he would find new uses for his left hand now that his right one was gone.

"You must put on your best robe and neck kerchief," Madame said. "When you see who it is, you will not be sorry. I'll have Jocko come and groom you, fresh as a daisy. I must say your paleness becomes you, Mr. Sebastian. You are handsomer than ever. No wonder it is that the women fight for you!" She touched the top of his head, as one touches a little boy, to commend him.

He turned away impatiently. Everyone felt pity for him, and pity is cold curds, indeed.

"Wake up!" she said, in mock harshness. "Demosthenes' tongue was tangled, was it not? Yes! Caesar and Alexander had fits, did they not? Yes! . . . Why, Napoleon, the Liberator, had fits, now! And you grieve after one hand. Shame, Mr. Ratcliff. One hand is plenty to hold a horse or a woman with. It's all in knowing how."

She spread on the floor a small square of carpeting woven of silk and goat's hair. It was rich and red. (She had brought it from France and had never spread it for any but brides and corpses, though she did not tell Sebastian that.)

"Who is this calling?" he demanded. "I think I have a right to know."

"You will welcome him—I can swear to that," she said. "He is from the North originally. He wears a tail coat and has Boston manners. You will all but fall in joy about his shoulders when you see him. And I will *not* tell you his name, begging your pardon, Mr. Ratcliff."

In spite of himself, Sebastian felt a vague and delightful impatience arising within him. Mayhap here was his stage-company partner, with the backing of Uncle Rafe.

Madame set a brace of shining brass girandoles on the low dressing stand; their swinging prisms swung and tinkled as her weight moved about the room. She went to the door and tongue-lashed Nerissa, the chambermaid, to come and wipe the dust from the bases of the girandoles. There was not time to polish them now.

"I have told you to keep these knickknacks dusted, Nerissa," she stormed. "I will have you flogged, and then maybe you can remember."

The girl came in meekly and ran the feather duster over the brass. A little fume of dust rose from the turkey feathers bunched and fastened. Nerissa was slender, and her face had a smooth, polished look. A red kerchief was wound about her head, and she had liquid eyes. Now and then she would roll her eyes at Sebastian, and her lips would part in gentle smiling.

Madame set tall white candles in the brass stands, and their unlighted forms were mirrored in the glass with Nerissa's face admiring her eyes and hips and the long turning of her hands on the feather duster's handle. Madame brought in jars of roses, opened this morning. She brought in pink lilies and spikes of rosebays and wine-red mallows. And there was a large blue ewer of fleur-de-luce blooms, Lebanon's favorite posy.

Nerissa giggled when she dared, the laughter coming shyly here in the Ratcliff gentleman's room. She showed all her teeth in the mirror between the girandoles, and tilted her throat and pursed her lips and lifted her brows, every time Madame's back was turned. Madame laughed and chattered incessantly till Sebastian got fidgety and all but told her to keep quiet, if she pleased. Here was the slender-hipped, tight-breasted Negress, and here was Madame, fat and too old for love, never showing cares of her own. Suddenly it came to him that he was fortunate, indeed, for all his lost hand! He was not a slave, able to hope for no kindness farther than a kind master. And Madame—her hands had a loving way with the flower blooms. Doubtless, under that mountain of fat, her heart was, or had been, female and loving, tender and remembering, and in its time it had doubtless been troubled because of love, or the lack of it. Madame's face was grotesque in the midst of roses and dead candles. Suddenly he knew why she always laughed: it was her shield against ridicule. She laughed at herself before anyone else could think to. She knew herself to be ludicrous and a misfit at anything but roasting a lamb gammon or rolling pastries penny-thin. At least I am no monstrosity, he thought soberly; leastwise I do not weigh a quarter of a thousandweight.

These casual women brought Lebanon to this room, and she was stilled here with him, quiet as a portrait out of Paris, rich as a piece of Cyprian cloth of gold.

Madame's cheeks quivered in her haste, and there was a little dew of perspiration in the edges of her hair. Finally there were flowers everywhere—purple altheas and short-stemmed stonebreak and even rushlike leaves of green sedge for greenery. The room was cluttered in fragrances, and now the knotted rosebuds in the paper on the walls seemed a foolery. You could smell the flowers beginning to die, graciously and in lingering beauty, in the close warmth of this room.

Sebastian bestirred himself to think who the surprise might be. Aunt Maria's brother, perhaps, or Lucie's Aunt Irina who had been in Italy for ten years. One would think Madame was decking this place for a foreign prince!

And now she was putting up fresh lace curtains and knotting them back with bow knots of riband. She pushed Sebastian's bed far up into the corner, jarring his wound till he cursed under his breath. Against the wall she set a broad-armed chair Jocko had brought in from the hall. Now and then she halted and stooped, grunting, to gather fallen flower petals from the crimson carpeting. Her tongue went incessantly, cheerful, telling off little tasks for Nerissa, the chambermaid: "Set this there, and take that out, and then come back and arrange these things in order. . . ."

"This place looks like a seraglio," Sebastian said, tempting her wicked wit.

"You'd not be homeless in a seraglio," she said, "not even with only one hand," and he laughed with her though it was a poor joke. She was healing to him; she taunted him with his hidden hurting, and so brought it to light that it might heal cleanly.

"Jocko!" she called, when the last rose petal was picked from the carpet. "Wash him now, for callers, and put on his best nightshirt and robe and kerchief. . . ."

Madame and Nerissa went away, Madame leaving her mirth behind. The pleasant sounding of her laughter stayed with Sebastian.

First of all Sebastian asked Jocko for a pain pellet, and the black man handed the little vial from the window table. Sebastian swallowed two for good measure. The opium had a happy way of removing his pain and nervy megrims and of bringing Lebanon more near. He was already somewhat wearied down. He could not seem to regain that strong, lost blood, and the stump of his arm was still a little fevered. He lay thinking of the opium trade, and the half-merchant-captains-half-pirates who smuggled the stuff from Calcutta and Bombay into the China Seas.

He hoped the caller would visit but briefly.

Jocko busied himself with Venice soap and water scent, scissors, towels, face paste and tooth powder and stick. First he washed Sebastian's hair and beard and curled them expertly on tongs heated in a brazier.

Sebastian asked for a draught of the red wine from the bottom of the washstand, and Jocko poured a tumblerful. Thereafter Sebastian lay dreaming awake whilst the black man's hands went softly along his person, washing and rubbing, readying it for a caller in a tail coat and a top hat. The pain pellets and the red wine and his own weakness contended gently in his veins, so that Lebanon's face came and went, and Lucie was here sometimes, too. As Jocko rubbed astringent flower water on his back he fell fast asleep and in a sudden flash of nightmare saw Lucie naked and beheaded like a hog for a butcher.

He waked, moaning a little. I dreamed of her so, because I aim to break her heart, he told himself.

"That's all right, suh," Jocko murmured soothingly, over and over. "That's all right, suh."

The caller would be here at eleven of the clock, Madame had said, and it was drawing on to that. He looked up at the pendulum clock on the wall. It had a cluster of red roses on its glass face. He had thought he would ask Madame if she would not part with this little bell clock for a sum. Lebanon would like it for her shed room. Its hand told lies, but it was a pretty thing for a blank wall.

Sebastian's beard was washed and shining. His hair lay just so now, sweet in rose oil. Jocko would have touched Sebastian's white cheeks with a hare's foot red with French carnelian, but Sebastian cursed at such effeminacy and would have none of it. "A little, suh, just the leetlest touch to make you shine. All the genmuns does it when they fixes up. . . ."

Sebastian agreed to only a very little, for he could see in the hand mirror that he looked a yellow-skinned corpse.

At the tick of eleven of the clock he was braced in the tall-backed, broad-armed chair and fit to lose his stomach from nausea. His head was giddied and his eyes dulled and drowsing from the pellets and the wine, but his face was lit in irritable curiosity. His wounded arm lay in a black sling of China silk. A bright silk-squared quilt was laid across his knees, and he dragged the quilt part way up to hide the arm he nursed. His eyes haunted the closed door, waiting for the comer. His memory had exhausted itself thinking who this might be.

Suddenly the door opened softly and Julia Birdsong stood there, dressed in smiles and a new panne velvet of a rose color with black sattin bands. Close behind her was Mr. Marye, the minister, in a tail coat and a top hat, doffed now in his left hand. And there was Uncle Rafe, seeming rough and uncouth and ungroomed, for all his best clothes. And there was Uncle Luke, nervous-lipped as always.

And there was Lucie.

A halo of meshed tulle hooded her hair, her body stood in a dragging, wide-spread gown of white mousseline de soie, frail as plum blossoms. In her hands there was a loose burden of white garden roses, and in her ears were her mother's briolette diamonds that were to be her own when she was married to Sebastian.

Julia Birdsong made a pretty speech:

"Lucie wished to make up somewhat for your misfortune, Sebastian. . . . We thought this would be a sweet surprise and aid you in your recovery."

Sebastian had gone whey-faced. Rafe Ratcliff thought sure that he would swoon. Rafe laid a square jewel box in Sebastian's palm. The velvet of the box was warm from Uncle Rafe's hand. Before the ceremony was said, Sebastian would open the case, would pin his marriage gift on Lucie's breast. Since he had only one hand, Uncle Rafe unclasped the box and lifted out the fleur-de-luce of diamonds and pearls and rubies on gold. Uncle Rafe pinned the gewgaw to the white garment that covered Lucie's breast.

Sebastian hardened his mouth, and his eyes hunted through the room, as a beast's seek a near-by fastness when a steel jaw has closed and cleft his escape. Now the candles were lit, there in broad daylight, and the roses were opening more and more from the heat of the hearth. The candles smoked in a sweetness of bay and honeywort compounded in their wax. Sebastian saw a flower shatter soundlessly on Madame's blood-red carpet. It was a wild flower from Madame's spring garden and did not like walls and hearth heat. The falling of its petals seemed loud and heavy.

Beyond the door the Negroes stood, and curious guests who were stopping at the tavern. Sebastian saw a fat man's red jowl, shaven clean as a dead pig's carcass, and a woman with a black lace shawl about her shoulders and a fluted cap on her head. Beyond the tall light of the window he saw a bird wheeling in an idling journey. He took it to be a bunting that likes hot sunshine and winters in warm places.

His head was reeling, though he held it so straight on his shoulders. I should have thought, he was thinking desperately, I should have known . . .

Lucie took her place beside his chair, her eyes nearly so bright as the briolette diamonds in her ears, and the Ratcliff fleur-de-luce on her breast. She laid her hand on his left shoulder. There was a smile on her mouth.

"I have no ring," he said, speaking in silly desperation, looking into the minister's face to make his unspoken appeal. His eyes and his thoughts were fogged.

From his inner waistcoat pocket the minister held forth a small circlet of mined gold.

"Everything is arranged, my son," Mr. Marye said.

"But Lucie . . ." Now Sebastian's voice was hard indeed. "This is no time . . ." She only smiled and clasped his good left hand in her two hands. Her hands were icy cold, too, and shaking like his own. It gave him a strange sort of comfort, now he knew that she, too, was terrified.

"Dearly beloved . . ." Mr. Marye's voice began to drone its solemn words of eternal marriage. "We are gathered together here in the presence of God . . . and these witnesses . . . to join together this man . . . and this woman . . ." This man bowed his head a very little. The floor was unsteady below his sight. His face was like pale stone, still and stern. He could feel Lucie's hands pitifully endeavoring to warm his good left hand. . . .

There was a wedding feast at noon. And such a feast!

Madame and all the kitchen slaves had been up and doing since three in the morning, they said. Besides beef, there was mutton. And there were geese and ducks and chickens, and partridges floured and buttered and spitted and roasted until they were gold crumbles of sweet meat. There was a lamb gammon dressed in wine and delicately boiled. There was all manner of meat which Madame could procure on such short notice. At midnight she had sent Josephus to the river fishermen. The fish, larded and gently baked in waxed paper hoods, were delicate-fleshed and flaky. There was all manner of wines and hot spiced mulse, and a jug of jargonelles preserved in refined sugar, and there were broad platters of cold cuts laid out in a sauce of mint leaves and sour red berries in syrup. There were salt nuts from Southern Sea Islands. There were even common flitches of dried venison smothered in cream sauce with whole peppers grated over them.

Cubi, the baker, had been at his big oven since before dawn, doing the little queen's cakes with currants, and the peach tarts glazed in sweetened egg white and cream, and the molasses cookies and the butter teacakes, and finally the Bride's Cake with roses twined all about it. In its heart were buried a silver thimble, an iron shoe, and a gold heart—for the guests to tell their fortunes by.

Sebastian found the gold heart in his slice of cake, for Madame had thrust it in a certain place and marked the rim of the cake pan with a flinder of straw. When the cake was done, the icing was marked unerringly so that Lucie would know how all the fortunes lay.

Sebastian kissed the heart, true to a gentleman's form, wished lightly upon it, or pretended to, and gave it to his bride to keep. So had Lucie's father wished upon this selfsame gold heart, and so had his father.

Sebastian was laughing now, for the guests were gaping as they gape at all grooms. Everyone had taken wine, even to the ladies— though they were handed only small snifters. Sebastian stood his turn with the best of the men. His head was light now; he laughed; he was foolish—and even a little happy.

Even when, unthinking, he reached for the gold heart with the forgotten stub of his right hand, and waked his wound to infinite throbbing, the pain was soon submerged in wedding mirth.

"There is nothing so happy as a wedding," Julia Birdsong said.

"It is the prettiest wedding we ever had in this old tavern," Madame said, jouncing everywhere, in and out among the tables, and seeing that all were well fed and that all wineglasses and tumblers were replenished. The slaves were merry in the kitchen, too, getting their share of drink and rich food. The oleanders leaned into the open, blowing windows, their leaves rustling like unfinished leather. Beyond the windows, tethered horses whinnied and stamped their hoofs to go.

A little past noon the Wednesday coach came in, and every new traveler must come and eat and drink and wish well to this bride and groom, this man and this woman who had been joined as one.

Suddenly Madame screamed out: "Never has he kissed the bride!"

"Sebastian!" Uncle Luke roared.

And Uncle Rafe pulled Lucie forward from behind a high-backed chair.

She was blushing, and her hands wrung one another. There was more excitement in this room than she had known in all her other days compounded.

"Show them, son!" Uncle Rafe said loudly, and Sebastian stood, reeling a little, and caught his wife against his breast and showed them all how to kiss a woman, and with only his left arm about her, too.

Lucie had put aside her bride's mantle of meshed tulle. She set her arms about his head, laying them in a warm circlet on the pillow sham. Madame had laid out a sham of Irish linnen, trimmed in point lace. Across its breadth were embroidered love words, "I will ever love but thee."

"Poor sweet," Lucie told him. "I knew you would hate pity. But no one could hate love, could he? I'll never pity you. But I swear I shall love you madly. 'I will ever love but thee.' "

Her fingers trailed across the words that ran away under his head.

"I love you madly . . ." she whispered, her face pleading for love.

He stroked her cheek with his left forefinger.

"Poppet, you are sweet," was all he said.

There were tears in his eyes.

"Was it too much for you in your weakened state?" she asked.

"No," he said, his face pale and taut in a sudden pain.

So his lost hand pained him—aching and easing—for a long, long time.

Chapter 7

LEBANON WAS BUSY with many things these late spring days, and a good thing she was. All the bedding in the loft had been beaten and sunned, all used quilts washed and folded away till cold weather again. The walls were washed down in lye suds, and the floors scrubbed clean to every crack. When the floor skins were hung in the sun on the sapling fence about the garden patch, they glistered and brightened. The hardest matter was to wash the feather beds. Joel helped her lift the sogged, heavy things over to the fence, and they dried in the constant bright weather.

There was the garden to plant, perennial things to grub about and manure, seeds to sow in loamy earth in a corner and set in rows when they were big enough to stand alone. Lebanon had a flasket of good seeds wrung in little separate cloths, dried from last year—all the way from pumpkin to pipe tobacca, yet scarce any spring passed that Crease did not bring some other seeds home, plain or fancy. Lebanon had saved and dried seeds from a Seville orange, and the things came up and stood in a row like little swamp bushes, only more shiny than most, and of a leathery toughness. Each year the cold killed them back, not the root but the body. They were tall as the fence now, and bore real orange blossoms sometimes, but never had fruit come. The cold always got there first.

Lebanon was all aquiver for Papa and Joel to come home. She wished to hear from Sebastian's hand. She had longed to go into Birdtown herself, but she would not. He was entangled with the Birdsongs there, no doubt, upstairs in a fobbed and painted room with bed drapes and window hangs.

Now her heart found itself treading a high place in spite of her sober reason. If he were able to stand and travel, she knew he would come home with Papa and Joel. She would not count too strongly on his coming, for then suppose he did not! However, her inner judgment convinced her that he craved to see her face as much as she wished to see his. When Sebastian came back, she would boldly tell him that no heart can endure such partings and absences and uncertainties. Why *could* they not go West, if they had the iron? If Sebastian wished to marry Miss Birdsong, well and good, but if he did not, let him say so like a man. When Papa left this morning, Lebanon was scarce a lady, for she said: "Tell Sebastian that the whole place is scarce itself without him." That would bring him home to her, if he anyway wished to come.

She went to the front doorway again, the last of a hundred times. She had looked for the cart since noon—foolishly, for never did the men come home till dark.

The cart came plodding home behind old Buck.

Papa's old hat and Joel's coon cap she could see, but not Sebastian anywhere, not even sprawled in the back, as Joel sometimes rode when he was tired or lazy.

She said to herself: By any fool's reasoning, it is too soon after his hurt to allow his traveling so far as this.

She was herself though when the cart came into the side yard. She stood at the edge of the shed, her hand on the weathered post, waiting. They did not call out to her. Buck plodded on to the lot. His old head was low. When Joel loosed his belly buckle old Buck shook his head as though he shook away miles and dust and weariness. It was a longer jaunt than it used to be. He went toward the water trough.

"You tell her," Crease said, going off into the thickening dust toward the house.

Joel went on up to the house, too, wondering how to break the news.

Lebanon was putting supper on the table. The fire was bright, replenished with a seasoned pine knot. The hominy boiler had been rubbed till you could comb your hair in its shine. The floor was sweet from being scrubbed. The brass candle sconces shone like new. There were flowers in a honeysuckle basket across the breast of the chimney piece.

This will be no joke, thought Joel, though I must tell it like one.

Lebanon set on the biscuits and sat down to eat, too. The goose stood rich and crackle-skinned, hot from the spit, in a crockery trencher in the middle of the table.

"You'd never guess who got tied and tethered in town," Joel said, reaching his plate for Lebanon to help him to greens.

"Who?" Lebanon asked carelessly. "Offhand, I'd say one of the Retty girls. They wanted to get married worse than anybody I ever saw."

Crease kept his eyes down as he gnawed a goose wing. He did love the taste of roast goose, but did not dare more than a bite or two of wing.

"Sebastian Ratcliff," Joel said, laughing a little to help out.

Crease went on chewing the goose wing.

Lebanon's fingers braced themselves on the knife handle.

Before she could say, "You are joking," Joel went on:

"Been married two weeks. It was Miss Birdsong, like we heard. They stepped up the wedding on account of his hurt." He went on trying to help her.

"I forgot to light the candles," she said. She went to the fireplace to bring a lighted flinder of wood. "There's more gravy here in the drip pan if anybody wants it," she said. "Doubtless they will find happiness together. . . . We'll be having new potatoes by next week," she said. "The garden is in prime shape, if one of the old biddy-hens does not find a crack. That reminds me, there was one coop I did not cover, and it looks like rain tonight. I will eat later."

She hurried out the back door.

Joel went into the shed room for a fresh tobaca twist. Crease went on eating, though he had no heart for food.

She stood in the dark, leaning on the rails of the barn lot, hanging her weight by the clutching of her hands on the top rail. The wind had risen, and her skirts blew in the wind like the careless skirts of a hanged woman. It would rain presently; one could smell the rain close and hastening closer. The chicken coops were long since covered over, in boards and sacking, so the old hens could sleep safe from the pounding rain.

She looked up to the blowing sky. Scudding drifts of rain clouds lowered. The trees were loud-boughed in the blowing. There was no sound of any bird. Only the pigs tossed and grunted in their shelter;

the cows and sheep had gone up under the shed. Lady sat on her haunches, questioning Lebanon.

The rain began to fall in big drops. She walked off down the back path toward the swamp, knowing she would not go far or stay long. Blackness and bog, hidden ways and quietude were what she craved. The rain began to beat soundly all around. The thunder rolled, like tobaca casks thundering down a wharf. Her skirts stuck to her legs, her hair was plastered flat, and she walked on toward the swamp.

The hard rain stung her flesh, the wind wrenched the cloth of her skirts and pulled her steps sideways. Walking was heavied and slowed, for she was wetted through. The rain beat upon her this knowledge: He had not loved her, nor ever did, and certainly never would now again. He had not so much as sent her word that he was wed. The blood was scarce stanched in his wrist before he was wed to Lucie. A fine bridal embrace she had from him, no doubt!

She blew her breath hotly into the cold. She spat into the rain, as an Indian spits toward a white man's steps, to show his contempt.

She turned toward home again.

Back there was the old carved juniper-wood stool in the chimney jamb, where she used to sit and warm herself when she was wearied. Empty and inert her flesh seemed to hang now, sickened and languid, wishing for a stool by a fire. Back there was the hobbly wooden floor. And she thought of setting in glass windows and putting up new-carved four-post beds; she had thought of dancing on that floor as Sebastian's bride, with forty yards of gold lace flickering about her ankles and swinging free!

As she passed the barn lot she could hear old Buckingham's tender gums rooting around the feed trough. The rain had slackened and ceased.

She went into the house and took off her wet clothes; wrapped in a dry shift and a warmed quilt, she sat cumbrously on the little stool her mother had carved. The fire leaped and chattered like a living creature. Lady shook and shivered and licked her fur free of rain. She had stood the storm with Lebanon, never understanding why.

Now and again so great a pain would come on her that she hated him. I loved him so, she thought, I loved him so. Sometimes her face would light a little and she could guess a solution to his action: Did he think her careless, and so fell out of love with her because her gun had taken his hand? Did he think she stirred the gunstock so that he could not marry Miss Birdsong?

Then sometimes her face would still, counseled by her heart: He loved me when I saw him last. I know it. He had no need to tell me so. He loves me now. He will love me forever, as now, in the only way he is able to, more quietly, but never less.

When morning came she went to the well for water; she shucked corn and fed the chickens and other fowls, dropping the yellow, dried kernels on their heads and bodies clustered about her feet and crowding on her boot toes. There was some comfort in going and doing and working hard, and now she was glad for every duty.

Crease and Joel never mentioned Sebastian's name again. But the little dog would whine when she saw and felt Lebanon so troubled; and when she whined, it was as though she howled in a hushed tongue for Sebastian to come again and stay here. When Lebanon sat, Lady leaned her head on Lebanon's knees; she sighed and licked Lebanon's still hands with her small, pink tongue.

Crease and Joel never named his name again to one another or to Lebanon. In her face, as the days grew in number, they could see how deeply her heart had been set on young Ratcliff. And he knew he was to marry Lucie Birdsong, all the while he was here in this house, eating their meat and bread and partaking of their friendliness.

Crease knew nothing to say, so he said nothing. No need to say: "He is not worth your tears, nor ever was." To Lebanon, Sebastian still would seem worth a full life's grieving. He had not held himself to his own mark of honor, it would seem. Sometimes one must drag himself to a high level and hang on by the very skin of his teeth. It is a difficult assignment to climb high and take a long, broad view.

Such things Crease wished to tell Lebanon, and he did not know how. Anyhow, if she were to learn them, she would learn them alone, he decided.

Crease told a lot of little things, and all of them when added up did not mean much. Yet Lebanon could hear many things unsaid beside the fire. She could feel Crease's love about her heart, the stronger now because she had been hurt. She could feel Joel's young hatred, unvoiced but loyal, for the man who had shamed his sister's heart. This was home, and these hearts were nearer to hers than other hearts. It had taken a deep hurt to cause her to know it, but nowhere else could she find such loyalty of blood. It was a shame she so craved to leave. She could not bear the leaning of the trees where she had walked with Sebastian, she could not endure the scent of the swamp since he was no more here with her.

She thought a hundred times of that grandfather who had come West in a sailing ship, claimed a knowledge of letters, stayed a jump ahead of his pupils by hard study, wore right black pantaloons and maintained a careful calm and decorum, tutored in a good family, and then a better one, amended his manners as he went along, till he could bow and kiss your hand like a lord, read verses like a bishop!

Like Nowel Fairgale, she wished she could go from this place, as he had gone from England and found him a place of honor and a good wife in a new world. He tutored a little hunchback boy for two years, and his indenture was sold to a barrister and he taught three small daughters of a barrister. Nowel Fairgale married the oldest, and her name was Evaline.

There was a burial stone in the graveyard in Birdtown. Sometimes Crease walked through the place to see the new graves. His mind was turned to morbid things like graves these days; maybe he was growing old. He had an idea in mind to move Lollie's body to town, so she might be companied, and not forever alone out there under pines and bright space. If he sold his land and moved to town, he would move Lollie, too. The graveyard in town had a handsomeness about it that would be proper for the dead. There were old stones, greened and darkened, the deep-cut words shallowing under rain and wind. Old oaks leaned, their boughs hooded in moss that was never pulled down; the place was shut apart in veiling. About some of the lots there were borders of yew, and in summer bright patches of flowers showed where a woman's hands had been, loving dust and ashes long after death. In one place a woman had enlarged a grave to the likeness of a heart, and violets grew there, enriched from death below. In spring one could smell a sweetness of violets all across the burial ground.

Where another man would have loitered at the tavern bar, Crease slipped off to the burial ground to pick a new place for Lollie and for him. With Ratcliff money he could move to town and make a lady of Lebanon; all that is required is money, and a fine-grained body and a gentle heart. He would buy her silk clothes aplenty and hoops and false hair and powder boxes—if he could make himself willing to give over his land. And he could. The old place would not be the same, anyhow, when the Ratcliffs brought in the logging crews to camp, and the shining saws sang in the swamp. He would build a new house of English brick and buy a silver teapot for Lebanon. He would choose a plot in the burial ground and then he would be fixed for the rest of his life and for eternity.

Chapter 8

IT WAS NOW TWO MONTHS AND SIX DAYS since Sebastian's wedding day. Lebanon decided she would go into Birdtown again. She had pulled her heart together somewhat after the lashing it had taken. She wished Sebastian to see that her heart was not broken, quite. Far off she might see him, going down a sidewalk, his fine English-made boots quick on planking or cobbles. Or maybe the Ratcliffs were not in Birdtown now.

The sawmill was ordered and the woodsmen booked; Joel said so. Soon there would be the swaying fall of the trees, the stunned silence thereafter, the mill saws whining. Old cypresses topped and quartered would fall like dead hogs. There would be money aplenty in return, Papa said.

The Ratcliffs would be here in the swamp lumbering, coming by the house for beans and pone and squirrel pilau.

The salt was out and the Ratcliffs had eaten the last of the refined sugar. She would trade the gator skin she had killed for Sebastian. The egret feathers were lost somewhere that awful day. Not till days afterward did she even remember them. There were more wool packs in the loft than the Fairgales would need; she had three dozen eggs saved, and could spare a ham and shoulder in trade, and perhaps a kag of lard. Whilst she was going, she would take in a little shelled corn to be ground to meal at the mill.

Buckingham was old and lazy. His hoofs dragged through the sand toward town; never would he hurry till he scented home again in returning. He would make the way home again in two-thirds the time he took to step it away. Crease had traded fifty gator hides for him when he was young and newly broken to the rein. Now he knew the way home without so much as the pull of a bit in his mouth, for he went nowhere but to the hitching rack in town and home again. When Crease bought him and the red-wheeled cart, he was the master-proud of him, but driving home to Lollie the horse drooped more and more. By that time it had so sunken in Crease's eyes that he lied to Lollie and said he gave ten gator hides instead of fifty, and even at that Lollie said he had been taken in for fair, and secretly Crease agreed with her.

To Lebanon he was better company than another woman, and Crease and Joel would not have parted with him for a thousand silver dollars. One could talk with him, and he would give a right answer by tilting his head or shaking his mane or staring solidly ahead. It was as though he understood every word; the Fairgales would swear that he did understand. He did his work of a little plowing and a chance journey into Birdtown and was as much a Fairgale as Lebanon or Joel or Crease.

"Do go on!" Lebanon slapped the reins on his rump. He was named Buckingham for the Palace; his former owner had said he was straight from the Isles, being lately personal mount to the King's Equerry, and Crease believed it. Obeying for so long as Lebanon might be looking, the old horse humped along the more quickly to fool her; but in a moment he slumped again into his low-headed plodding.

Little plums were green in the thickets. Now the plum thickets and all taller woods were loud in sudden flights of birds. There were brown thrashers, fidgeting wrens, and mewing catbirds. They were all busy at house-raising and family-making—timbers of straw and joists of fine, white rootlets, walls of stolen lamb fur and gold flax-wort fiber, and roofs of close-held wings. There was an array of bird nests home under the eaves of the loft. Now and then, when Lebanon was younger, she had brought one in and set it away. Twenty-six of them she had collected, sheltered from weather now, ruining in long decay.

Riding into town, she remembered the old bird nests along the eaves of home, hidden in the attic, lost in childhood. Would she ever now again lift down an old bird nest and fondle it as a child? It would seem unlikely.

Yonder stood Birdtown beyond a last wall of pines. A veil of smoke hung, risen from chimney and smithy and tavern.

She found a snubbing rack under the oaks and tied old Buckingham and left him to content himself on handfuls of hay. She brushed her skirt free of his spring shedding and walked toward the tavern. She would see Fernald first, and then she would attend to her trading.

"Come along, Lady," she said.

Straight up to the bar she walked. Off in the gaming room one could hear cards flicked and shuffled, coins spun and stopped under a palm, spasmodic talk and mirth. But this long room was bare, for it was an in-between time, later than late breakfast and not nearly so early as early dinner. Only Fernald was in the room. She laid her palms firm and flat on the counter betwixt them.

"Pardee!" he said softly. "It is you."

She tried to put into a few words the desperate thing she had come to say. She found her face beginning to quiver past her control. She looked in Fernald's kind, dark eyes and she thought she saw pity. His hands went suddenly up and sleeked his hair slowly, as though he found pain there.

"Could I have a little glass of brandy?" she asked.

"Yes. But why?" he asked. He watched her face in curious surprise. She returned his gaze, and her fingers danced on the dark counter.

"You shall have it," he said indulgently. "And at noon you will eat with me. Madame has red snapper matelote and snow pudding, as well as all the usual. She told me so."

There was an inner room behind the bar. Lady was sniffing along the floor where a mouse had walked last night. The room's high-set window was thickened in dust. It was never opened or washed. Back in the little room Fernald kept the ledgers at a slanting desk with a high stool to sit on. On the desk there was a candle near to burned down, showing he worked nights.

"I wish some words with Sebastian Ratcliff," she said. "Would you fetch him to that room?" She pointed beyond Fernald to the cubbyhole where Lady had already gone, sniffing.

"You have no words for him," Fernald said suddenly.

Her head drooped a little.

"Have you now?" he pressed, persuading her against folly, stretching his hand to stop her fingers from dancing.

"He is buying my father's land," she said.

"He may be buying your father's land, but that would have nothing to do with you. He is a bastardy sort, and he has a wife. I do not need to tell you that. Further than all that, his wife is illed. What word could you have for him?" he asked her, speaking a little roughly.

"None," she said, holding tightly to the edge of the counter.

He poured her a drink. He led her into the small inner room and pulled up a deep-armed chair cushioned in red plush, tufted and worn.

At this moment, Abigail, the cook's least young 'un, stuck her plaited head inside the door and said that Madame wished Mr. d'Aussy to come to the kitchen. Fernald could guess what Madame would say: How much did we pay for eggs last? Are there four barrels of flour in the storeroom, or three?

He left Lebanon with the glass of brandy filled before her.

In passing through the long ordinary he saw the Ratcliff table already set for the men's dinner. Goblets and plates were turned down against dust. The cruets were new-filled and shining. Short-stemmed red roses were lolling in a round maslin bowl in the center of the table. Fernald tightened his lips. He would show them. He and Lebanon would sit in the ordinary, too, at three of the clock. When the fashionables ate, he would take Lebanon to eat, too. Only first he would tell Madame he was expecting a lady guest to eat with him. Next he would go down the street and have Miss Lily Ludgate outfit Lebanon in a gown and flowered bonnet and something to go around her shoulders, to be laid aside carelessly at table, of course, and lace mittens and perhaps a brooch. Red would go well with her coloring. She would look fetching now in a black silk gown with a scarlet guimpe.

He had lived forty-eight years without a woman. Now, if he could, he would take Lebanon Nowel Fairgale and show any Ratcliff gent what he had lost.

Madame was giving Abigail's mother, fat Josepha, orders on a saddle of venison for late supper.

Would Mr. d'Aussy be so kind as to bring her up a bottle of white wine with which to baste the venison? She had mislaid the key to her cellar, and Fernald had the only other key.

Lucie was laid by a sick headache and long nausea.

She was weeping again, and why she did not know, unless it was that she could not persuade her poor stomach to hold so much as cool water. Mama had got out all her medicaments and had bought others, but nothing seemed to avail—neither ginger tea nor cold bread toasted, nor anything anybody could name. The old physician said there was but one happy cure to this contagious disease. He thought it was a laughing matter. Lucie hated him for laughing. Even Sebastian thought it might be just as well if the matter were taken more seriously. He was long since up and about, but the heavy-scented air of this close-drawn room sickened him a little.

Lucie was not one to complain loudly. She lay with her face turned away, scarce answering words that were put to her.

"Do leave me, Mama," she said miserably. "Quiet will help more than anything."

When Mama had gone from the room, wounded past speech, Lucie called Sebastian. She held her eyes shut under the damp camphire cloth. She held the bottle of smelling salts in her left hand.

"I want only you," she said.

"Yes, poppet," he said. He came near to her side. His arm was yet in its black sling, for till now it throbbed if he hung it downward. He touched her cheek with the back of his left hand.

"Go out and take the sun for a while," she said, thinking of him, or appearing to. "Don't trouble yourself over my feeling ill. I'll feel much improved once noon is past."

"I'll not stay long," he said, easing himself from beneath her gentle thumb, and glad enough to go. "Try to fall asleep. I can go and see the harness maker while I am about it. Everything you have done in this town, you must be constantly overseeing it."

He went through the gloom to the door. When she heard his grasp on the rattling wooden knob, she called him again.

"Sebastian!"

He turned, his hand clenching the doorknob.

"Yes, poppet?"

"I'll think of you while you are gone."

"And I of you," he said, telling no lie. It was the parting she always gave him to bear away with him.

He closed the door softly.

He considered that a hot toddy would dispel these morning megrims. Lucie's illness had almost got him to where he was sickened each morning, too!

He went slowly down the narrow box of stairs, nursing his arm against a jolt. It was a tedious task, this careful lameness, this learning of a new manner of doing all things. He was beginning to be clever at ciphering with his left hand. What was it Lebanon had said? "Habit makes us strong or weak." It was that last morning when she was poling the boat into the swamp, and he had offered to do the poling if he had known how. But he did not know how.

Whenever he thought of Lebanon, it was as though a knife turned in the flesh of an old hurt. But what to do? There was nothing he could have done in all those things that had fallen out, except to work hard now and leave the outcome of all things to high Providence. He could have sent her a note, but would that not have shown some slight disaffection to Lucie? Lebanon would not wish him to be careless of his wife.

He was growing a fine and strong affection for Lucie. She was good and kind and soft-voiced, a gentlewoman in all her ways. She thought of others before herself. She would take no advantage, fairly or unfairly. She would not speak temperishly, no matter the provocation. She had been trained to hold her tongue in strong government and her head high, and her life according to firm daily rule. Furthermore, she was his wife.

He walked down the long ordinary and saw the Ratcliff table already set for three o'clock dinner. There were red roses in a brass bowl. He took a rose to stuff into his cravat. He would take it up to Lucie for her to smell. Perhaps its freshness would somewhat revive her.

Fernald was not to be seen at the bar. Sebastian struck the counter with a blow of his left hand. The rose shook in his hand.

"Fernald!" he called sharply. (Heaven knew they were paying enough to have a little service in this place.) Fernald would be in the little dark counting room doubtless.

There in the dark of the little door he saw her.

Her face was the face of a woman now, pale and passive, and unspeaking until he spoke, deferential and gentle.

"Lebanon . . ."

He called her name brokenly.

"Pour me a glass of that." He turned his left hand toward a squat Burgundy-colored bottle on the shelf near her hand. She lifted a down-turned goblet and poured some of the liquor into it.

"Enough," he cried softly.

He lifted the glass in his left hand.

"Health and happiness," he said gravely, no japery, no lightness on his tongue, a simple wish-you-well—the only thing he could say.

From the kitchen they could hear Madame Lateuse's high cackle of mirth. From the courtyard they could hear a horse nicker and move his hoofs restlessly.

"Fernald tells me that your wife is illing," Lebanon said. "I hope she is soon improved."

"She is with child," he said, carefully guarding both Lebanon and Lucie from any hurt in his words.

"I wish all the three of you all happiness." Lebanon looked straight into his eyes.

Sebastian measured a pour of liquor, larger than the first. He downed the fiery, sweet courage.

"Our thanks," he said, "the three of us."

She saw the red rose thrust carelessly through the tightened loop of his cravat.

When Fernald came back to his counter, there was Sebastian Ratcliff, but no Lebanon. Sebastian sat at a little table before the bar. His head lay forward on his good left arm. Lax and ungainly, he lay as though asleep. When Fernald touched his arm, he pleaded a pain in his head and dizziness, for he had been thinking that he could have told Lebanon the truth of his marriage with Lucie. Yet he had left things as they were, for he could not bring himself to speak of it unless Lucie could have heard every word he spoke. Though this monstrous misunderstanding had come betwixt them, still the air betwixt their faces was clean and sweet and untroubled. They both felt it so.

It was that very afternoon that Lebanon told Fernald these words:

"You always said you had a foot for wandering. You always said you wished to go West more than anywhere else in the world. Well . . . so should I."

The last words died on her lips.

He laid a sudden hand over his eyes.

"Dammit, Lebanon Fairgale. What are you saying?"

She held her face steady, as though he might give it a blow from his hand.

"I might be a little wild-hearted," she said, telling her faults honestly. "But I am a good cook and housekeeper. I would be an obedient wife."

"I would tame your heart." He leaned nearer her face. He put his hands about her head.

"If traveling West is what you wish," he said, "we will take a long journey West together."

He wished to kiss her, to see what kissing a woman after so long would be like. But he would not ask for a kiss now. Westward he would stop under a green tree and he would kiss her truly.

Chapter 9

"MY MOTHER IS DEAD," Fernald said. "My little sister is lost some-where—dead, too, maybe. If I ever loved any other woman, now it would be finished and forgotten."

"Did you ever love any other woman?" Lebanon asked, knowing better than to ask.

"No," he lied softly. Mayhap Lebanon knew he was lying.

He put his hands about her head and drew her face down to his shoulder where the faded green of his jacket was scented.

Such was their marriage.

For a long while Fernald must have loved her, never guessing his own heart. Now she was his, for, in the first place, she had offered herself to him; and in the second place the binding words of marriage had been spoken in an immaculate silence, for all to hear, before the tall glass windows and the sober face of the parson's wife.

For twenty-five years Fernald had lived mincingly, on frugal food and no pleasures, saving silver half-dollars, double eagles, and notes in little stacks.

Now he could go West if Lebanon wished, or North or East. He could open a fancy bar in any place and serve gentlemen, and Lebanon could wear Irish lace and go to chapel and send her children to dancing school. Here was their freedom with a head and tail to it and four legs to go on. They could do anything they pleased. Suddenly Fernald was sick of life in Birdtown, though he had been contented enough till now.

He bought Lebanon a cloak of black velvet with a lining of red silk. The cloak had bound slits in its front for her hands to come through, and it had a ruff of pleated silk. He bought for her a bonnet that had a high crown of nothing but roses. The finery out of Miss Lily Ludgate's Shoppe comforted Lebanon greatly, as did likewise the ring upon her finger which Fernald had given her from his dead mother.

They traded for tarred tenting; for a cart with a steady floor of cypress planks and heavy bracing of iron. They traded for a dappled mare named Miranda, neither too young for wildness nor too old for long travel. She was a crump, born so, and so came the more cheaply. Yet her crippled foreleg caused Lebanon to love her more than if she had been born perfectly formed.

In the back of the cart, under the tarred tenting, they laid away a new iron boiling pot, a skillet and a gridiron, an oven pot and a saucepan. These would be enough for any eating. They could cut three pronged sticks and lean them together over a fire, and spit a gobbler to roast over oak coals. They took along a corn grater, salt, and side meat, meal, and dried pease, a shaker of mixed Indian spices, a trivet or two to keep ashes out of the hominy, a little sack of lye, a loaf of soap, a kittle to hang over a fire, though it might be a thousand leagues west.

They carried bedding and the brass-bound chest that was Fernald's. Most of their clothing swung on hooks under the tenting— a dusty way to go. What was too fine for dust was folded in Fernald's chest.

They could think of no other need, though traders tried to talk them into more buying.

Folks asked them: "Where will you be stopping, D'Aussy?"

And Fernald would reply: "We do not know ourselves. The Californias, maybe, or west of there . . ." Then everybody would laugh, envious and well-wishing.

It being late spring, and green grass everywhere, they took no provender for Miranda. She could crop her dinners this summer, and by winter they would be settled. Then they could buy hay and corn for her.

At the back of the trek cart was a feed trough, and they piled needfuls into it.

The cook pots clanked and jostled one another roughly, complaining of their nearness. Under the seat the musket and tinder box were safe, and the gunpowder and bullets. At Lebanon's feet there was a willow basket of ready food that Madame Lateuse had provided for them, tears on her fat cheeks. For a wedding gift she gave them a gold double eagle and a French china tea set—a rose-bowered creamer, sugar bowl, and a teapot and cups and saucers. Lebanon stuffed each piece in wood shavings and linnen wrappings. Her great-grandchildren would handle this china, along about the year 'thirty or 'forty next century! Lebanon smiled to think of such foolishness.

Lady went with Fernald and Lebanon westward.

Crease was not told of it till it was done. Fernald sent old Buckingham home under a strange hand, with a penned announcement of his marriage with Lebanon:

"We have decided to be wed and go West. When we are settled we will send word. Do not fret after your daughter's happiness, for I will conscientiously attend to it. Lebanon wishes you to know she grieves to leave you without a farewell, but time presses on us.
"Yr obt and faithful svt,
"FERNALD NAPIER D'AUSSY."

Lebanon sat high beside Fernald. She noticed the little crump had stray marks of silver across her flanks.

"Madame d'Aussy—that was Lebanon Fairgale," Fernald said, trying the sound of her new name in his own hearing. The sound of it startled her a little.

When they remembered their hunger, Lebanon served the food from Madame Lateuse's willow basket, her best and biggest basket with a hinged double lid. There were rissoles of chopped lamb, breaded and fried. There were beaten biscuits, syruped carmelites and figs and gold cheese.

Wind swirled over the little cart as though it were a roof. Heavy dark came down. They had found a little piece of water. Fernald laid a fire. Fireflies carried their lanterns everywhere.

They had eaten and it was time to sleep. Lebanon spread a bed under the tarred tenting. Lady saw nothing strange in sleeping in a house a few feet long and a fewer feet wide. Here was a man she must learn to love, since Lebanon loved him.

The next day they found talkative ferry-keeps at portages over black rivers that flowed slowly southward. Post houses were far apart, and in some cases taverns were dangerous stops.

Lebanon carried some of Fernald's moneys hung to a little gold cross betwixt her breasts. Some of the moneys Fernald carried at the bottom of his tobaca pouch, each piece wrapped so it would not jangle against another piece. Some they carried in their sock feet and some in pockets sewed inside Fernald's pantaloons and inside Lebanon's underskirts.

There was newness all along the way.

In one little place, while steeple bells tolled a fair, Fernald bought for Lebanon a blue cashmere gown because her eyes were so blue, and a cotta of red velvet with jet beading bordering its armholes. It had an upstanding collar and a swinging hem. He bought her, too, a pair of black cheverel boots with velveteen tops, and pearls strung on a cord that would loop three times about her throat.

In another place, where the little dock was washed by the Big Gulf itself, he bought her a Bokhara shawl; it was knotted of silk and wool in shades of mauve and rose coloring. Now Lebanon had shifts of linnen and underbodices of fine muslin, fichus of starched lawn and lace—and no tedious spinning and weaving, either. All you did was lay your money on a counter and point your finger. Fernald had a gift for trade. He had storekeeps dusting off hidden chests and bringing out things saved back for rich men. No calico for Lebanon. Now she had a glove box for gloves, and a rouge pot for rouge, and a trinket box for jewels. Now she had a gilt-handled hare's foot for rouging her cheeks. Sometimes now when she diked her skin in such fineness, and Fernald treasured her in his arms, she felt a scarlet-heart, for true!

Fernald bought nothing for himself. He still wore the faded green velveteen jacket, and the only newness about him was the new great-coat he was wedded in, a silk cravat, linnen shirt, and a double-breasted buff waistcoat.

The days came and went in a multitude of surprises. They were a week from home, a month, and two months. She had no time to consider if she were happy, and no one asked her. She had no complaint against Fernald as a husband—and no one to complain to. His caresses were gentle; he took thought to little things, day by day, and drew her affection more and more to him. He showed toward her a fastidious behavior in all things, so that she had no occasion to think: Sebastian could be kinder. Fernald showed his person fastidious care: he pomaded his hair so that it curled about his collar most becomingly. He brushed and scented his beard carefully. It was contenting, this being married to a gentleman who gave her beautiful things for herself and who was careful of her feelings.

One evening in a bright-candled tavern, the tavernkeep flirted mildly with Lebanon, and she was secretly affronted that he should consider her rouged cheeks an invitation to sin. Fernald was more than commonly wise; he said his wife was wearied, and they went to their room at the end of the corridor. He quickly packed their things and they slipped out the back way to the cart and were gone, to sleep under the stars. It cost Fernald a paper note to a slave, as a bribe to get them away in secret, but it was worth it to avert trouble.

Lebanon was much quietened in these days of new marriage. If they came across a tavern—of good repute, that is—they put up in style, if only to enjoy damask hangings and a wine-scented ordinary. Some nights Fernald would not come to sleep till three of the morning, and then having taken more drinks than were good for him. Lebanon would sleep with the horse pistol on the candle stand and the door barred. When she was waked from sleep to let Fernald in, she smelled his breath and thought: The path of a bride is not all pink posies.

Lebanon could begin to feel that softness that had showed in Lucie Birdsong's face. Yet why should she remember that white wench here at the back side of nowhere? Now Lebanon's face and throat were soft from cucumber cream, too, and white from strawberry juice and lemmon. Now she also was powdered and scented and spoiled. Sometimes she felt like a fool.

"You are the most beautiful woman ever I laid eyes on," Fernald would say, smothering her mouth in a kiss. And straightway she would feel beauty warming her till she was beautiful indeed. She would take his hands and look him hard in the face and say all her thanks in no more than the shining of her young eyes. To him that was thanks enough.

Fernald had paid in advance for this side room with a fireplace in it. Fernald was out with the keep. A woman, the keep's wife, had laid a fire and brought in more fat pine wood. The smoke boiled. The woman stood wringing her hands a little. She wished to talk—that was clear.

"My husband says that you and your husband are going yet farther west," she said. Her head was high above a faded calico hubbard. She carefully studied Lebanon's velvet wrap and the red riband tie in Lebanon's hair. Her voice was as soft as a lady's, a little high-pitched and with a silver tone to it.

"Yes . . ." Lebanon hesitated.

The woman stood, not knowing what more to say.

"It is fine weather we are having these mornings," she said.

"It is, indeed," Lebanon said, smiling.

"We came West," the woman opened up, wiping her reddened hands on a faded apron. Her tongue knew good words and an English way of saying them. "We came from Virginia. . . . They told us there were fortunes West. . . ."

Her face was pale and haggard; her hair was drawn into a tight knot with one knobbed pin to hold it. Her eyes were still blue, but a paler, subtler blue than when she was young in Virginia.

"Forgive me if I weary you," she smiled deprecatingly. "It is not often that nice women come through. My papa swore that I should rue leaving home. I often wonder if I do and am not aware of it."

"Leastwise, you would never admit it, would you?" Lebanon spoke sagely. "No more shall I, if ever I am sorry."

They looked at one another, and they smiled one smile.

"Please have a chair," Lebanon remembered to say. "It has been a long while since I knew any woman to talk with."

"My thanks," the other woman said. She wore no six ruffled petticoats over steel stays. Her thin figure showed through the faded hubbard, but she spread her flimsy skirt and dropped a curtsey.

"I never turned my hand at home," the woman said. "I never so much as washed a kerchief. And now I gut the game and wash the grooms' wear, and plow the garden patch and hoe it. . . . If Papa could see me now!" She spread her hands, laughing, and folded her fingers in one another again.

Next morning Lebanon saw the woman again whilst she served breakfast. Her name was Roanoke Carter, as Lebanon took pains to ask. She did the scrubbing before dawn, before the lodgers were up. The meats for today were already floured and larded and spitted across the hearth, dripping fat into the drip pans. A world of work there was to such a business as this! Roanoke was worn thin as a weathered rail.

Lebanon put a rude question to her:

"Your pardon, but why did you never have children?"

It had occurred to Lebanon that if she had children in the West, Fernald could teach them their letters and manners.

"God's will, doubtless," Roanoke Carter responded. "That is what my mother would say, I feel confident."

Her mouth twitched a little at its corners. She laughed a lot, more than was necessary to carry any point but courage. There could not be much to laugh at in her life.

A God's mercy you have no children, thought Lebanon. What could you offer them?

Fernald said her husband, Brewton Carter, was a tippler, harsh to the point of blows when he had too much. Before breakfast he drank, and before dinner and before supper and after all three meals. He was a loathsome lot, Lebanon thought, when Fernald pointed him out. Bloated and pink-faced, he lounged in a big chair by the fire, a smudge of tobaca spittle on his beard, a hound at foot. Now and then he gave the meat spit a hard turn, which was about all the labor he did in a long day. Roanoke brought in the firewood and the water from the well; she cooked and scrubbed and washed. She took the names of the people who stopped, kept the records, sent orders for merchandise.

The morning they left this tavern, Lebanon decided she must ask this Roanoke a question, even though it might affront her.

"My mother was from Virginia," she led off. "She went to Georgia with my father, and lived twenty miles from another roof, went to town scarce twice a year. I have often wondered whether she was happy or no. If it would not seem too bold, I should like to ask you has ever the thought occurred to you that a man's love is soon over?"

"Love?" Roanoke laughed. "I used to ask myself if I loved Brewton. And I used to tell myself that I *must* love him. There is no one else I would have worked so hard for. I doubt love was made to be happy in. I remember . . ."

There was a little pause. Roanoke's eyes went far off through the open shutter, where there were trees and space.

"I remember once my mother showed me the birth gown she wore when her children were born. It was of plain stuff, and simply seamed. They tell me it is a torment to wear one. . . ." Roanoke's voice sank away to nothing.

"How long since you were in Richmond?" Lebanon asked, to break the silence.

"Nineteen years, come Michaelmas," Roanoke spoke as one makes response in church meeting.

It was at that moment that Lebanon knew she would never see East again, nor Papa and Joel, nor the old roof sagging over home. . . .

Roanoke set free in Lebanon's mind a question that had troubled her more than you would think. She had thought that Lucie Birdsong was lady-tongued because she was forever kept on a sattin pillow, so to speak, pampered and dolled. It was no wonder that Sebastian had chosen her for wife instead of Lebanon. A woman will have a softer tongue if she is forever cottoned in a happy manner of living as now Fernald had laid about Lebanon.

Yet here was a woman nineteen years from Virginia, with softness in her throat and charm and gallantry.

Good blood runs true, Lebanon decided; Lucie's son will hold his shoulders back and his face toward trouble, but so shall my son! Like many another truth, this she had learned alone, putting two and one together to make five. But Roanoke Carter taught it to her.

"Will you write me sometime, when I let you know where we are to be?"

Lebanon thought this woman was as near a friend as she was likely to find.

"By all means," said Roanoke, "happy to serve. . . . It would be a pleasure to receive a hearing from you. The time that has passed since my name was called by the post!"

"When we come back East again, we shall surely stop and stay a time," Lebanon promised.

Roanoke's eyes took on a faraway look. Then she laughed.

"It is a pity you could not settle near to us," she said, "but truth to tell there is little opportunity hereabouts."

She had set down two heavy wooden buckets of water. Cold water had splashed on her hide moccasins, and the hem of her skirt was draggled in wet.

"A happy journey," she told Lebanon, holding forth her roughened hand as though it wore a lace mitten.

"Be sure to post me," Lebanon pleaded, looking back, as though she were finally now loosing her father's hand.

Miranda's hoofs went steadily westward.

It seemed to Fernald that Lebanon had quickly learned her lessons from the fashionable, cheweting wives of travelers.

"You are the finest lady ever I saw anywhere," he would tell her proudly. "You always held your head like an empress, and I saw you take a flogging at Sebastian Ratcliff's hand without flinching."

"Don't call his name to me," she said gently. It was still a pain to her, the sound of his name.

"I wish I might have a child," she said, the trees slowly receding eastward, and Miranda wearying a little. It was midafternoon and they must look for camp, for they were here in between likely stops.

"All in good time," Fernald said.

"A child gives your life back to you," she went on, as though she were wishing for a lost chance.

He said no more.

Fernald was thinking he must find and buy a parcel of land and be more than a common tapster at a bar, if he was to get anywhere and live in any but another man's house. Through these next few years they must work hard and hoard and build a little house, adding a room as they could, and then a wing of rooms. They must buy further tracts of land as they were able, beyond their first holding. So it is that fine houses grow, and big names.

Now he was going West to find such a holding, to build the beginning of his house. One room it might be at first, but sturdily built. They would first set in a monstrous fireplace of stones; later he could buy the marble mantelpiece. As years went by they would lay walnut floors over the rough pine planking. They would add new rooms and new roofs, and when the house was finally done, the fire in that big room would burn where the first fire was built on their first hearth.

As they went west day by day, Fernald asked more shrewdly concerning land for a new holding, richness of soil, nearness of water.

After seventeen weeks he turned south from a road that went through low coast land and showed Lebanon a piece of land that pleased him. To eastward it was bounded by a river thick in water hyacinths. To the west, higher pine land lay. The land was level, thick-matted in fields that had never felt a share. This was good black land, made for rice and corn and cattle. It was rich and cheap, and there was a water spring in among myrtles. Fernald bought warrants and the thing was done.

Chipmunks played in and out among the cart wheels. "Company for dinner," Lebanon said, and threw a piece of johnnycake where they would find it.

Fernald stood on a slope that went down into the river. Long ago a haphazard wind had planted water oaks here to arch a way to the water. This was the place, Fernald said. North, two miles off, the Big Pike went, east and west. From here, if the air were still, one could hear the faint rumbling of bridge timbers under the passing of a wooden-wheeled cart.

He stood under the trees and named this place "Cockaigne." Built it might never be, yet here was the place for it. By lifting his eyes, he could see galleries green in vines and the whited slave quarters. He could hear the clanging of the stable bell, he could see dust rising from the far fields in summer plowing. Now there was but a crowding of trees and pensive garlands of gray moss nearly touching the earth.

Here was a vast loneliness. Lebanon shivered the least bit and called brightly to Lady, to make a sound in the ghostly air. She could hear the oaks leaning, though they made no brushing of boughs, for there was no wind. Lady knew better than to chase the chipmunks, but she whimpered, begging Lebanon to allow her to forget her raising. "No," Lebanon said.

Down on the black breast of the river they could see ducks settle. Near by Miranda was cropping the new grass of home. She was tamed to them now, and they did not stake her at night. She wore a brass bell, which tinkled softly wherever she fed, day or night.

"When you have heard drunken men call God's name carelessly as I have, this silence is good on your ears," Fernald said, being brave. "I was sick of tavern life."

A bird whistled. Lebanon tried to cheer Fernald, for he seemed disheartened over his trade, and it was too late now to be disheartened. There were no more gold guineas betwixt her breasts, and no more notes in her petticoat pocket.

"If you ever craved music here, that bird's whistle sounds as much like a flute as anything I ever heard."

The bird whistled once more and hushed.

"We'll have music aplenty in time," he said jovially, "and anything else we crave. People will be coming West in droves before long. You'll see it. We'll be the early birds and catch the fortune."

"Don't be afeared for me," she said. "I was never lonely."

Her face glowed in solemn fidelity to him. She felt a pity for him, for he had been accustomed to busy rooms and a lot of talk.

"Listen to the frogs," she counseled him. The frogs were speaking down there in the river shallows. "Mourn! Mourn! Mourn!" the oldest frogs said. But the young ones were crying, too, and they said: "Sweet! Sweet! Sweet!"

She told him what the frogs were saying, and he took her hand as though he were lost in this new world where strange tongues spoke.

She built a fire and made hot pone, heated water and fried meat and eggs they had bought in the last town. When the food was ready, she called him from where he had walked down the slope a little way. Lady had gone with him studying the horizons.

"Come on and drink a hot cup and eat some bread and meat," she said.

She stooped by the fire and filled his tin plate and put a pewter spoon on the side of it; she poured a cup of hot water and flavored it with molasses and a little vinegar.

"I'll set a partridge trap off there tonight and give you a better breakfast," Lebanon promised.

It was near night. Birds were coming in toward the river, to sleep near water. In a thorny thicket of crab-apple trees to the leftward, a joree was making small talk in plaintive tones, saying: "She thinks . . . she thinks . . ."

"He will never finish telling on his own wife," Lebanon said. This night Fernald needed cheering. It was a far piece to any bright bar, and it is a hard job to make jests with no more than a bird's talk to go on.

"They love houses," Lebanon said. "When our house is built, they will live near as they can to us, and they will scratch in the earth like little black-and-tan chickens. They will love this piece of earth, and so will you and I."

The fire was burning down, and he threw another length of fallen log to it.

"This place is already thick-settled," she said. "It is just that we have not met the old settlers."

She meant the loons and ducks and possums and panthers and coons and rabbits and the rest of the animals.

"We could begin the lean-to in the morning," she said. "I understand every trick of a lean-to. We'd best have that in case of wet weather, unless you are content to sleep on in the cart. We could set up the lean-to and then raise the cabin over that."

He rose and poured another cup of hot water from the new copper kittle.

"That would suit," he said. "That way, this fire is the hearth already."

They sat a little time by their hearth that night, he smoking perique, and she saying careful words to tighten up his slack spirit. He was afraid he had done the wrong thing—she could feel that. But it was done now.

So it was a roofed home to them already, with a dog sleeping on the hearth, a copper kittle sighing, and their hands together. Miranda's bell called the night hours like a night watch all night long.

They began to fell trees next morning—first, saplings for a lean-to.

Lady chased a rabbit till her tongue lolled, and then she was sick of him. Lebanon went hunting along the river and with only a little trouble brought in a young buck and spent the rest of the day jerking meat over coals. She had ridded and washed the meat at the river.

They had a roast venison haunch for supper, and they had enough jerked meat to feed a big family, turned and dried and salted down in strips.

In not so many days Fernald rode over to talk with the tollkeep, and he brought back a hen, thirteen half-grown biddies, and a pig. The tollkeep was named Poake, Simon Poake, Fernald said. He had a pretty wife, Fernald said, and grown twin sons.

"They have stores," Fernald said. "We'll not want for anything."

Lebanon was more cheerful than common, for Fernald was slow taking heart.

"A man needs such a little," she said. "With the start of chickens and the pig, we couldn't very well ask for more and not show greed. All a man honestly needs is a musket, a tinder box, and a salt jar."

"And a woman," he said, and held her hand the more tightly. The days were past when he would love her desperately; after this, he would only love her faithfully.

Chapter 10

A MAN MUST BUILD A HOUSE for himself, and a woman must make it a home. Timber and stone and planking are not the only matter that go into a house. Also there must go the pulse of the brain and sweat of palm.

A little lean-to was enough of a task for a town-made man like Fernald. Fernald could make a profit on a hogshead of Port Royal any time. But he was a very dupe at this business of building a house on his own land. Often Lebanon's eyes would go about his face in wonder that he could be so helpless over a dulled ax head or a gummed cook pot or an adze mislaid to rust in the grass. His land was bought, his house was tall in his mind, but a time is required to hew out one plank, to say nothing of felling trees for the walls. There were arts she would need, once the house was walled and roofed and shuttered.

Before they had the logs halfway up, Fernald spoke of paneled corridors, corridors paneled in black wood from Terra Firma and rosewood from New Spain! They could go and lodge with the Poakes, but they were impatient to be in their house.

Lebanon was vaguely troubled all the day because she was not Madame d'Aussy or Lebanon Fairgale any more. She had striven to make herself what he wished her to be, flicking imagined soilure from the plush bodice of a bed jacket. Now he needed a strong woman to help him lay out his house and keep it for him.

She laid away the sattin and lace flounces and velvet-topped boots. She borrowed a buckskin jacket and worsted skirt from Priscilla Poake—till she could tan a skin and weave a skirt—and she went to work.

Now she was somebody new and she did not know her own name.

If the toll taker, Poake, and his two grown sons, Erwin and Estis, had not come over when they could spare a day, cold weather would have come and found Fernald and Lebanon still felling.

"How a woman wears flounces year in and year out is more than I can see!" Lebanon said, to hide the regret she felt to lay away all the pretties under cover in the cart. Sattin is fine for a bride, but hide boots better for a wife, she decided.

"You seem such a little older. It seems such a short while," Fernald would tell her lovingly.

"It seems a heavenly long while to me," she said, more than once, telling no lie.

They laid the hearthstones for the house when the time came. She had a steady strength of body; she could heave near as well as a man on the end of a felled tree. The house grew little by little. Simon Poake and Erwin and Estis Poake were brawny, and this man from East was a good customer. Besides all that, they were lonesome to be with other folks. Once a week the mail coach went through—one east, and one west. The horse change was in Mercierville. Except for pedlars' carts and horsemen and the military and gentlemen's coaches, there was nobody to see or hear talking. Sometimes a week would go by and never a coach or horseman or pedlar.

Even Lebanon was glad to ride Miranda over to the Poakes', two miles, to sharpen a tool for the men or borrow this or that. Priscilla Poake was a good-natured sort; she did not say much, but that much was kind. She and Lebanon got to be friends, as lonesome women will.

It was a long time before Lebanon knew why Priscilla Poake kept lodgings and fed and slept passengers from the coaches when they would stop. She had three extra rooms to her house. Priscilla did a lively business with such as would do business. She was lonely to desperation, and disenchanted in what she wished her life to be.

For a long while Lebanon found Priscilla Poake no different from many other women—a brighter face, maybe. She would lift her skirt shyly, if Fernald were thereabout, and show a lace flounce's edge. She had a pretty face, her eyes deep-set, with darkness about them that gave her a quaint appearance. Her lips were red as anything, and she was always about to smile. Her hair was always coming down around her collar like a baby's soft hair, yet she had no look of frowsiness. She had little feet, and womanly shoulders and breasts. Her hands had a way of touching lightly a man's hand or thigh or head, as though she thoughtlessly petted him.

Erwin and Estis, the Poake twins, were a sight to see. Not even their mother knew who was who, if she could not see their eyes and the twist of their lips. They were much taller than she, and she had a coy smiling way with them. She was no little stripling, but her sons were still taller than she, for they were six feet and four, and a long way from lean. They were nineteen years old, and as gentlemanly men as one will find, though they came from common people. There had been a girl, their sister, but she died when she was ten.

Erwin had a loud and hearty laugh, but Estis smiled in place of laughing. There was a deep bond between them. Sometimes they would turn toward one another and would march off to some project of their own, with never a word. Each was handsomer than the other, in this way or that. Erwin's black and shining thatch of hair stood and glinted in sun or candlelight till a love-hungry woman would scarce take pains to keep her hands out of it. Estis, for the most part, kept his hair wetted down and calmed. Erwin would look one straight in the face, but Estis was shyer and would go on working with his big, stubby hands if he was listening or telling something.

Lebanon liked to cook the iron pot full of squirrel pilau and the oven pot full of buttermilk biscuits if the Poakes were helping Fernald. "Thank you, ma'am," Erwin would say, his mouth crammed with brown rice and young squirrel. Estis would smile— to show his thanks, too. No use to say your thanks twice over, his smile would say.

The more Lebanon saw of the Poake twins, the more she wished for a son of her own. They had their father's rough, dark good looks and their mother's softness and charm. She did not know that they worshiped the dark earth she trod.

They had two guitars from a pedlar, and one picked out the air while the other beat the accompaniment. Some nights Priscilla Poake would ride over to go back home with the men, and it was a gathering right! Fernald would reach out his old flute from the bottom of the chest and play. . . .

> *Lean thy head upon my heart;*
> *The sea is still tonight.*
> *The billows break upon the lake,*
> *The lonely moon is bright.*

All about their plot of land, Fernald had gone with the land agent, measuring with a wheel marker on the wheel of Miranda's cart. At the last the wheel came to rest where they had started out. Fernald took pleasure in this measuring off his share of earth, to keep it to die on and be buried in. Such as Fernald and the Poakes must stay with their land in cold and heat, never leaving it unless it be to go deeper into it. There is stock to be protected, seeds to sow or reap, something to do for the land every day of every year.

The first seeds they planted on their land were greens for late summer eating. With Miranda, Fernald plowed a patch and Lebanon broadcast the seeds, a gift from the Poakes. They were precious to Fernald and Lebanon, but they came up like greens anywhere. If they had had manure for the ground, there would have been a difference, but the greens were pretty enough anyhow, softer, thicker than grass.

The late summer went. Fernald complained hardly at all when the blisters in his hands changed to bloody sores and healed hard afterward. With the Poake men helping, he found a certain pleasure in the woods. It was a new satisfaction to learn to judge a tree's height and the set of its boughs, its girth, its texture and hardness. He would lay his palm on the body of a certain tree and say: "This one." Then there was nothing to it but to chop it down.

The trees were notched and laid in, set to ride securely against a Barbados hurricane careening in from New Spain. Twelve feet up the walls went, log by log. Then the gable ends went up, ridge-poles of young cypress riding lengthwise. The hewing of clapboards was a wearisome task. Some days it seemed as though the thing would never be finished. Once Fernald said he would just as soon lodge with the Poakes and farm the land from there, but Erwin was too eager. He looked at Fernald hard.

"Lord, I'll trade you, Fernald. Estis and me could make this land stand up and sing, with a wife betwixt us. Ma would lodge you and Miss Lebanon for a little bit of nothing. Lord, yes, Fernald, I'll trade this minute." His hands were hard on a green pine slab.

But Fernald had already changed his mind. He could be as good a man as any, when put to it.

Finally Estis laughed belatedly, letting Erwin do the talking. This much he said:

"If we're to have a wife, you let me do the picking, Erwin." Minutes later he looked in Lebanon's eyes, in merry, secretive foolery, and she thought of how hard young love is, remembering the bitterness of parting from Sebastian. Then she decided it was well indeed that she was fast-married to an old and sensible man like Fernald.

Many nights the stars looked in through the ridgepoles, and some days thunder cracked and rain came in a hurry and flooded the floor of the house abuilding. Yet foot by foot the clapboards were split from oak and poplar, were hewed by ax and wedge from blocked tree rounds of weathering cypress, were fastened home under poplar poles.

Now Fernald's hands that had shed blood on the timbering of his house were gloved in gristle and callused as a hound's forepaw. Finally there was but a narrowing space that let in starshine, and then on a certain night the roof was dark, sealed from the sky and the rain and cold of coming winter. Not in their time nor their children's time would these rafters rot.

"We locked them in a long hug, these logs," Erwin said, showing his teeth and brushing his hand over his young beard.

Their clay chimney was five days abuilding. Clay from the riverbank, stuck with twigs and moss to give it body, turned to a pale gold as it dried. The door place was hewed out, and the door would soon be set on wooden pins through leathern hinges. In time they would have hand-hammered iron hinges; in time they would have window places cut and greased paper for light by day, and shutters to fold in at night. They would lay a puncheon floor.

Erwin and Estis brightened the house, inside and out, with limewater. Lebanon liked this newfangled, French way of whitewashing things. As winter came, and if trapping were lucky, the floor could be covered in furs. Already the list of things she needed from Mercierville had grown to the length of a foolscap page—the loom and the spinning wheel, the cow and the calf, the iron traps, the new needle and linnen thread, the alum and the copperas . . .

Fernald took more joy in his house because Erwin and Estis coveted it so much. He had hardened his hands so his children would not have to do so. He would clear the land so it would not have to be done twenty years from now. The well was to dig, the garden patch to rail in, the crib to build, the lot to fence. Lebanon's chickens roosted in the low trees. On a still night the young rooster could hear his father crow at the toll house and would answer in a shrill all's-well. Lebanon kept the fowls so full of corn they never craved to go back to the place they called home.

One day Lebanon was singing across the yard toward the spring, with an empty pot in her hands. Estis jumped and whirled her away from the path. Much too late she would have seen the rattler coiled there, not a foot from her ankle. Estis crushed the snake's head with the side of an ax head, although for a moment it was a guess whether he could dodge the striking fangs and kill with the first lick.

Fernald said he was browsing around where he had no trading to do, but if one looked at it from the snake's viewpoint, he was well within his legal rights.

Now in the very last of summer the mosquitoes were so thick that Lebanon had to buy netting from Priscilla Poake's commissary, and veiled it above their sleeping pallet where they slept. They were forever hearing of yellow pestilence to the West, and there was no relief from that Thing but flight.

The thought of the Pest troubled Lebanon a little. It came through the air and settled on a place, and there was nothing to do but get from that place with all possible dispatch. Those who tarried to nurse and bury their dead died too.

Now and then pedlars would come by, told of the D'Aussys' new house by the Poakes', and they would sleep by the fire—and bring news of things West and East. Old Mississip had run wild in the spring, Orleans was growing richer and wilder. Out yonder plantations were spreading out along old Mississip, and wharves were thicker. There were gambling houses and worse, and cock-fights, bearfights, and slave farms.

"When were you East last?" Lebanon would ask.

"Oh, last year," the pedlar might say carelessly.

"Were you ever in Birdtown, Georgia?" Lebanon would press him.

"Why, yes . . . why, yes, a six months back. Nice place to be," he'd say, and Lebanon would hush, because Fernald would not help her.

"This country is better," the pedlar would say, to cheer them.

"I heard tell Northerners were buying up a whole business of trees in Birdtown."

"Yes, that is so," Fernald said suddenly. "Name of Ratcliff."

"Why, now that is the truth. Ratcliff it was. Well, I be! You know 'em, then!"

"You never carry any such thing as fruit trees about, do you?" Fernald asked.

"Why, no," the pedlar said. "But I know a feller that does." He spat a blob of rich brown tobaca juice smack into a hovel of powdery ashes heaped at the end of the backlog.

They could always ride over to the Poakes' tollhouse and read the tavern sheet posted, but that was dull business. There were items on Mr. Adams and General Jackson, and Mr. Calhoun of Carolina, and Shall We or Shall We Not Recharter the Bank, States' Rights, and Can South Carolina Secede Just Because She Does Not Like a Duty on Foreign Goods? . . . But those were strangers' names, and dead deeds, far off and meaning little. This was news—this talk of the pedlar's, gamecocks in Orleans and painted women in Natchez, a five-legged calf in Pensacola, and five beautiful sisters, two of them twins, in a big white house in Mobile; their daddy keeps a guard awake all night at the door with a loaded shotgun, they say, and the young ladies climb down the rose trellises and their young beaux kiss the places where the thorns have torn blood. And the Pest . . .

Lebanon had never feared a wildcat or a rattler—that is, given the chance to see him before he saw her. But this talk of the Pest shook her. She almost wished she were back home with Crease. It was time a letter could catch up with them. Fernald had sent word home, but the mail was unsure. Some of the coach stops were little more than rum-and-lemmon brothels, and a canvas post sack is easily pilfered.

Lebanon grew nervous until her sleep was troubled, and she decided it was time to conquer such fears. The thing to do was to deny fear its way with her. Disaster would come or it would not come. At home with Papa and Joel she could die of the pox in a week. Past these fears her mind described to her there might be worse things which she had not guessed—like the coiled rattler Estis had killed. The Papist Fathers walked into the Pest with a smile, and if they were afraid, you could not guess it. So Fernald and Lebanon practiced merriment.

Their home stood where once was long moss veiling and the bowers of water oaks that arched a way to the black river. The chimney was of a gold color. The roof and walls were of bright new wood. The old oaks stood about. Quick, small tongues of birds chattered in the wild mulberries and cherries. Chipmunks were friendly as kittens till Lady thought nothing of chasing them any more. About the spring, till Lebanon fenced it in saplings, they could see fresh

deer sign on many a morning, and little cat tracks of badgers and
porcupines. Tame fowls roosted in the trees, wild turkeys went over,
their wings whistling, and wild geese and ducks came down on the
river.

Long before day, they ate corncakes and fried meat and went to
work. Lebanon's hearth was bright with new brass now. A pedlar
had sent a loom and spinning wheel by a trader's wagon all the way
from Orleans, though Fernald swore she would never see the things.

Fernald's ax could be heard ringing in the woods, girdling trees
in new ground, bringing down wood for fencing the land and for
shelter for stock. Through the high noons the sun was so hot overhead that he had to come in and rest awhile. He would lie and
watch Lebanon spinning for winter wear.

Lebanon went about the little house's small matters. She worked
the garden and had beet tops hand-tall and more turnips than Brad-
dock's Army could eat! She wove a chest comforter for Fernald, for
winter, and stirred a stew pot while she went on with afternoon
sewing. She had time for wishing while she worked. She wished for
sheep, if ever the cow was safely bought, but she would not mention
sheep till she saw the cow. She would use all the lamb's wool for
baby things.

Erwin and Estis brought her a beehive with a swarm of bees, but
it was late, and she would have to sweeten them all winter. Proud
she was of them, though. On the middle day of October, Fernald
led home, at the back of the cart, a cow, lowing for her first calf.
Lebanon had prayed the beast might be cream-colored with white
markings somewhere—and so she was. Fernald named her Juno,
and Lebanon considered it a likely name. More and more, as they
learned how matters stood, Miranda and Juno stayed together. The
two bells never strayed far out of hearing, and Fernald built for the
animals a shelter below the spring, and they lived there, eating dried
shucks and meal from one trough.

So the months were tolled off, and farther and farther the trees
were girdled for a field. The fireplace was manteled by a hewn
board, and now they had a bed place of forked poplar logs and cross-
pieces of cedarwood and a spring mattress of woven roping. Erwin
and Estis were clever with a barlow knife and any kind of wood.

There was now a shelf by the door, for a water pail. There were chairs aplenty for Fernald and Lebanon and all the Poakes to sit in —polished wood of walnut, with seats of split hickory withes, or plain poplar chairs. There were two low stools of pine. Now and then Erwin and Estis would take a day off and come over and work on the corncrib, or split rails for a fence, as though this were their own house.

Once Estis turned a red face toward the gourd he was carving.

"Everything is different since you and Fernald came to live close," he said.

Lebanon felt like an old woman before his face. Still her hair flared as it used to do when the swamp wind fondled it. She felt somehow matured, straitlaced, and forced to reason every matter through for herself.

"We will always try to be good neighbors," she said.

Estis looked toward her, wearing his heart in his eyes as Lady did.

Now she had pewter plates and smoothing irons, spoons aplenty, steel knife blades, copper pots and brass skillets to go with the little kittle from Birdtown. She even had a new lamp and oil for it, for occasion, though that seemed foolish, indeed. She went and spent a day with Priscilla Poake and helped dip candles and made some candles for herself, by her own labor, and was as proud as though she had brought Fernald a gift.

Fernald would sometimes think beside the fire till he fell asleep and must be jostled into bed by Lebanon's tongue. He would break perique into bits into his palm, crumbling it for his corncob pipe, and bitter-sweet drifts of smoke would coil and vanish above his head as he sat so, thinking.

Lebanon would be knitting a worsted stocking, the leg lengthening to be as long as Fernald's leg: or she might be spinning.

There are few words, or none, to tell fully what they thought, those two: set into plain little A's and R's and X's, their thoughts would not amaze you, and perhaps they would not even interest you; yet I am convinced that what they thought was important, just as the secret things you set your mind on are important.

They said little.

Fernald would be thinking: Here are warm hearthstones, toted one by one from the river. Not a chimney stone of India jadestone could be more comforting. No marble could have a prettier cheek than the dull clay of this chimney we built. No windows of finely spun French glass could so shine as these walls with firelight papering them in a thousand designs. No gold-colored zargun glass from Persia could burn brighter than the copper cook pots which Lebanon keeps shining like a bride's ring. No Isles of Japan quince could seem finer in my mouth than the greens and late corn Lebanon got to bear, somehow grew, and cooked for me.

Fernald had found his Cockaigne, though it was not exactly according to his specifications.

Next time Fernald went to Mercierville he brought her a little saint for the mantelpiece and a thin copy of that man Byron's poems, to see what she would say when he read them out to her. . . .

> *"So we'll go no more a-roving*
> *So late into the night;*
> *Though the heart be still as loving,*
> *And the moon be still as bright.*
>
> *"For the sword outwears its sheath,*
> *And the soul wears out the breast,*
> *And the heart must pause to breathe,*
> *And Love itself have rest.*
>
> *"Though the night was made for loving,*
> *And the day returns too soon,*
> *Yet we'll go no more a-roving*
> *By the light of the moon."*

Lebanon's eyes were not on the book in Fernald's hands, but on a far distance there near to her face.

"Who was it wrote that?" she asked when Fernald hushed reading.

"A man named Byron, a lord of England," Fernald said.

"A lord of England . . ." she repeated softly. It was as though Sebastian had hailed her across a widening gulf.

"Read it over again!" she pleaded, wishing she knew her letters.

Chapter 11

IT SEEMED TO LEBANON that she had liked the building of this house better than living in it. Now that the time was past, she remembered those days when she and Fernald were first in this place, with a musket, a tinder box, and a salt jar. Now she hungrily remembered the lean-to that had stood here in the middle of this room, its air odorous in pine, and a low fire before it.

It may be that Lebanon's first discontent grew from her being within walls at all. There was this and that which discontented her and Fernald. One of the first times they had cross words at all was over nothing, and they were both ashamed of it. Now and then Fernald would speak of a bitch—and he did not mean a female dog. The sound of it was strange on his French tongue. That first time they quarreled he said that Priscilla Poake was a good-looking bitch, and Lebanon took offense. (He knew what she was, and Lebanon did not.)

"I don't like to hear a woman called a bitch," Lebanon flared, and there was a somber tone in her voice.

"There are bitches that do not walk on four legs nor howl," Fernald said, holding up his end of the log. There was a grating of pepper on his tongue.

Lebanon reached her hand and laid it on Lady's head. "This dog shames you," she said. She spoke as though Fernald were a little boy with no raising, and Fernald resented that most deeply.

"I'll not have a woman called a bitch in my house," Lebanon said.

"Then what will you, my fine lady?" asked Fernald, reminding her that this was *his* house, for his money had paid for everything in it and the land under it.

She went off to the cook table and washed a pot she had left to soak.

They had been a year, and a little over, in the house. Often now when she felt a tightness in these set timbers of home, she would tell Fernald of a wish to take the musket and wool cotta and follow a trail for deer—whether she killed one for fresh meat or not—sleeping before a new fire on a dry rise in the wild with a wind wall of pine for shelter and the chattering of the forest instead of these shut-in, dulled walls.

"You'd best keep home," Fernald would say shortly. "You'll be as wild as Dan'l Boone's woman, first thing you know."

"His woman was not wild," she said. (But she thought: Maybe she was too tame, and that is why he was always leaving her!)

Fernald would never consent to her unnatural desiring. The wild woods were no place for his wife. In the second place he was amazed that she could languish for any reason, now that she had this house to keep. In the third place there was deer sign, any morning, by the spring—if it was deer she craved. And in the fourth place they had jerked meat aplenty to feed Nap's Army, if ever it should march again.

Lebanon despaired of telling Fernald what she felt—of the smothering feeling that the clean air of the woods would dispel; or was it walking alone that did it, and he not too near in a close house? From toddling time she had gone on hunts with Crease and Joel and the hounds. As she oldened she was not much less than a lesser man with them, in a sheepskin coat and a fur cap and toting home her share of game.

"That was no way for a lady to grow up," he would say sourly, if ever Lebanon mentioned it. "You know it as well as I do."

"I know nothing of the kind," she would flounce back. "My raising was as good as your own." The bride's nights are over when a man taunts a woman with her blood, and his best happiness is done when she replies to it. Crease used to say a man and his wife never had an honest-to-God quarrel till they got onto each other's families.

Sometimes she looked at Fernald in wonder. He thought he knew so much! But he was a master fool in many things where she could have taught him better. Where had he lived all his life to know so little? He did not even know to warm an ax blade before chopping with it in cold weather. He did not even know to chew poison-ivy leaves to keep hot blisters from his own skin. He did not know to drink strange sage tea for fever, or cinchona broth for a chill.

She knew it was not becoming in her always to be saying: Did you not know that? But Fernald would as soon picket Miranda by the hind foot as the forefoot, and saw no reason why she should not be hobbled in a thickety place.

The first time Lebanon lifted away her hat the better to hear, Fernald laughed at her, and never believed that the brim of a hat can muffle sound about a body's ears. He saw no difference in sign of the cat tribe or the dog tribe. He would mix bear and cougar and lynx tracks as one, if left to judge for himself. He would not know a mink's trace from a weasel's, nor a badger's from a skunk's or a porcupine's. If Fernald were set down in the woods he would be dead in a month—if he lived that long.

He was little to blame, of course. He had spent his young years in playing hot cockles and toddle-top, in flipping cards in a game of corners. His feet had moved in quadrilles and arabesques while hers had tramped mile on mile, tracking a certain buck. Gentilities were as thick through his young years as sand spurs through Lebanon's. He had lessons once on a viola da braccio, and could play the flute till now. Till now his hands were that daintily turned that they seemed forever curved to fit a fine-stringed music piece. Yet he would not know tonic root from birthwort, or creeping myrtle from sassy bark.

The whole thing had taught Lebanon this: She had had to pole the dugout while Sebastian lolled like a Mogul in the prow. Sebastian knew no more of wild things than did Fernald. Therefore Fernald was as good a man as Sebastian. Doubtless she would have grown temperish with Sebastian, too, shut up a long year and a half in four walls, with nobody but the Poakes to know.

Now and then she would sit on the cypress door block if the mosquitoes were not too troublesome. She had learned from Priscilla Poake a better remedy of pine tar and pennyroyal. She would sit, her back to the doorjamb, and she would look away eastward, a long way off. From the gathered chimneys of Mercierville the smoke rose, clustering thinly, telling of houses and smithies and platemongers.

For Lebanon that smoke was too near. If she had her way now, she would wish for no neighbor but wild deer. Often she was troubled by her own restlessness. Fernald could feel her discontent and hated it.

"You have no notion what you want," he would say.

"Maybe I do not. But I am certain it is not a bobbinet bodice nor a bijou jacket."

She thus threw back in his face all his gifts which now she could not wear. Likewise, it was a taunt of his taste for niceties. Still he groomed his mustaches and beard and wore bright waistcoats when he went to town.

Once he went to the Poakes' late in the afternoon to have a little corn ground. He stayed the night, because it was late. When he came home in the morning, Lebanon said nothing, for she knew nothing to say. How could he wish to sleep under another roof without her? How could he have fallen asleep—for she could not! They might have had their little ripples, but still . . . but still . . .

When Erwin Poake asked her to go with him to shoot squirrels next day, she went, and when Fernald learned of it there was torment to be paid up.

There was growing disorder, and Lebanon kept on thinking when she should have stopped her thoughts dead. She resolved to say no more sharp words to Fernald, no matter what he should say.

Once she got out the old crimson bodice and spangled skirt and put them on to eat supper in. She fringed her front hair and piled her back hair high on her head and stuck a blue riband bow in the knot. She creamed her face and powdered it and rouged her cheeks. They were sitting at supper, and Fernald was pleased, though he was too stubborn to say so or to kiss her.

Then who should come to the door but Erwin and Estis Poake! They stood dumb-faced in the door, looking at Lebanon. She asked them in, and they sat and talked, though any fool could feel Fernald's displeasure. Never in all their lives had they seen anything so beautiful as Lebanon seemed to them!

When they were gone, Fernald was in a torment.

"So you were expecting them!" he thundered. "You expected me to be gone, doubtless. And what if I had been gone, what! A pity a man must keep close home to keep his name clean."

Fernald stamped and shouted. He was scarcely himself, for he had drunk too much of the mulberry morat. Lebanon's eyes blazed. She tore off the bodice, scarce troubling the buttons.

"I did this for you!" she said solemnly, holding tight her tongue with her teeth.

"You are a liar," he said.

She told him he was mean and little then, and wept half the night because of what she had told him. He never believed her, and she never forgot.

Lebanon worked at skins of deer, cutting and sewing a short skirt and a pair of leggons to thread about her legs. Such things are a guard against a snake's fangs for one thing, and keep out cold for another, and cover nakedness for a third. Once wet, deerskin can be a cold bother to the skin, but it is soft to deal with in sewing, and about as good as anything for general wear.

Fernald did not like Lebanon in skin shirts and tight skirts. When pedlars came out of their way by this house, he was ashamed when he saw his wife's stockings showing like any poorest out-trader's wife. He said this and that about the garments, and as women will, Lebanon took it amiss and thought he was thus berating her raising and her old home, and she became more firmly determined to wear these garments to the end of her days on earth.

"I dressed up once in your clothes," she said, "and you remember what I got for my trouble."

"Served you right, too," he said.

Then they were both angered and hurt again, remembering.

The more determined she became, the worse he got about nagging, and there they went. Fernald went more and more often into Mercierville. Lebanon grew the more quiet, living carefully to herself in a little silence.

Sometimes when men hallooed in the dooryard, and Lady ran and barked madly, Lebanon would open the door reluctantly, if Fernald was not there, and would have little to say at all. She would not ask the pedlars in, and the Poake twins felt her discomfiture if they went to her house when Fernald happened not to be there.

"She is afraid of him, I do swear!" Erwin would say.

"Reckon he is mean to her when nobody is there?" Estis would ask.

The six-foot-four twins came more often than ever, and half the time they came and sat with their hearts all but falling out of their eyes. They did not care if they should make a fool of Fernald. And one could never blame Lebanon for being glad to see them, because she knew she should not be glad.

There was a Fall Fair in Mercierville, and Fernald asked Lebanon to go, too, but she declined because it was a far way, and she was shy, and Fernald had been bitter-tongued. Fernald rode off alone, fobbed and sleek.

Lebanon had not believed he would leave. She wished him to take her in his arms and say: I am sorry for all our hard words, and as for my part, I shall not quarrel with you again, because you are the most beautiful woman ever I laid my eyes on.

He never told her that he felt twinges of conscience about it, leaving her that first time. After that first time the feeling was much lessened, and finally it disappeared.

Lebanon thought: This is the first time he has left me, and in a way it is the last time he will ever leave: after this I shall not care so much. When Fernald was gone, Lebanon rode over to the Poakes', because she was left out now, for sure. Priscilla told her she was a fool not to go.

"When your husband asks you to go somewhere, always go," Priscilla said.

But Priscilla had not gone with her husband and sons.

"Somebody had to take the tolls," she said. (But who would care if the river were free one day and night?)

"I doubt old slow Poake would ask me any more now, anyhow," Priscilla laughed.

She seemed not to care at all. She tossed her head and reached her white arms to tend her hair.

"Fernald is a good husband to you, is he not?" asked Priscilla, slyly sizing Lebanon's face and figure.

"Finest ever," Lebanon said. "I have never had the least cause for complaint."

The way she said it you knew she was sad and distempered.

"May you never, then!" said Priscilla, lifting down a bowl from a shelf.

Priscilla went on smiling. One by one she broke four egg-yolks into the bowl and beat them all together. The whites she set aside to whip to froth later. She was making a pudding or a batter.

In these moments that Lebanon first knew Priscilla's character and trade, a cool wind blew around the corner of her heart, the cool wind called jealousy. She remembered Fernald's tales of Priscilla's bright sayings, and how trim she kept her hearth, and how smooth her feather beds always were. There were many nights when Fernald stayed at the Poakes' now. He would bring back the ground meal next morning. If ever she chided him with staying so often at the Poakes', he would be sour about it.

"What if I do?" he would ask. "You are glum and say nothing. You will never talk and laugh like other women. You show all too plainly you do not like my company when you run off to the swamp for a deer or a cooter."

Then Lebanon pulled herself up. He likes gaming with the Poakes men, she told herself. I will not allow jealousy to come into my heart. It is too great torment.

"Fernald is a fine man," Lebanon said, to say something to this woman whom she suddenly hated—for no reason except that her heart told her to hate Priscilla Poake.

Yesterday Fernald had brought over Erwin and Estis and told Lebanon to go and shoot squirrels if she liked. He was going to help Simon shuck corn, he said; and the boys were due a day off. . . .

"Does Simon generally take much time off at the Fair?" Lebanon asked.

"I say he does," Priscilla laughed. "This is the third day he has been gone, leaving the whole load for me to carry."

Lebanon clenched her hands softly together. Then Simon Poake was not at home yesterday, and Fernald said he was. Fernald said he was helping Simon shuck corn.

"I wish I had gone to Mercierville with Fernald," Lebanon said. "I suppose I will always regret telling him I would not go."

She looked away off toward Mercierville.

Priscilla's sleeves were rolled up, and her full-fleshed arms showed as she worked with the mixture in the bowl.

"I thought I'd beat up a light-cake," she said. Her basque was tight over her high bosom. Her face was flushed, beating the dough with the long-handled wooden spoon. As soon as she could, Lebanon said her farewells and walked back toward home. She took off his ring and dropped it into her apron pocket. Before she got to her door block, she put the ring on again.

Fernald did not have anything more to say about the twins coming over. If he had a hard word for her, Lebanon would stiffen her hands on whatever they might be holding, and her eyes would fill with a sad and bitter light.

Fernald excused his little trickery with women, as a man will. Was it his fault if women found him nimble of foot and gallant at handing them about in dancing measures? Could he be blamed if he liked to toss Priscilla about when the twins beat their guitars in a dance tune? Was it his fault if she took his hands, and kissed his lips for good luck, so that he could not forget the kiss?

Not for anything on earth would he have hurt Lebanon. Yet now to him his own house was dulled and dark, well-nigh sullen, when he came home to it from the glass-chimneyed candles and merrymounts of Mercierville.

There was a small ugly tale that grew out of Mercierville.

On a certain night the tavernkeep considered that Fernald and his wife chose one another too often as partners. The man's name was Patrick Margate, and his wife was named Cassia. Looks flashed, and Margate took out his pistol from its holster and laid it before him carelessly, so that everybody could see it.

"If you don't have a taste for pistols, we'll use short swords," Margate said.

"But Patrick," Cassia Margate said, "this is all a hideous misunderstanding. You don't wish to challenge Mr. d'Aussy. We only this night discovered that we are fourth-degree cousins. He was telling of it. We have mutual kin in Augusta and Memphis. A Jameson married a Miss Laughran and their daughter married——"

"Oh, I never knew about your kinfolks," Margate growled, contemptuous of his wife. "Maybe this dandy will fight to prove it. A good man ought to be willing to fight for a cousin in Augusta. Or Memphis."

"Oh, never do, Mr. d'Aussy," Cassia pleaded, although it would have been better if she had said nothing at all.

Fernald had stood saying nothing while that woman pleaded for him. His hand was on his holster, but he did not draw his pistol. He leaned hard on the table. A man must rise when he is challenged, though he may fall down again at once. Fernald did not quite fall down again.

"Do men have wives where your mother brought you up?" Patrick Margate asked Fernald, because he saw he could.

It was as though he had spat a tobaca wad straight into Fernald's face. And Fernald still stood with his empty hand on the pistol holster, his eyes full of tears.

"We out here be most particular of our wives," Margate went on, rolling his tobaca cud and enjoying himself in the eyes of the onlookers. "Next to a man's knife and pistol, he values his wife most highly."

He put his fingers like claws on Cassia's shoulder and marched her through the silent crowd to the door. He slapped her where she sat down, and he laughed, and then the crowd laughed, relieved. He turned, when he was at the door, and swept off his hat and made a deep bow toward Fernald.

"A good evening, Mr. d'Aussy," he mocked. "I leave this gathering to your graces. My respects!" And in only a slightly lower tone he said: "Watch your women, gents!"

The room rocked with laughter.

Priscilla Poake heard of the contention, and it was her pleasure to tell Lebanon.

Lebanon turned her face away a little as Priscilla spoke. She wished to say: "Hush! Oh, hush!" She knew that Fernald was a finer gentleman than Margate or his friends. She wished to go and shoot the tavern up, call out the men and tell them off. But there are some things you cannot fight.

"The less said the better," she murmured to Priscilla Poake and went to talking of another matter.

Priscilla studied her face the more closely. ("She is the hardest, coldest woman ever I saw," Priscilla told her husband.)

The twins came over, turning their wool hats in their hands, standing on one foot and then the other.

"We'll go and wear that Margate to a very frazzle betwixt us, if you give the word," they said.

Estis did not smile now. His chin was a man's chin. They had good fists.

"We can whip all that crowd," Erwin said.

Lebanon spread her hands and laughed. "It was nothing. Nothing. . . . It all has been much enlarged," she said. "I'd dismiss it all. Everybody has had too much to say about it. Fernald says there was nothing to it but talk. . . ."

Things got no better. The way to cause a man to drink all the harder is to call him a fool, a weakling, and a criminal against his family, and people said all those things of Fernald. Most of Fernald's trouble came from the fact that he did not work enough. He would come home reeking of wine, his pretty waistcoat soiled, his twilled pantaloons spotted, and his silk stock flowing. Lebanon took off his boots and beat up a pillow for him to lay his head on. If he was much disturbed inwardly, she gave him a pinch of calabar-bean powder to cause him to sleep off his drunken megrims. She handed him a cup of mulse to wash out the bitter taste and tame his nerves.

She pitied him at such times, and she despised him, yet she hid her feelings even from herself. She would go and curry Miranda where the saddle had worn since Fernald had put it on, yesterday or the day before, or the day before that. Unless some kind man that loved horses had unsaddled the little mare at the hitching rack, she stood saddled while Fernald was in town. Somebody would set Fernald on her back and she would plod west with him, or he would have a blinking interval and climb to her saddle, and slip, and climb again.

A worse worry than his drinking was his spending money as though it were spring water, always flowing.

Sometimes they quarreled bitterly now. They quarreled over Miranda, when Fernald loved her as much as Lebanon did. Or they quarreled over whether beans should go here, and pumpkins yonder, or the other way round. Fernald stayed longer in town, and Lebanon grieved. Sometimes she thought: I will leave him and go back home to Papa. But East was not home any more, and she had no way to go home, and she did not wish to leave Fernald, for Fernald was part of her, the greater part.

Now Lebanon had full excuse for trapping much as she might ever desire. Fernald would not know if she stayed ever so long by the river. Sometimes he was gone for as long as a week.

The winter of that third year deepened, and Lebanon got furs aplenty, black and shiny as sattin, or streaked in silver, like Miranda's flank. Before Hallowmas she had hollowed a dugout, burning it out slowly as she had seen Crease do long ago, heaping and tending oak coals in little places on the wood.

When the boat was done, Miranda dragged it to the river's edge for her. Lebanon shoved it out across the sand, and it rode bravely and truly on the slow current. She drove a stake to tether it to shore. Here in this west country she required a longer pole, for the river was deep in places. It took time and careful reckoning to ride this river, and long practice; otherwise the river was little different from a swamp current. Before another summer she learned to catch the currents rightly; she learned to judge deep water and shallows. Soon she could ride this river as she had ridden those lost swamp waters, Crooked Arm and Lebdebby Slough and Dead Man's Water.

"I should have stayed East," Fernald complained one day.

"I should have gone on farther westward," he complained another day. (He should be any place but this place, it seemed—and here he was snagged properly, with a wife to feed.)

"A good thing you never had a child," he would taunt, because he himself was in pain. "God knows His business. . . ."

For that, Lebanon could have wept, but she would not let Fernald see her tears.

"I think I'll ride into Mercierville," he would say, rising from the table with a look of deathly weariness on his face.

"Go, then," Lebanon would tell him, but her eyes glowed.

Time went along: sometimes it hastened, sometimes it slowed.

Lebanon cured fur pelts. With the Poake twins she cut and laid a rail fence about the dooryard. She hoed winter cabbages and set wild-plum seedlings close into the house in a little nursery. She spun and twisted worsted and hanks of cotton and linsey-woolsey, as always.

Fernald no longer brought her gifts from Mercierville. He brought only himself, sodden and piteous. Rightly speaking, he did not even bring himself, for Miranda brought him. Twice travelers found him ditched and roped him to his saddle, and so he came home like a half-dead man from a war, drooling and weeping and saying he never had a chance.

"You have a chance, any time, any new moment," Lebanon stormed. "Turn down the next glass. Keep away from Mercierville. Stay here with me, and we will pull things around together."

Her words had little weight. He was sick of words and wished to be away from her. Something had eaten into his heart until his cravings were stronger than himself. He was led by them as a broken-spirited hound is led, belly low and tail drooping. Lebanon knew herself heavily to blame. Never was there any matter that had only one side to it.

Somewhere along in these days another cunning came to her. Now and then she knew happenings before they came to being. A voice would speak with her, and first she would cast its prophecy out, accounting herself too old to be troubled by unheard voices. Still the voice would wheedle her against her will. Long ago she could smell rain far off. Many a man can do that. Long ago she could smell game and name it. But now this further sense was more keen and more deeply grown. Standing against the wind, near a run, she could swear deer were on the browse a little way beyond, before she could catch the least sound of their hoofs. These little knowledges were somewhat of a curse, for by such a sense she knew that Fernald was trafficking with Priscilla Poake.

Once Priscilla told her of losing a ruby stone from a finger ring, and before she gave the matter any thought at all Lebanon said:

"Look in your meal barrel when you go home."

Priscilla went home and looked in the meal barrel, and there in the first handful of meal she picked up was the little ruby stone.

Lebanon had known the stone would be there, though she could not have told how she knew it.

She could trap a weasel because she could guess the tracking he would make this night. She could foretell rain or sun for tomorrow by a feel in her bones. There was an inner hidden ear within her head, an understanding of things, a certain knowledge.

She was sure a child was growing before she had any reason to suspect.

She did not tell Fernald of this certainty. He might consider her peculiar—and she was shy of this child, somehow. She did not sicken. She trapped as always.

After a time, there came the sign.

Like a wild thing she took the secret to the woods with her. Fernald was gone a week in Mercierville and the house was cold. Lebanon and Lady lay in the woods, with a wild fire for company. She thought of Sebastian back there among clattering cobbles and boardwalks. Now he might be with Lucie Birdsong, beyond stifling window drapes, eating from silver trenchers. Would he have been like Fernald in Mercierville while the child grew within her?

Not till later would she tell Fernald of it. This was his possession which she hid within herself. Would he be displeased? . . .

A new and forgiving affection took hold on her heart: I shall tell him, and this will make all things straight betwixt us. I am cursed by moods and contrariness. Now things will be different. In many ways I have failed him, and I could not seem to remedy my failings. If he has failed me, neither could he remedy it. This child will remedy every crooked matter.

Chapter 12

LEBANON HAD FERNALD write to her father of the coming child, and how happy life was in this new country, how pleasantly situated she was by all considerations. Crease never saw the letter, for there came to Fernald notice that Crease Fairgale had departed this life, having passed away in his sleep of a stomach malady.

For a reason she did not know, Lebanon had Fernald write to Roanoke Carter of her father's death and the child's coming, and after some months there came a missive from Roanoke Carter, scribed in blue ink and trailing curls and loops, and she spoke of "deep happiness" and "unheard-of delight" and "a little son" and "a little daughter" and "your dear father" and "your old home" and "your fine husband."

Roanoke's letter, read and reread by Fernald, steadied Lebanon's feet more than you would have believed possible. "Write to me soon," Roanoke pleaded, "and tell me whether it is a son or daughter and what his name shall be. I shall knit for him a pink wool feckit and post it along if ever I have the time. My respects to your honored husband and your dear self. The pigs are fattening proudly and we shall have hams aplenty. The corn is prime. The sky stands still above us all, and I commend you to the mercy of Him who suffered for us so that our sufferings, whatever they may be, may seem small by comparison when we think of Him."

The child was born in the year 'thirty-six.

That was the year the comet came and did not destroy the earth, after all. There was a conflagration in New York City, and bloody talk from the abolitionists.

There was a lot happened that year. One of the longest railroads in the country was opened from Wilmington to Weldon in Carolina. One hundred and sixty-one miles one could ride, and turn around and ride back again! This South country was opening up and filling in.

But all that was dull news in gazettes and tavern sheets. Jefferson was dead, and the Liberty Bell cracked a year before when it was tolling for Chief Justice Marshall. There was many a mouth that hid behind a hand and said this country would go back under England's wing if things got too tough. It seemed a bad thing for politicians to split a dozen ways—when there was only one country to serve: Republicans, and Aristocrats, and Aristocrat-Republicans, and Republican-Aristocrats, and Democrats and Hellfire Republicans, and on and on. . . . The patriots spoke out, though, and held things together: from the Philadelphia *Aurora,* the Columbian Museum, the Augusta *Courier,* the Savannah *Republican,* the *Georgian,* they preached what Jefferson or Washington said, and men still got up in the Senate and told where they stood on a question.

Lebanon, of course, could not read the bulletins, and when Fernald and Simon Poake began to talk of politics, she and Priscilla always started up a whispering about new yeast or sage plants or a rose cutting.

Lebanon did not see much of anyone any more.

In the last week of the secret life within her, she tended traps miles from home. Fernald had gone into Mercierville, and she loaded musket and tinder box in the dugout and, missing the down current, rowed upriver, past graybeard points of land and whited sandbars and tupelo swamps. She made camp by a brown-water branch that crept softly into the river there. She caught six quail in the old snare in half an hour, and loosed four of them again. She set the fishing line and lay waiting, stretched on the coarse white sand of the river bar. From here she could see if a fish jerked the line. The two slain quail lay cooling in a pannikin of cool water, picked and ridded. When the fish were caught, there would be supper aplenty for Lady and Lebanon, and ashcake left over.

The stirring of the child troubled her comfort now and then, but she gave that trouble little mind, save to wish the child might be born this hour, so that she might lay eyes on it at last. The child's growth had been no great burden. An ungrown woman might squinch and shed tears, but this was only a little weariness, a differing ailment such as a head cold or a case of megrims might be.

Somehow the child's presence with her had imbued Lebanon with a sort of sadness. Carrying a child will sometimes burden a woman with the ponderous woes of all the earth; such a pregnancy is somewhat like a fulsome growth in a man's mind when he brings to birth a thought or a deed that will color some number of centuries.

In these days it was never game that Lebanon sought, but the throbbing healing of earth and sky. It seemed to her eyes that game was seldom near her house, with settling grown so common. Meat was plenty still, but now a man must trudge a mile, or maybe two

in heavy weather, and never jump a deer. Were they leaving their
ancient runs and salt licks, and facing westward as the shaggy
buffalo had done awhile since, as the Indians were doing?

The earth was still thick in Indians, in the Floridas and all along
the Mechikan Gulf. They were still thick as fleas but not so thick since
the big Creeks made their last stand at the Great Bend of the Talla-
poosa, twenty years back. The Indians knew it was not much use.
All the old counselors had said from the beginning that the white
man's skin was like a pest to the red men, a pox of cruelty and
cleverness and strength, and no use to fight it.

The Indians kept much to themselves, coming and going at the
trading posts, but still on any border one could hear of murders done
in a red night, fires eating the roofs of white settlers, and here and
yonder a wholesale massacre.

If Lebanon had an Indian woman to help her in the house,
maybe the whole matter would have been changed. If anyone had
asked Lebanon about an Indian woman or a bought slave, she
would have said no. You love a pewter plate the more when you
have washed it a thousand times; you grow to understand a chair
when you have oiled its rungs year on year and mended a spoke in
its back; you are at home on a floor that you have scrubbed time on
time. Lebanon would have said that a woman cheats herself if she
does not know her own house intimately.

Often Lebanon had wished to go West, too, as the Indians were
going and the hardiest of the adventurers. They could once more
load the trek waggon with Indian meal and jerked spittard, they
could head Miranda West, with Juno tied to the back of the cart,
tolling a new journey. Lady would be there at her feet, too. In the
house there was now no such pleasure as they had known when it
was but a dream about them: the waggon's shade, the green-breath-
ing lean-to, the thick walls rising, the ridgepoles laid to jail away the
shine of stars and winds of night. Never since the roof was closed
had she thought the house so fine a place to be.

When the child was born, could they not go West again and find
that place which was lost to them here since the roof was laid? She
asked Fernald of going West.

"Gad!" he said, "If I went in any direction, it would be East again. Our moneys are sunk here, and you know as well as I that we must endure it out. Your discontent is in yourself. You will not be happy, for you will not allow yourself to be."

And Lebanon would ponder and ponder as to what might be the matter with herself, since she was so different from other women, contented East or West or North or South.

Yet sometimes the days were sweet in Lebanon's face. If Fernald did not drink too much, or stay too long in town, if he would chop the wood and show a little care for this house and her, there came a sudden acknowledgment of affection between them. "We two are against the world, and it against us . . ." Never was Fernald to her what Sebastian might have been; but then neither could Sebastian have been to her what Fernald was.

Fernald felt no great bitterness any more. But what mad folly had ever caused him to see a white-pillared house in this tree-thick wilderness? Why, this country was how many hundred miles from the East; who ever would come here into this desolation but a mad trapper or a man with a crime on his hands? Let fools come West; the smart men stayed East and established themselves. And here he was sloughed past rescue. And Lebanon forever speaking of going farther west. . . . If he had never listened to her long ago in Birdtown, things would be very different now! He had been happy tending that little bar, buying and selling (and drinking secretly at night) sweet liquors. That was his fitting work. What could he be expected to know of this lowly labor of breaking a field to his will? He had listened to Lebanon. And she had willed him West, following her own will as she had always followed it and always would. Sebastian Ratcliff had proved himself the smart one, and Fernald the spoony! So Fernald declared to himself, over and over, and took another tope to drown any thinking at all. Of course, it was not on all mornings that Fernald felt so bitterly toward Lebanon. He felt so only on those days when he had the desperate feeling of a dog drowning with a stone tied to his neck.

But here was the child coming, a burden or a comfort, and he wished it would come on and be done with it. Lebanon's disposition was certainly no better. There was some male pride in siring this child, yet he had wished to see Lebanon standing in a high hall, commanding slaves and wearing violets on the shoulder of her muslin house dress.

Lebanon stayed much by the river, within close walls of trees where squirrels barked unafraid of her, where ripening broom made a roof for the singing of crickets. Even on rainy nights she would lie out, the wet slipping down her glossy roof of pine needles. She would lie beneath the bear pelt, she and the unborn child, and they felt the thudding of raindrops on the pelt's thickness. She had a rock-walled hearth by the river far from home, and none but the heaviest rain could out her fire; even if her fire were outed, she had dry-hot tinder aplenty, and a fiery flint in the tinder box.

Fernald blamed himself not so much as one small jot that he stayed so much in Mercierville and so little at home. She would not stay at home, and she heavy with child! She had little to say to him. For Fernald there was too wide a difference in this gloomful house and the bright-candled tavern in Mercierville. What if he had slipped down from flirting with women of class and manners to the low company of gaudier females with louder mouths and brighter eyes and bolder hands, and little heart left—only a body and a crying hunger, like his own?

Yet if these women seemed to fail in contenting him, they would try the harder till one would weep to see the sight. Lebanon scarce chided Fernald. She looked briefly on his leaden eyes and loose tongue. He had given up his search for strength and means to build a white-pillared mansion. He suffered no grief over its loss, so far as she could judge. Fernald was a least bit afeared of Lebanon's quiet, so deep nothing could get past its barrier and find her out. Fear of his wife helps no man's love for her.

In truth, word had gone slowly about that Fernald d'Aussy had married him a woman that would poison him for a little bit of nothing—for she was a wild, hate-tempered woman, they said. Not that Fernald didn't need poisoning, they'd say and laugh, though he was scarce worth the apothecary's charge.

They had not seen Lebanon, so they the less fairly judged her. She was a strange sort, they heard. Simon Poake said she never came to his wife's house much any more, and she would be off in the swamp if you went to her house. Kind enough his own wife would have been to her, Simon said, telling her receipts for sugar loaf and shortening bread, pumpkin spice or berry mulse. They could traffic in babies' bibs and a sock's turning, and how to make a linsey-woolsey skirt keep its hang. Any woman needs the lend of another woman's wafer iron now and then, or such a matter, the candle mold or the extra smoothing iron, and four women can quilt a quilt in a tenth the time it will take one woman to do it.

But Lebanon had little to do with his wife any more. She was a queer sort, Simon told people in Mercierville. She would look on one sullenly, and would go with scarce a leave-taking. His boys, now, Erwin and Estis, they thought the sun rose and set in her. They would fight for her, but he had in a way told his boys to keep away from her. You know how folks' tongues are. . . . You cannot watch your sons too closely, and Fernald d'Aussy was seldom at home.

He had warned his boys, he said, and they blushed to the roots of their hair, as though they were guilty, indeed. They looked at him solemn as owls. You would think there was indeed a rain and lightning-flash history between them and Lebanon d'Aussy, as maybe there was indeed.

Never did Simon Poake have the least intention of harm when he said those little things about Mistress d'Aussy.

If Lebanon had gone into town and been one of the people, they would have seen that her eyes blinked and rolled and shut down and opened like any other woman's, that her legs walked her about where she wished to go, that her tongue spoke English, that she would fondle a lost child and help him find home, that she would wrap an old man against cold even with her own cloak, that she would feed a sick hound, and note a bird flying.

But Lebanon stayed home, and her name was a whisper and a wraith; "The Frencher's woman," they called her.

She was sufficient to herself, and they were not, and whether they knew it or not, they felt the lack, and blamed such a one as her for it. There was a worse thing whispered, and Fernald innocently gave rise to the whispering. This was how it happened:

Fernald rolled in like a hoop, as they say, and put in for a night of it at the Mercierville tavern. He stayed in the bar, sitting and whirling England Notchaway around and holding her on his knee, and she with a bosom like a feather pillow and with two warm hands with nothing to do but soothe him. He kissed her, but he would have liked her kiss the better if she had not made so strong a return of it. Men are peculiar creatures. Then she wished to go on with more kissing, but suddenly, to show his male power, he pushed his hand into her face and held her mouth away, to show himself the greater of the two.

"I'd best be home kissing my wife," he said, more to tease England Notchaway than to state a principle.

"Fernald," she pleaded, her mouth muffled under his palm. "Fernald, kiss me . . ."

"I'll have a son this month, sure," he said.

"Now if you go remembering her, I am wasting my time," England said, her eyes glowing sullenly. "Let me go," she said. "I was looking around for a man, and I thought you were one."

"I am scarce a man," he said. "I'd be a beast if I had good sense. My wife likes the beasts better than me. She will stand an hour to hear a lynx yell. She lives days on end in the swamp. She has a cave, like a wild she-thing, and lies there, days on end. . . ."

He was drunken, and yet he meant no harm to Lebanon's good name; he was only nettled and spoke of it. He was innocent of calumny. And others were innocent, for they only carelessly believed what they thought they had heard Fernald say. But they talked. And they talked.

Finally it came to be said that Fernald d'Aussy was wed to a woman who consorted with beasts in preference to her husband and home. He had said so himself in the tavern. It was not likely that Fernald would hear such talk. If he had heard it, he would have hotly defended Lebanon.

Fernald could feel pity spent on him, and others gave him pity when he was sodden drunk, and he supped on pity. A strong man will have none of your pity. He wishes only good will or admiration. Yet Fernald liked the taste of it. He came to feel a strong sense of his own rights. He talked and japed and said too much and not enough. If he thought of Lebanon, he understood her no more than these men and women of Mercierville to whom she was but a name. Fernald little suspected it, but he was coming to hate Lebanon.

Fernald might storm at her: "Why are you forever lying in the woods? Is there a Poake there, maybe?"

Yet he knew different. He was only trying to pry from her some hint of her differentness, her distinction of heart. He hated her for her silence, her air of high nobility, for she seemed to spurn him as coarse and less than she. It was but that she spurned men as being less kind and sensitive, tender-eyed and intelligent, than the wild things.

Lebanon grew the more quiet, stayed the longer beneath the lean-to far up the river. She kept there a cache of meal and salt and jerked meat: she had fresh fish to eat when it might please her, or quail snared or meat killed in some other place, for she would not fire a musket along this reach of sanctuaried earth. Above her the cut pine boughs leaned, shielding her head from heat and rain. Lady would eat a mess of stew, drink river water, listen to the squirrels' talk, and be content under the look of Lebanon's eyes. To Lady this was no peculiar home: as in a happy marriage, Lebanon was hearth and roof and long sustenance.

The fire burned faithfully, if given but a little length of log now and then. The trees hummed a long summer song. Lying on the earth, Lebanon could nigh swear the earth's great form moved solidly beneath her, as a very breast, as mighty arms cradling her. Such was her bright place to walk in.

The child was born quietly as any wild thing—with only the little dog to stand watch, with only the listening trees to attend.

Suddenly Lebanon knew her time was upon her, and it was fifteen miles of poling between her and home. There were three more weeks to go, or two, but she would never go them. She gathered moss and made her bed. She filled a pot at the river and warmed it so there would be water to wash him in when he was born. There was bear grease in a little pot, and that would do to soothe his new skin against the harsh air of this world. She readied the knife to give him his freedom from her. After that there was only pain and more pain, and retching pain, till pains crowded to strip her limbs of flesh. Yet this was sound pain, manful and clean, for the child caused it.

After the pain there was a weariness such as old mountains must know, and old rivers running clean among the bones of earth, and plains heavy under a thousand years' dust. She was sinking into lassitude as a sogged chip sinks gradually home under flowing water —for there is no other such tedious labor.

Suddenly Lebanon opened wide her eyes, hearing the cry of her child. It was as though the sky had shouted at her.

When she was done with the knife, she bound his body in a strip of fawnskin she kept in the shot pouch. Having rested from her labor, she laid him in the prow of the dugout and turned homeward. He was wrapped in her own shirt and swaddled in a bear hide, and shaded over by a willow basket turned bottom upward above his face. She laid him on his side so that if he spewed he would not choke.

Lady's head rested on her forepaws, and she did not see Lebanon any more, for she was watching this child, this new thing, this bundle in a bearskin. And there was now more love in her eyes than she had felt for Lebanon, though that would have seemed impossible heretofore.

Though separate from her now at last, the child seemed all the nearer upon her. He was a dark very marvel to her arms. His head was softly furred as are all wild things. His limbs were birth-pink and more soft than the fur of young beavers. His eyes were cloudily dark and opened seldom. When she thrust her finger against his palm, his paw curled about it as might a young coon's, and she could near lift his curved weight by the pull of his small man fingers. Never had she caged or tamed a chickaree or a coon or a badger. Lebanon liked these things better in their own homes, free there, and she free to visit them. Yet here was a wild and young loveliness tamed already at her heart, to feed fearlessly at her breast, to take its care from none but her hands.

She held him near to her all the hours of the day and night. He lay at her breast while she fed the fire, dipped water, stirred mush with one hand. A woman needs no more than one hand, anyhow. When he was a little older she would put him on a backboard, like the Indians.

He was three days old and her milk was plenteous for him when Fernald first saw him.

When Fernald saw the child, its small, dark face framed in a wrap of beaver, she felt pity for him. A light came from far off into his eyes, and there it grew and grew till it was washed in tears. His hands became cold, and they trembled as they took his son to hold.

"Pardee," he said softly, "and I was gone and no father to make him welcome."

Wine scent was strong in his mouth. He laid his head forward on the bundled body of his child and wept.

When word of the child's birth got to Mercierville, men whooped coarsely and told their wives and one asked if the thing had claws, or if it might have fur within its ears.

Lebanon never heard their words or their laughter.

She never told that this child was not born in this house, that the wide sky and deep earth had first welcomed him. It was so unheard a thing to bear a child in open woods, so Indian-y a thing to do. She would never tell how Timothy was born: it might lead to idle talk of her, she thought, and she would have no least improper whisper ever to touch this child or his mother or his father, or anything in all his life. Fernald must, once for all, turn down his glass after this.

When next Fernald rode to Mercierville, he remembered his old way of gift-making, and brought the child play trinkets of shells and plaster, and a wooden doll with jointed legs, wired to step and sit; and a painted china doll head for Lebanon to sew and stuff a body to. In his mind he brought a plan for a trundle bed he had seen carved of polished cocobolo, with two small angels hovering in its hood. They could copy the cradle from his mind. In the old days he would have bought the cradle, but now the wind whistled through his pigskin purse. Now Erwin and Estis would have to make the thing!

His breath did not smell of wine when he came home this time. Not one drink had he downed—and the town marveled. Even the tavernkeep was the least bit jealousied. His own son had died aborning, and never had Cassia managed to have another one.

"My father's name was Timothy," Fernald said to Lebanon. "Would that suit?"

"I do so think Timothy would be a fair name for him," Lebanon said. "And then Fernald added to it, too, for you."

Fernald looked deep into her eyes, and he kissed her forehead as one might kiss a saint's forehead.

Finally Fernald said:

"A good wife you've been, Lebanon," and he said it no more grudgingly than a shy man will.

"Why not," she asked, "with so gentle a man for a husband?"

Fernald wrote the name in the old Bible, with a blue-ink bird flying forever past the little words, hovering them.

Timothy Fernald d'Aussy, borned Aust 20, 1836
Son of
Fernald Napier d'Aussy
and
Lebanon Nowel Fairgale d'Aussy

There was his name now, set fast in The Word. But secretly Lebanon called the child foolish names—pigeon and jackstraw and toddle-top—as fond mothers will.

Now this house was a bright place to walk in. Here she was housed in happiness with a home to tend and a man and his child to feed and make clothes for. Here at last they had stumbled upon treasure under careless footing.

Chapter 13

TIMOTHY GREW CARELESSLY as a solitary windflower will grow in a sweet place, in seeming indifference to cloud and sun, yet taking wet and warmth and earthy richness to himself. Like a bright green weed, his sap of life came from beyond himself, asking no careful nursing. Yet he received every care.

There was a little lump in betwixt his shoulders. Lebanon greased it most carefully, that first day when she saw him; she greased it a thousand times, her hand flowing down across it. But the lump did not lessen. Each toe was perfect and secure; each finger was properly set; each finger nail, not as large as one of your nail parings, was perfect. But the little lump was there. And as Timothy grew that lump grew, in just proportion to his little size.

Forever this child was cock-of-the-walk, astride Fernald's shoulders or Lebanon's hips. If Timothy spewed forth salted hominy when Lebanon had chewed it in all care for him, and ladled it into his mouth with her own fingers, then he had no more hominy unless he should deign to ask for it. After that, Lebanon would syrup the grits or sugar them, or do any other way to please him—for she and Fernald greatly preferred Timothy's tastes above their own.

Fernald brought home from Mercierville a jar of sugared figs from Araby, and Timothy howled for more and more of the things till his small belly was outraged from such a load of sweetness it could not carry, and his bowels loosened like a creek at freshet time and his fever rose till Lebanon was distracted, and Fernald sat and gripped his hands and prayed as never he did before, asking God not to take this little one this time. Timothy's child taste had no more judgment than to eat a whole jar of Araby figs, and they had no more judgment than to give him his desire no matter what it might be, so long as they could contrive to furnish it. Lebanon would say to Fernald: "There will be those many years when he will cry to us, and we won't be here. When he is old and in trouble, in body or in heart, he will call to us then, and we can give him no answer. So we will do for him now, while our hands and backs are young; we will content any desire he may feel now, and he will remember when he is old."

So Lebanon would think, and Fernald with her.

It greatly disturbed them that there should be that small defect in Timothy's spine. They would not speak of it to one another save to say: "It is nothing, it will go away. He is perfect in every other way."

Lebanon bore Timothy through the woods when he was but a few weeks old, when he could first hold straight his head on the supple length of his spine. There was nothing of a weakling about him. His back curved, of course, knotted somewhere there in the bone, but he held his little face straight, and his neck was delicate as a woman's wrist. His little face was dark-eyed, like Fernald's, and his lips were pinked and smiling. His brow was like Lebanon's, and his eyes had the flashing quality of her smiling. His head nodded unsteadily when he first went awalking with his mother, but in time he could follow the flight of snowbirds, or turn his cheek to hark to the chirruping of a cardinal, blood-red in dead brush.

Before one would think he was old enough, Timothy pulled to his feet about the chairs and stools that the Poake twins had built for the room, carved finely of walnut and pine and cherry. The Poake twins loved Timothy till he would have been sadly spoiled in any case. They made him jointed dolls and a hobbyhorse and polished blocks of wood and anything they thought he might have a craving for.

Timothy's knees were knobbly, his stance uncertainly proud. Now and again, through no apparent fault of his own, he would flop to his bottom when he tried to stand, and Lebanon's heart would fail as she thought: Do you reckon now he cannot walk, nor ever will! Then Timothy would look to her in pained surprise, asking her to explain this monstrous chance that had undone him tall-standing. His mouth would crumple from its smiling, tears would blot his laughter. Lebanon would catch him up to comfort him: "It was but a fall, littlest!"

She would go on thinking: A hundred years from now it will be 1937. Will heaven still be standing then? Unless a comet or earthquake tears the whole business down! Wonder what folks will be about then? Living in houses of Paris glass, no doubt, and wearing silk to Monday-morning breakfast. A pity a woman cannot live always, so she can see the guimpes and bows her great-granddaughter will delight in, the beaux she will torment, the way she'll pile her hair and perfume it. They will be able to look back on me, yet I cannot see them at all. Mayhap Fernald will someday have a painting of me done on a plate of ivory so that Timothy's son will know what I looked like when I was young. They will be born in the same way, by sweat and blood. They will be swaddled in point lace or mull and will be given raspberry cordial for cramps. They will have fevers and winter colds and the Pest will afflict them in cities, as it always has. There will be ten thousand like my Timothy, little and dear to their mothers. They will not fear for wars and tumults; a time of long peace is ahead. The States are settling in their places, and Jackson tamed the Creeks once and for all. There won't be any more wars.

Timothy's eyes were soft as Fernald's, his hair was silken and fly-away like Lebanon's, his jaw was Fernald's over again, the uplift of his nose and brow were like Lebanon's. Fernald found a likeness to his mother's dead face in Timothy's face, and Lebanon thought she saw her mother's face again. Never was there such a warm, sweet-tempered winter, never such a spring. Their spirits knew little gloom now. Sometimes an unacknowledged jealousy would torment one or the other of them: He cares naught for me but loves his father entire. He loves his mother, and takes little after me. But for the most part glad content filled their hearts and their house and all their days. Down into the muggy dog days of that year their happiness walked with them, and the child grew beneath the fond watching of their eyes.

Lebanon used every poultice and stupe on the lump on Timothy's spine, but it did not lessen, and he could not straighten that knotted place in his back. His face looked up at them in a coy, believing look, and to see the little knotted back would make them ashamed of their own straight spines.

Early Timothy began to walk, staggering the length of the room, proud laughter in his face and laughter on the faces of Lebanon and Fernald. "He is so quick at everything, I fear me he may die," Lebanon told Fernald.

By the time of summer, Timothy was learning the calling of words. "Duff!" he commanded when he wished the water gourd brought to the level of his mouth. "Murmu!" he shrieked when he wished Lebanon's arms to be about him. "Favwa," he called Fernald. And never before had Fernald heard so sweet a sound from a human mouth, unless it was that time long ago when Lebanon offered herself to him, to marry him and go West with him so they could find a fortune. A fortune they had found, too!

Timothy's speech was a marvel upon their ears. Erwin and Estis Poake would smile broad as an ox's behind to hear one of Timothy's strange little words fall like a trinket.

"What is my name, Timothy?" Erwin would plead, jouncing the child on his knees, riding him a-cockhorse, letting him rummage in the pockets of a jacket to find a bluestone marble or a wooden pistol carved last night.

"Twin!" Timothy would say soberly. He called Erwin twin and he called Estis twin, and their laughter rolled to the roof over the simple jest.

If he but knocked his head on a chair rung, Lebanon all but lost her calm, so fierce the blow seemed to her own flesh. Fernald was even more the fool. He brought a black bear on a chain, to amuse Timothy before ever he was breeched. The Poake twins laughed till they all but rolled. Lebanon, womanlike, felt a monstrous dread that the thing might grow willful one day and bring harm to the child, but Fernald said no, he was tamed and young and safe enough. They named him Erasmus, and he ate fish and oats or anything. Timothy did love the sight of the bear waddling about the back door, gnawing the stake that held him tethered, as a dog gnaws a bone.

Lady had a high-bred conniption when she first saw the thing, and thought, What on earth is the world coming to when black bears come in the very yard and are not shot down! But she soon settled down. Timothy would bounce up and down on Lady's back till she could scarce bear it, and she would have to crawl up under the low bed to be away from him. He pulled her ears and her tail, but she would not whimper though pained.

But best of all Timothy had brought a new Fernald into being. Now he went seldom into Mercierville, and then only to sell an oversupply of lard or salt meat or eggs or potatoes, then only to bring home gifts to his family. He had not touched liquor since the first time he laid eyes on his son. Fernald brought Lebanon gauds and trumpery now. Now and often his tongue would slip and he would call her "Honey-pot" or "Trinket," as a very lover might do! Lebanon would pretend never to note the love word, but, womanlike, it would so enrich her love for him that it is no wonder her face burned like a light in a dark room! This is sane happiness, she would tell herself. My love for Sebastian was always impossible and insane.

This manner of living was monstrous contentful. Here was the child, and Fernald worked at anything needful. This year's corn was near a failure because of a big wind that laid it flat in June, but the hogs were doing well, and the garden patch was favored by heavy rains. Lebanon had a heavy catch of pelts from last winter, and they had plenty to trade. If hard cold withered the greens patch, it thickened the fur for the traps. The earth withheld one palm and extended the other. Somehow, by one means or another, they would always be safe.

Fernald had taken new hope in all of living. The pride he took in his son! He brought home a Dillworth's Speller, a squeaky slate and numbering beads and a New Testament before the child was eleven months old! To Lebanon, because she was the child's mother, he brought a basket of purple figs and green leaves, painted on stiff-ened cloth, and she hung it on the wall over the fire, and it was a new beauty to the room.

Lebanon purposed to learn her letters and number work when Fernald began to teach Timothy. They had held various cravings for themselves, but now they wished things for Timothy. In Paris Timothy could learn to paint canvases, Fernald would promise him-self. In Germany he could learn the stern beauty of pure thought. In England he could learn theology and how to pray and how to build a cathedral, even. In Salamanca he could learn surgery. It was a great care upon Fernald's mind, wondering where to send Timothy that he might learn most.

"Across the ocean?" Lebanon said softly. "Fernald!"

"He could sail from Baltimore. It would take three or four years for him to learn——"

"Baltimore!" Lebanon repeated, saying that word more softly still.

"When he comes back, the green on any tree will be velvet to him, and he can tell us all the poets ever said, and why; he can prove a geometry theorem in sand with a little twig in his hand. He could preach, or teach in a university. . . ."

Suddenly Lebanon felt old and discarded as a worm must know his doom when the butterfly first stirs deeply.

"He will be ashamed of me, Fernald. I do not even know how to read and write. I would not even sit in the last row when he preached. . . ."

"Oh, he would be proud of you. He would say: 'Gentlemen, this is my mother. . . .'"

That is how they talked.

Lebanon made a muslin coat for the books, and using every care, she tried to study out the markings in the books, but soon she decided herself too old and laid away the books in their black muslin jackets till Timothy should be old enough to begin to learn with Fernald. Timothy would just have to go without her to Europe, to a university. She would go down by the river and think of him.

Even now Timothy played with the painted number-beads, running them through his fat fingers, and gnawed his fevered gums on them when he cut a new tooth. High on the shelves Lebanon set the tea set from Madame Lateuse, and the brass and crystal lamp, and the ivory saint stood under the painted picture Fernald had brought her last, there above the fire. People here to West much favored likenesses of the saints, and it was a pretty for her mantel, and Fernald had brought it to her. As for it reminding her to pray, she had needed no strong reminder: that is, there had been nothing hard to be prayed over.

The room was now bright and gay; Lebanon had drapes of red calico at the windows the twins had cut out on a rainy day, and the brass cook pots stood about the shelves, shining like new sun if the firelight struck them. She had learned a lesson from that china tea set with roses and forget-me-nots on it. Timothy had cried for it, and she had allowed him to hold one cup to please him, and splash! the china went, and now the handle was gone and the cup rim nicked; the thing had fallen on a bear pelt, but it was that dainty, still it had broken. Lebanon could have cried, but that she counted Timothy of more value than the cup. She turned the handleless side of the cup away from sight on the shelf, and the nick scarce showed. They had never dared use the china, anyhow—it was too precious for hot tea or cold mulse.

Of nights, Fernald would hold the drowsing Timothy in his arms and would read from the old Bible—where Timothy's name was set in the middle, in The Family Record, where Fernald's and Lebanon's marriage was recorded; Fernald had brought the old book from East, and their record was firm and secure in its fat middle. His mother had given the Book to him when he signed papers for the Horn voyage long ago. The child drooped heavily on Fernald's breast and slept, and Lebanon would listen as though Fernald's mouth spoke the very words of God. These *were* God's words, with Fernald but reading them over again! Sometimes the Poake twins would be there, and they would listen, too, holding their heads still, a little sideways, as at a political rally. Never would they tire of the heavy words of Holy Writ. (The Poake twins were fiercely loyal to the D'Aussys, in spite of what their father had implied. In fact, the more he said, and the more their mother pouted over their visiting the D'Aussys, the more the twins were determined to be friends with them.)

Always Lebanon would sigh a little when Fernald softly closed the Book to, and hushed from saying the solemn, golden words of God—slow-flowing words telling of the seven lamps of fire burning before the heaven-high throne—and the four angels at the corners of the earth, holding all the winds of earth. It was a wonder to Lebanon how the angels could gather those prayers—those feeble, breathless prayers—and keep them in vials. Did God keep them to reply to later, as a tradesman will file an order and send it on in due time?

Deep summer came and the air stilled.

Along about that time the little bitch sickened suddenly.

Lebanon bore Timothy on her arm to the river to take fish from the trap for dinner. Lady frisked along ahead, leaving Erasmus, the bear, to lunge on his chain, wishing to go, too. Lady danced across the earth as always, touching her paws only lightly.

Lebanon saw no thing go wrong suddenly. They walked to the river—she and Lady and Timothy together, as they had done a thousand times. They walked home again, the fish basket heavied on Lebanon's other arm.

In an hour Lady huddled in at the back door, crawling feebly toward Lebanon, swollen so that she could scarcely crawl. The swelling was greatest on her jaw, but from there poison of some kind had spread mightily through her body.

Fernald was off past the corn patch seeing to some matter, and there was no time to call him.

Lebanon set Timothy down to toddle and took the kitchen knife and slit Lady's jaw where two little darts of fangs showed on the little dog's tough white skin. Then she poured in spirits of turpentine, as good a blood bleach as there be.

Lady did not whimper under Lebanon's hands. She shivered and held her head closer to Lebanon. She lay on the pallet Lebanon laid for her near the fire; she was shivering from some deep ague of the blood.

Till her eyes were swollen shut, she held her eyes fast set in Lebanon's. Now and then she would turn her head restlessly toward Timothy's prattle. It was as though she grieved to leave him alone in this world's great danger, and she not here to protect him.

So long as she could lift her head, she licked pityingly at Lebanon's hand as though she were saying: Do not grieve. This must be. It is neither your fault nor mine.

Her breath came short and more short. Her legs began to twitch, suddenly, now and then.

Lebanon could not judge what thing had so poisoned her. There were the pricks of fangs—two red dots like a quill's stickings—but whether they were a scorpion's or a snake's, who could say? Lady was a healthy body—maybe she would over it, Lebanon told herself passionately, refusing to give up hope. If the swelling would abate, Lady might live yet. She knew nothing to do further than the lancing and the drench of turpentine.

Lebanon looked toward that ivory saint, set there like a doll. Lebanon was not brought up to say prayers to a little blessed figure. If that saint had power and good will, it could see this little room— it had looked down on this room for a long while now, this room should be its special care; that saint could see this little dog laboring beside the fire.

Lebanon turned away from the little saint and her eyes sought the heavy rafters that held up the roof. She looked down at Lady's swollen head and bared teeth and panting sides, and since she could not bear the sight, she looked back to the dark rafters again, and after them to the sky.

Her own breast was laboring now, to bring forth a prayer:

"You saints—You, God, there—You know I cannot say the

proper words. . . . It is so little to ask, when you ask for a little dog to live. You would never miss this one small thing, living or dead. . . ."

Timothy watched Lebanon, his mouth fallen open. Never before had he seen tears on his mother's bright face.

"God!" Lebanon called the more loudly. "You've got to let this one little dog live. I will do anything You say after this. I will not forget. I have not got another friend like this beast."

Lady raised her head piteously toward Lebanon and rolled sidewise to lay her paw on Lebanon's thigh.

The little dog was dying now and swiftly.

Lebanon set her arms about Lady:

"It will soon be over," she said. "It will soon be over."

She laid her face in the struggling fur; in long stroking she soothed the dog's shudders till the shuddering ceased.

Chapter 14

DEEP SUMMER CAME UPON THEM, and the air stilled yet more—for the great earth was now in travail with fruit and grain, tuber and bearded weed, cypress ball and pear. Dread murmurs came from Orleans. Even out past Orleans and the river, the Pest was rampant in Louisiana, among Indians and whites. Carts began to come eastward, rumbling over the wooden planking of the bridge at the Poakes', willing to pay any toll if the Poakes would let them through. The carts found scant welcome as they passed eastward. Only physicians and the fathers of Roman faith and the Quakers and preaching Methodists—in fact, those men with strong religion of some sort —had courage to face that thing out. Tavernkeeps spurned money from people coming in from the West, and constables kept their distance and said: "Move on! Move on now! We mean no harm— but you move on!" Little families cooked mush in a pot over a campfire and hurried on eastward, hard as the horse could take them. Judges set town limits, and guards at the limits, so that no stranger could come in, and the waggons made tracks out around the town. And still that Thing's feelers spread, as though the very air itself bore the blight. There were hundreds dying in Orleans.

The air of day was thunderous and heat-heavy. The air of night was black and evil-seeming. The earth cried for rain. The sky was brassy and cruel, cupping the world in close, hot terror. The mosquitoes were never worse. Lebanon could not go out into the dark toward the outhouse that they did not swarm on her, for all the grease and pennyroyal juice. Carefully she kept Timothy inside the barred and shuttered house by day and night. Fernald and Lebanon left the house only to feed Miranda and Juno and the chickens and pigs, to dig a few potatoes for dinner or gather a few greens. Not for a pretty sum would they have gone onto that Pike yonder.

Late in a night there was a thudding at the door. They could hear the whimpering of a child.

Fernald would not open up that door, and Lebanon would not ask him to. Dead silence was in this room, and beyond the door there was no sound but the steady whimpering of a little child. A fist thudded strongly at the door again. Fernald rose softly; silent as an Indian he went to the door. That fist thudded again.

"Go away!" Fernald called loudly. "Go away! We never open our door after dark, no matter who comes."

A woman's voice spoke out there in the hot dark.

"We are from the East," the voice said. "My father is illed in Orleans and we are traveling there. My child is fevered with his gums, and I was wondering if you could spare me a pinch of purge. The ferrykeep's wife—Poake is the name, I believe—said you had a child in the house and that you might help out. Her beds were all full, and her medicine exhausted. If we could stay till morning, we'd pay you handsomely enough. Your own child might be illed one day, and far from home. I'd take it as very gracious of you if you should consent to help me."

Lebanon stirred her head suddenly. She had heard that voice before, and never any doubting it. That was the woman . . . the woman who was from Virginia. . . . That was Roanoke Carter who married that slovenly tavernkeep.

"Lebanon, I am Roanoke Carter," the voice called. "God will

bless you if you aid me. He will bless your little son. The woman at the bridge said you had a little son."

Lebanon held still her tongue. This was Fernald's house, and if he opened the door, he would open it. If he held the door bar and never lifted the latchet, the door would remain shut.

"Fernald?" Lebanon whispered, knowing no more to do than to call his name and to tell him she was his wife and beside him, and a little behind him in any decision he might ever make.

"Yes?" he replied, whispering through the dark.

They desperately sought agreement, each with the other. Neither of them knew any word to speak. And each was thinking: To be so cold-boweled might bring worse punishment upon us than the very Pest.

Fernald's hands were tight on the door bar as he lifted it.

The woman came in to the fire, and neither Fernald nor Lebanon remembered to speak any word of welcome. Roanoke's husband followed her in, saying not a word. His face had a blotted, sodden look. Lebanon buttoned her house dress quickly, pushed back her hair in a knot, stirred up the fire. Fernald got off in the dark and fastened his breeches front, and set forth chairs. Lebanon stuck two candles to the fire when it was burning fairly.

The door was closed again, against the Pest.

Roanoke Carter and her husband, Brewton Carter, seemed as though they needed a little pity.

"You'd best turn round and go back East," Fernald counseled Brewton Carter. "You don't want to go on to Orleans now."

"My father is illed there," Roanoke said. She was more gaunt and hollow-eyed and piteous than when they had seen her last, when she was trudging under an armload of firewood or two kitchen piggins of water.

The man was much the same, no less gross-seeming, no less fat; the only difference was that now his face was piteous, too. His red beard was a bush about his mouth and chin, but his eyes were clear and anguished.

With one hand Roanoke Carter laid off the little black bonnet that sat like a dead-winged blackbird about her head.

When the fire had brightened and the candles were steady-burning, Lebanon brought medicine, both town-boughten and of her own concoction—all of Timothy's teething remedies, all the things she used when his bowels were too free or too tight, or his body fevered, or his appetite slackened.

The child was still whimpering, its face under a corner of its mother's cloak.

"She is not greatly illed," the child's mother said, holding the corner of the black cloak in her hand, her face torn betwixt a desperate lie and love for truth.

"Forgive me," she said suddenly, her lips firm.

Roanoke bowed her head on the bundle hidden under her cloak. "I never dreamed this would be your house," she lied bravely.

Lebanon respected her lie, her courage, and her cowardice.

Roanoke began to weep, slowly and in difficulty. It was then that Lebanon and Fernald knew.

Lebanon stood a moment as though death held back her steps. Then she took one little step forward and took the child from Roanoke Carter's arms.

"No man ever escaped the will of God," she said, "so no need for any of us to try."

Timothy was yonder asleep in the bed, one arm lying careless over his head. Beside him lay a pretty-poll Erwin Poake had carved with a face to it, and wooden hair painted gold, and a pretty face painted white, with lips and cheeks of red.

Close to being the size of that wooden doll was this poor child which Lebanon now held on her lap where she sat on the low stool. This was little more than a mummied doll that whimpered ceaselessly. Its face was shriveled, and its arms and legs drew as strongly as its weak strength allowed in spasms of pain.

Now Roanoke was past weeping. "I was desperate," she said; "I had no place to go. Not one soul would sell us so much as a gourdful of cool water for this baby. Our child must die because of the cruelty of human beings who have children of their own and yet would not help us. The Poakes would not even open the door. I asked them who lived hereabouts, and they said your name."

"You are from West, then?" Lebanon asked suddenly.

"We had to leave Ulster," Roanoke said, "where we were when

you came through. We were starving there, and finally the very house burned down over our heads, and I was big with this child. Then as now we had nowhere to go. . . . . It was such a terrible time—such a terrible time. . . ." Her voice sang the words like a refrain.

Roanoke looked woodenly at Lebanon and hushed speaking. When she had drawn several breaths, each no easier than the last, and since no one else would say any word, she went on speaking:

"We went to Orleans, and were doing well, and then the trouble started. Brewton wished to stay there, and my tongue flogged him into leaving. If the child had been given one drop of cooling water on the way here, one purge powder, one stupe on her bowels, it would have meant a difference, I know it. If we could have found a physician anywhere at all, something could have been done. We should have stayed in Orleans. There the Sisters and the Fathers go bravely into any home and nurse and wash and tend sickness. Young men volunteer to nurse and laugh about it as though it were a battle. Women are not too afraid of it; they have seen it come and go, year on year; they know it takes the ones it wishes to take. They are hauling them out from Orleans like beef hides—like dead and rotting beef hides. . . ."

"Roanoke!" shouted her husband, the first word he had said. He slapped her cheek quiet, but there was worship for her in his eyes, and he took her hands and held them as though they were wounded and past help.

Timothy stirred yonder in the bed and turned on his other side, without waking. Lebanon would not look his way at all.

"What did they advise doing, if it struck?" Lebanon asked. Without thinking she began to soothe the child's whimpering by jigging her heels softly up and down so that her knees should be a cradle rocking; she put her hand on the child's poor head and soothed its hair as a little girl pets her doll.

" 'Keep merry!' they said," Roanoke replied. " 'Keep merry! Keep merry!' " Her high voice trilled off into broken laughter.

Lebanon went and got out a small lancet and breached the child's temple and allowed it to bleed. A man can do no more than try;

let out some of this filthy blood, was the first thing she knew to do. The harder the emergency, the harder you must try.

"Hold your heart still," Lebanon said. "She is in the hands of God. We will see if we cannot break her fever, and then she will begin to show improvement. I would not give up entirely until I must. In fact I would not worry now, for I do think your baby looks better than when you first brought her in. See?" She stroked the child's gaunt cheek. She ruffled the child's tousled hair, and her saying so gave the child somewhat a better appearance, as though a cool breath had taken hold once on these little laboring lungs.

It was then that Fernald preached for the first and last time in all his life. He said some of those words Lebanon liked to hear read out of the Book:

" 'Let not your heart be troubled, neither let it be afraid,' " he said. "That is what the Bible says."

They were all suddenly dumbly soothed.

For a wonder Fernald was not ashamed of himself. He went on talking: " 'Ye believe in God, believe also in me. In my father's house are many mansions: if it were not so, I would have told you. I go to prepare a place for you. And if I go and prepare a place for you, I will come again, and receive you unto myself; that where I am, there ye may be also.' "

He hushed, though he knew the other words. That was enough preaching from a sinful man.

Lebanon carried the child in the crook of her arm as though it were her own. She mixed a clyster and a blister and warm oil to rub life back into the clammy limbs of the little girl baby. She put a purge into the little thing's lips, and it scarce had strength to swallow. It was no more tempted by its mother's breasts. Its back was straight as a forearm bone, and beautifully formed.

"You must get yourself together," Lebanon told Roanoke. "Fernald, heat her some milk to drink. Her milk will never agree with this baby if she's all nervy and tempestuous. Now get calm, Roanoke, for before you know it, she will be hungry and you in no condition to feed her."

The child's father could not think of a word to say, but he held Roanoke's hands.

"What is her name?" Lebanon asked, to say something.

"Her name is Virginia," Roanoke said, "for where I was born."

So they sat about that fire, and when the child soiled a garment Lebanon burned it and took a garment of Timothy's and bound the baby's shriveled haunches in it. Brewton Carter watched his wife's face and looked away again and looked back.

Brewton was looking into Roanoke's face when he saw her pale yet more and her head tumbled aside, and since she was of small build and light-boned, he reached and took her in his great bearish arms and held her there like a baby, in his arms beside Lebanon's fire. He did not know that his breast rocked back and forth a little as he held her. When she waked from her faint she opened her eyes and found herself in his arms.

"Brewton?" she asked, as though to be sure it was he.

"Rest yourself. You are exhausted," he said. "Virginia is in good hands." And he rocked a little, never knowing it, holding Roanoke in his arms.

The baby whimpered less, for Lebanon had given her near to half a man's dose of laudanum. Her fever still was high, and her mother only a little less near to madness.

Now and then Roanoke's hand would reach and cling like a claw to Lebanon's sleeve.

"I lied to you," she pleaded. "I lied to you. Never did I lie before."

"I'd not give it leave to worry me," Lebanon said. "Doubtless I should have done the same. The Pest rides the wind, they say. If a filthy wind rides down on us, we could not prevent it."

Maybe Timothy had always been in the palm of God, for all mother care and father pride. They had taken care of him through every hour. They had built fast a roof against a hurricane, yet no man can build against the pestilence. It takes those it will take— it leaves those it disdains. Not one time did Fernald or Lebanon think of fearing for themselves.

"There will someday come payment to you for your kindness of this night," Roanoke said, speaking from the warm encirclement of Brewton Carter's arms and breast.

"We ask no thanks," Lebanon said. "You hush now and go to sleep."

"Hush now and go to sleep," Brewton said, his mouth in Roanoke's hair.

That child lived, that Virginia Carter, thirteen months and two days old.

"We'll go home and face the rest of the way out," Roanoke said, her face and hands and eyes worshiping this place where her child had found life again. There is no doubting her love for that child, and there is no doubting her love for Lebanon d'Aussy. She took Lebanon's right hand in her two hands and said her thanks. "I will slave and send you a gift," she said. "If I knew and could, I would do the hardest thing there is before you to do—I would do it for you so gladly."

"Wonder what that hardest thing will be I must do," wondered Lebanon aloud.

"Oh, you may never think it, but there will be one, though I do not pretend to know," said Roanoke brightly. "Doubtless you have had everything easy to your palm, but it seems to me that every woman has hard things sooner or later." (Roanoke was judging Lebanon still by the plumed bonnet she remembered and the wide velvet skirt, and here were the crimson drapes at the windows, the painting over the mantelpiece, and the fine polished pieces of furniture everywhere.) "I will somehow provide you," Roanoke promised, "if ever a hard time comes to you. I feel we are much more than sisters now. I somehow know that I will someday help you. I will not forget," she promised.

"Sisters . . ." Lebanon said. "I never before had a sister."

There was much more standing there unsaid betwixt them, their faces held still as words they did not know how to say.

"We will meet again," Lebanon said suddenly. "I feel it."

But there was no gladness in her words.

Roanoke rode away, she and Brewton and the pale child, freshening for life again where death had all but shrouded it. It was Roanoke who looked back now: "Write me," she called. "Remember. . . ."

"Fernald will write you for me," Lebanon called: "but I will tell him what to say."

Fernald had set down the post directions most exactly.

One can guess the happenings that followed close on this turn of the wheel. Timothy sickened. Lebanon gave him a purge powder. She held him close and felt his flesh grow hot under her hand, and cool, and hotter again.

She called Fernald from the corncrib where he was clearing out and mending against the autumn harvest. The crops had never done so well that he could recollect.

"Timothy has a little fever," she said, never meeting Fernald's eyes. "It is a new tooth growing, doubtless. He has still some jaw teeth to come in."

"God be merciful," Fernald whispered, losing his voice for the moment.

"Be calm," she said, her own voice shaking.

They worked with every knowledge they knew. It was so far to Mercierville, and only Priscilla Poake's ministrations this side of Mercierville. Fernald wet a cloth in cold well water and wiped Timothy's brow and legs and wrists till one would think he would wear the skin away. He went on dipping and wringing the soft old linnen rag, renewing the water and steeping the cloth in coolness to ease Timothy's fever. Lebanon could scarce do anything for putting the little fellow in fresh, clean garments. This was the Pest for true. There was a scent here that named it by its right name.

Fernald seemed more upset over Timothy than was Lebanon. His breaths came near to sobs, his hands shook, and when he was not wiping away the heat from Timothy's body on an old white cloth, he sat with his face in his hands. He would go out and come in again and go out again, and it seemed as though he could not bear this thing happening to his son.

Never had Lebanon been so dumb of sight and blind of heart. Finally Fernald came in and leaned on the doorjamb. Sweat stood in little stopped rivers on his brow; his lips were blue and quivering. All his body was shaking now.

"I am afraid I cannot stay up any longer," he said. "You must go into town and find somebody. You must go by the Poakes' and get one of the twins to help you take Timothy to town. Go in a hurry," he said. His face had a sullen, yellowish tinge.

Lebanon rose suddenly, and never did she forgive herself for not having seen poor Fernald's agony before. He had tended this child with her these past hours, and she was so concerned over Timothy that she did not see his father's face. Fernald had been the man not to tell her, for he, too, was more concerned over the child on her knees.

She laid the baby on the bed and went and grasped Fernald's hands and helped him to the bed. There was not one word to say, and if there had been a thousand words, her tongue could not have pronounced them now. She held his hands hard and took him inside her arms. She helped him to the bed and laid him down, offed his boots, and dragged away his outer garments. He moaned and then held quiet.

Timothy, lying carelessly sidewise across the bed, wailed ceaselessly. Fernald closed his eyes.

"Bring me some rags, any old matter. I cannot rise any more. I think I am dying, Lebanon. Get back to Timothy," he said. "I will see to myself."

Thin tears stole from his shut eyes and paced slowly past his temples and into his hair where white had fallen, and lay fixed. Fernald was no more a dandy. He had not dyed his hair brown again since Timothy was born. Lebanon knew how old he was, and that was all that mattered to him.

"I have been true to you," he said, "—that is, since Timothy was born." He was speaking brokenly, as though he were very drunken.

Lebanon laid her palm on his mouth, not able to bear a meek recital of a good man's claim to his wife's love.

"You always were true to me, and I know it," she said, and she spoke the truth, and he knew it and so did she.

After that he began to vomit and could not talk any more.

She gave him a bitter drench of powdered root and pummeled leaves, cathartic and healing and binding at once—for cold sweating and raging fever. She had not time to go for leaches, and could not use them till she got back with help. So she took the lancet and breached his temple vein, allowed the blood to flow, and bound it shut again.

Fernald writhed slowly, sighing, his eyes sickened and sunken.

"Murmu—Murmu—Murmu," Timothy wailed incessantly.

When they were quieted a little on their dosage of laudanum, she went to her knees a moment by the head of each one.

She had prayed for that little dog to live, and Lady had died. Now she could not pray. But every time her heart beat—and in between, too—she called God's name, or whoever might be up there, hoping He might heed.

"I will go now," she told Fernald, when he could scarce hear even the sound of her voice. "I will be back in a very little while."

She caressed his sick head and laid her hands close about his whitened hair.

"I will gallop Miranda all the way there and all the way home again," she promised Fernald.

Lebanon set the bridle on Miranda's head. She bestrode the little mare and set her to a long, broken gallop. Miranda was olding, too, but her hoofs would beat faithfully. In the heat, Miranda's flanks were soon greased and blackened in sweat. Lather gathered, and Lebanon would beat her palm on Miranda's head any time the mare slowed. "Go! Go!" Lebanon called desperately.

Miranda blinked her eyes and shook her head now and then: if she slowed, Lebanon felt as though the very earth were slowing. She galloped at last to the tollhouse, and there was Simon Poake in the door of the mill, to see what this fast set of hoofs brought. His wool hatbrim was mealy, and so were his brows and the hairs on the backs of his hands, and the wrinkles in his neck were mealy.

Lebanon dropped down from Miranda's back.

"I need help," she said. "Is Priscilla busy?"

"What's wrong?" he asked, coming out of the mill door and walking up toward the tollhouse. He eased off his mealy hat, and it went round and round in his hands. When she would have come near to him he called "Wait!" sharply and backed away from her.

Priscilla came to the back door of the tollhouse, her hands meshed in dough. "What's up?" she called, none too friendly.

"I need help," Lebanon declared stolidly. "Fernald and Timothy are illed and I need a physician."

"What ails them?" asked Simon Poake, hard-tongued, though he had a kind face.

Now she could know why Roanoke Carter lied. "He has a stomach distemper," she said.

"Is it the Pest!" Priscilla shrieked.

Lebanon turned her head once this way and again that way, as a slave eases his throat under a galling collar.

"Yes," Lebanon said. And she looked Priscilla Poake straight in the eyes.

"God's mercy!" Priscilla shrieked, her doughy hands going to her hair and leaving remnants of wet dough all about her face. "Get from here! Do you hear me? Get from here!"

Lebanon straightened her breastbone the least bit more. She thrust forth her arm and pointed her finger.

"I need help," she said, her tongue clipping like a lancet. "Have you lived so carelessly, Priscilla Poake, that you are so afeared of death? Look at me. I am not afraid of it. God hears me say it."

"Who are you talking to, anyhow?" screamed Priscilla. "Get from here. The audacity! The brass! You . . . you . . . you . . ." Her words tumbled and fell upon themselves.

Lebanon looked at her. Now was the time to tell Simon Poake what his wife was—yet what good would it do? It would not cause Priscilla to come and help with Timothy and Fernald.

"I wished you to come and help me with my sick," Lebanon said.

"Go!" Priscilla screamed. "Do you know what they say of you all over Mercierville? Everybody knows what you are."

Lebanon's heart cringed, but her shoulders stood faithful and her breastbone held true. There was no use to ask this woman for help —that was the simple and short fact. I could tell you some things they say of you, too, she thought savagely. "Where are the twins?" Lebanon asked, her body sagging.

"You are after them again, then?" Priscilla called, fear bright in her voice.

Simon Poake spoke up:

"The twins are in Mercierville, trading," he said. Anything to hush these women's tongues.

"Would you go and stay with them till I can go to Mercierville and find a physician?" she asked Simon desperately, since his voice had some kindness in it.

He grubbed his shoe toe in the earth; his meal-whitened face had a kindness on it, beyond any doubt.

"I cannot do it," he said, "and you know I cannot." He was ashamed for something, he did not know what.

Priscilla's arms were akimbo. Her tongue spit words in cat's anger.

"I should say you cannot," she screamed, too loud for any but deaf ears. "Come in this house, Simon Poake. That's what you get, being friends with that Frencher's woman."

Lebanon didn't argue any more. She knew she had to get to Mercierville in a hurry now, since there was no help anywhere nearer.

Chapter 15

INTO THE HUDDLED OUTSKIRTS of Mercierville Miranda hobbled. Lebanon's face was reddened, but about her mouth there was a little muzzle of white skin.

She tethered Miranda at the hitching rack, the first one she came upon. Miranda was wet as though she had waded water, and lather was worn into wreaths on her flanks.

A man setting a halter on one of his team of horses looked at this woman and the crump mare.

Lebanon was leaning on the little mare's side, vomiting—a stomach can bear only so much galloping under heat and terror. Miranda's head drooped. Her eyes were closed, and her black nostrils flared in the heavy intaking of her breaths.

The man looked at Lebanon one moment, then he breathed one black word and fled. Into the tavern bar he ran.

"The Pest," he whispered; his teeth chattered and his face was white. "That woman—yonder by the hitching rack."

The tavernkeep hastened to the door.

He called the name of God carefully this time. "It is that Frencher's woman," he said. The long room stilled.

The D'Aussys lived but twenty miles, the tavernkeep was thinking. Already Mercierville had kept indoors and burned sulphur and scattered herbs and vinegar and prayed all day in the meetinghouse, and set limits to the town east and west, so that nobody could come in. Many folks that had carriages and horses had gone east even from Mercierville. There was no case yet reported near to here. But here was a case by the hitching rack. Here was that Frencher's woman come to bring it surely.

Suddenly in the tavern door she stood—in the very door—the Frencher's woman herself, her hair awry on the crown of her head, her face bleached in desperate hope. To their eyes her face had the look of hell in it—no matter what any neutral eye might have judged it to be.

Lebanon looked toward the men, making her face to sit as firmly as she could.

"My husband and my child are sickened," she said. "Could you tell me where I could find some sort of physician or nursing woman?"

She leaned hard on the side of the door, wilting. She could feel hate around her, but a heart with iron in it does not run away from danger.

There were five men who were there that day in the tavern; two still sat at a little oaken table, two stood by the counter. And there was the tavernkeep who once hated Fernald for flirting foolishly with his wife, Cassia.

The two men at the table rose slowly and stood, arms hanging lank, faces stiff as dead men's faces.

The two men standing moved backward a little. The tavernkeep got his voice at last.

"Get out of here!" he said and flung his arm toward the door.

"I am willing to pay!" Lebanon said, her mouth as firm as his.

She stepped forward one step, then held still when she saw rage on his face. Never had he forgotten that night so long ago when Fernald had played with his wife.

The tavernkeep caught up a drover's whip that lay idle on the table, forgotten from the hand of one of the men.

"You get out!" he said in a low voice. He had hated this woman a good long while now. He reared the whip in his hand, to menace her if she took one step forward.

Suddenly she knew her body to be no mean thing, no frail flesh for such as he to taunt with a black whip.

"Strike me if you dare!" she said, and her eyes were near to black as his own, for she had lost her temper.

"Stinking slut!" he said, and he struck her as she had dared him to.

She stood looking dully in his face, refusing her hand the right to go and comfort her cheek and throat and brow where the long welt was rising. Her eyes were bright in incessant courage. Even now Timothy might lie dead, and his poor father with him. Dead they might be long before her return.

"Begone!" he shouted, as though he cried down many loud words her mouth was speaking against him.

She held still her tongue.

She watched him, for she held her face most still till pain could somewhat abate. A snake of pain ran and ran where that whip had fallen.

The tavernkeep dropped his eyes and turned back to the other men, who were cowering like thunderstruck cattle.

She felt the growing flame of the welt across her cheek, upon her brow, down her throat.

Miranda stood hitched to the rack, her eyes gentled and closed in weariness, her sides cooling; her belly was blowing still from the long, hard ride.

Lebanon took hold on Miranda's stirrup strap so that she might not fall flat on the earth. The pain was so harsh across her forehead that she must blink her eyes to see. Black bolts struck her continually across the eyes.

She leaned on the little mare's blowing side, and Miranda turned her head about to see what Lebanon could be doing, riding like a hallion so far, then leaning like an old woman here at her belly. Never before had Miranda been called upon to make such a ride.

Then it was that Lebanon felt a hand on her shoulder.

"I am going, I am going . . . I am going," she said, as a child might repeat repentance for his misdeed.

The hand lay still on her shoulder.

"You be coming on home with me now," a woman's voice said.

The woman thought that Lebanon must be a whore that had been run from the tavern for rudeness or behavior past standing. She had heard the lash, she had seen this woman come from the tavern door with the welt laid down her head like a wide red ribbon. She saw the woman turn with a bowed head and go to the little mare.

Her name was Sheba Johann. She kept house for a preacher who held school on weekdays in the Best Room.

Jairus Mountjoy was the preacher's name. He spent himself earlier and later than did even Sheba, for he would go and plow a sick man's field or dig a widow's potatoes for her. He gave a young man a gold eagle he had cherished half his life so the young man could go North and make a study of pharmaceutics. Sheba would quarrel roundly at the world putting so much on one man when all the others did so little.

There was a room in Jairus Mountjoy's house that was kept freshly aired and clean-sheeted for any that might have no other bed; the man with the pox had died there, and half a dozen women had borne children there. Long ago they had made it a rule that no man should be too foul or too low to sleep in that bright room— and somehow no man ever proved to be.

The shack where they lived was set in a grassy lane that went down from the main street. The other houses turned their backs on this house, and the pigsties of the finer folks were to be seen from the little front shed of this clean-scrubbed shack. There were three little rooms in it—one for the stranger, whosoever he might be, one for Jairus to sleep in, and to preach in on Sabbath mornings and tutor in on weekday mornings, and at the back there was a little place where Sheba cooked and slept. There was a red-mantled couch at the side of the room where Jairus slept, when he slept; you could see his candle till dawn, for when he was finished with reading, he set the candle in the window to burn till dawn, to guide strangers there and let them know he was ready and waiting.

So it was that Sheba happened on Lebanon. Lebanon looked in the old woman's eyes, and Sheba's face had for Lebanon a look an angel's cheeks must wear when a lost child has found home.

"Come on home with me," Sheba said and set her arm about Lebanon's shoulder. Sheba saw the blood seeping through the whip welt.

Lebanon climbed toward Miranda's back.

"My husband and child are illed of the Pest and I came here for help," Lebanon said wearily.

"Why did he lash you?" Sheba asked, touching the flesh near to the welt. "I have ointment that will hush that swelling fast enough."

"I do not know why he lashed me," Lebanon said, and it was the truth. Never till she died did she know. "I will tell you good day now," she said politely and pulled the rein taut.

"Where is your place?" asked Sheba.

"You turn at Poake's Bridge, then south by two mile," Lebanon replied methodically. She cast her forehead high; the blood was running in a thin sheath down her brow and cheek and throat. Then suddenly she heard what Sheba had said.

"You cannot come," she said. "The Pest is at my house."

"I will be there with all dispatch," Sheba said. "I'm as good a physician as walks a street in Philadelphia—or at least I think so." Sheba even laughed.

"You wouldn't come?" Lebanon's heart thudded and stopped. "You'd not! You'd be a fool! I was a fool. I took in a child that had the Pest, and we nursed it back to health, and now God lets my man and child die of it and never cares."

"He cares," Sheba staunchly defended her old friend. "And who said your folks are dead? I walked into a drunk man's pistol butt once and the thing refused to fire at me though he snapped and snapped the trigger. I fear naught but the devil, and I can outsmart him any weekday morning. You go on home, and we will be there about as soon as you are. Turn at Poake's Bridge, south by two mile. . . ." Sheba clucked her tongue. "Put a big smile on, pet. They'll need it from you."

"Pest or no Pest, if ever I saw a woman need help that one did," Sheba told Jairus. "Not once would she even lift a finger to that awful cut on her face. That tavernkeep ought to be stocked for taking a lash to a woman, and I'll see that he is, whenever I can get around to it. She had done nothing but ask aid, from all I can gather. A mightily mean man he must be to be so afraid to die. If this day we die of pestilence, this day we die," she said, smiling as she got together medicament bag of polished leather, and a loaf of new bread just in case somebody might get hungry. "I'd best take along a piece of meat, too, don't you think, Jairus? And maybe meal and hominy and dried pease."

They got their apparatus of charity together.

"Come on, Jairus," she called. "The donkey's hitched and you yonder searching about for your Bible! It's there under the big slate. I can see it from here. Let's be gone. Never can I start out with you but you have lost something. It may be we will see Glory together this night. Giddup, Cherish," she called to the little donkey.

Chapter 16

BEFORE SHEBA AND JAIRUS got forty yards into the main street, they met the constable, Jabez Tare, coming their way. His peg leg was working fast down the cobbles, and he hailed them long before they came even with him. He had lost his leg in the war against Old George, and one could hear him grumble across a wide street because his peg would slip on a greasy cobble where a careless woman had thrown swill.

Sheba put her hands up to gather her unruly hair neatly under the sides of her cap. No use to show dudgeon or fear!

"Mercy or no," Jabez thundered and beat his peg leg on the cobbles, "this town will not harbor a case of plague if we know of it. If you go to that woman's house, it's quarantine on you."

Jairus leaned forward a little on the side of the cart. He had taken off his wool hat in deference to the constable. His face was lean and lined and meek. He leaned his face toward the constable, and his voice was low against the constable's bellowing. A crowd was gathering from nowhere, the way crowds will. Jairus put his eyes in the constable's eyes and began to talk, so low the crowd pushed to hear him:

"A pity the Almighty allows disease on earth; healthy men show it so little patience."

"There is an ordinance, sir!" the constable declared, strong-voiced in the might of ordinances.

"Damnation!" Jairus said, and Sheba sucked in her breath over her gums. (Damnation is no foul curse, Jairus told her later—it is a most common thing, following us all, and catching many of us.)

"Think of yourself, Jairus Mountjoy," the constable said, stamping his peg leg on the gray-cheeked cobble.

"Who am I?" asked Jairus, not unaware of the crowd's hush. "I am nobody."

"Then think of the rest of us," prayed Jabez Tare.

"You have done your duty." Jairus was firm. "Now I shall do mine. But not in the limits of your jurisdiction. You can tell the council so."

Jabez puffed back down toward the tavern, grieving after fool men you cannot save from themselves, even with ordinances.

"You say they're going down yonder past Poakes', into that Pest?" the tavernkeep asked.

"They are!" Jabez said, as though he held up a standard, for he was proud of Jairus, though he could not admit it.

Silence fell everywhere in that room. Patrick Margate for once had not one word to say.

When their donkey, Cherish, pulled their cart past the Poakes' house at the toll bridge, they could hear Priscilla wailing like a banshee. She was already piled abed, with a foot warmer of hot stones at her feet to keep off the first chills, and she was drinking cinchona broth by the pint. Her face was so swollen from weeping that Sheba and Jairus thought she had the Pest, too. They tarried not very long before the house when Simon Poake told them she did not have it.

They went on toward Lebanon's, and before they got there Sheba began to say the Beatitudes, pronouncing them slowly and carefully: " 'Blessed are the poor in spirit: for theirs is the kingdom of heaven. . . . Blessed are the meek: for they shall inherit the earth.

. . . Blessed are the merciful: for they shall obtain mercy. . . .' "

They rode into the arch of oaks where a wagon path lay. Beyond, the river shone, and the mosquitoes were beginning to buzz in the falling dark.

Erwin Poake came to meet them down that arched road, walking with his hands tight along his breeches' fringe. They were not dead, one could read in his face.

"You'd best hurry," Erwin said and slapped the donkey's rump. He walked alongside the cart back toward Lebanon's house which he had helped to build.

When they got there Estis had long since washed Lebanon's lash-bitten face in balsamic oil.

The twins stood about the room which they had mostly furnished with the slow carving of their hands. They seemed unafraid of the Pest for all their mother's weeping after them. They took a tubload of soiled clothing to the wash trough and began to wash there, like two women. The fire was lit under the wash boiler, the water soon boiled. They laid their broad hands into the Pest's nuisance as though it were no more than plow soil and common summer soilure.

Lebanon was greatly ashamed of herself that she could now relax and take rest. There was not much left for her to do, with so many pairs of hands doing. But she held Timothy in her arms, sitting close beside Fernald's head, and she spoke to Fernald again and again, and loosed her hand from Timothy's legs and held to Fernald's hands.

This room seemed far removed from her. These others were as strangers, indeed. She watched them, wondering a little upon their strange forms. This was her face, her hand; that was Erwin there beside the fire, and Estis begging her to lie down and sleep. There was the preacher from Mercierville, and never so kind a face, and Sheba Johann who was mother to a thousand people.

"I will hold Timothy and never take my eyes from his face, if you will lie down and rest," Estis swore.

But Lebanon would not.

Timothy had hushed his wailing. Now he lay snoring sharply, his breaths like quick puffs from a bellows. His eyes were shut and his limbs were lax.

Jairus took the child from Lebanon's arms.

"Let us lay him down," he said. "He will get his breath better flat."

Only when Jairus spoke would Lebanon give Timothy to that cradle which Erwin and Estis had carved together. There, far off in the cradle, it was as though Timothy were taken forever from her.

The little cluster of people in the cabin hovered before her while Timothy went down through the dark to the shore where maybe there is a boat such as Lebanon's dugout moored on a river. They watched him go, and it was as though his little breaths plucked breath from their own lungs and spent it.

Lebanon bowed her head on the cradle head, and it swayed once under her weight and straightened again.

Jairus Mountjoy held to Timothy's pulse till it was gone, and it was like a narrow ribbon fluttering in a dry wind.

Jairus' voice was gentle as a bell tolling. "You will not give under to this grief. You will hold your spirit firm. This is God's will. 'The Lord giveth and the Lord taketh away . . .' "

He motioned to Estis to help Lebanon away from the cradle, rocking under her tight-folded arms and hidden face.

Lebanon lifted her face once more. "He was so sweet," she said and stopped.

Jairus' tongue went slowly on:

"You will feel strength come from beyond yourself. You will feel it fill and overflow your heart. You will bear this because you are strong. You will bear yet more if it be God's will."

He looked hard at Fernald's darkened face while Sheba ministered to the sick man. Jairus took out his shambled Word of God and leafed it carefully, thinking what this woman might like to hear now, now that her little son was dead.

"Read of that woman that walked the moon," Lebanon said.

He found that part of The Word, for he knew where it was in the Book. He began to read, and the words went slowly in tall and lovely forms.

Fernald used to read her those same words, and now he lay so low to death that they could scarce catch his breath on a mirror. He was alive, Jairus Mountjoy said, clinging to that pulse—while

Sheba bathed and poulticed, stood and sat and worked incessantly. Lebanon's mind was clear, for she could still hear Timothy weeping out there in the deep cold. She went on listening for Timothy's tears, and she would listen for them for a long while.

Within her there were a thousand thirsts now, never to be healed: to hold him again, to hear him whimper and hush him against her breast, to see his eyes open mildly and close down again, sleeping in a long smile.

Lebanon could scarce bear to look in Fernald's face—and then she knew he would never discover this death. He was past knowing or caring.

Now she wished she were a fainting woman. It would be a mercy to sink into nothingness even for a moment.

She leaned her head on the back of the chair and closed her eyes. Estis' hand lay light on her hair, and Erwin handed her the water gourd and told her to take a drink of water.

She kept listening for the sound of Timothy's crying, and there was no whimper of it. Estis' hand was gentle on the top of her head. He was standing behind her chair, his fingers beginning to move in her hair, as one carelessly caresses a dog that is half asleep. Estis' fingers went softly round and round, moving like fern fronds in water, and the water deepened and warmed.

She fell sidewise, and Estis caught her head with his hands and gathered her up and laid her out beside Fernald.

"She's fevered, Preacher," was all that Estis said.

Erwin looked at his twin, sat quietly down on a stool and looked away into the fire.

The fern fronds stirred about Lebanon. Sebastian said, Do not grieve, Lebanon; I have never left you and never will. Why does not Timothy cry? If you will lift him up and blow in his face he will catch his breath. Fernald is lost and I am afraid. Roanoke, it can never be true. It is not true, Roanoke. Timothy is not dead, and Sebastian said, I will never leave you, never, never, never. . . . Sebastian was an old man now with a beard as white as milk and sorrow in his eyes. And he was weeping over her as he said, I have never left you, never, never, never. Yet where could he have been so long, to grow so old away from one?

And Timothy cried no more. She listened and she could not hear him crying. He must have gone with Fernald into another room. She could not hear him crying.

A far way off, a very long distance from her face, she heard a sound breaking, softly as a moon breaks on black water. Tremendous burdens lay upon her eyelids; monstrous weights lay on her flesh, pressing from it all but strong thirst. It was as though a still flame, now unfed, filled the space where her body had lain. She strove to cry for water, but a weight lay, too, on her mouth.

She slept again, and waked, and still this burden of silence and weight lay upon her. Sound was drained from her ears; nothing stirred within her consciousness. Her breast floundered desperately, for the thought came to her that she was dead—no loud decision, but a still one: I am now dead, and this is what death is like, now, time to rest, sounds of earth gone, forgetfulness!

Lebanon strove to lift her eyelids, so could she know if this was black death. Mightily she strove, tensing all the muscles of her being, straining taut her will. Her eyelashes struggled open a very little way, and she held them so. Broken light sifted down into her eyes. Sedately she held herself steady beneath a mighty weight, lifting the weight with but the delicate strength that lay in her eyelids. Steadily she bore upward the weight within her. If she let so much as one little muscle go, her eyelids would fall and stay forever shut. A little higher she lifted her eyelids, seeming to lift all earth and heaven. She stared, her eyes finding a little stretch of light, a space of wall.

She lay in a long wooden bed, and there were tall sides to it. There were candles at her feet, and there were candles burning behind her head, for she could see their light. Her flesh was shrouded in white. There were copper coins heavy on her eyelids, and cotton stopping her ears. She could hear a low voice saying steadily: "God, have mercy on this soul which we now commit to Thee."

Sheba stopped praying, opened her eyes, and unclasped her hands. It was for Jairus to build the coffin and dig the grave and say the sermon at the grave head. Whilst he dug the grave, she set the candles and said the prayers, because there was nobody else here to say prayers for this soul. The Poake twins were drooping out yonder beside an oak, saying nothing. They had helped Jairus to build the coffin and dig the grave; they could not help him preach or pray.

Sheba looked more narrowly toward the corpse's face. She blinked her eyes closed, then she looked again. The blue eyes of the corpse were fixed on Sheba Johann's face.

Sheba was thinking: I fixed those eyes under their coppers, I set the coins properly, and the lids were limp. If this woman's eyes opened, they did not open of themselves. The dead woman was watching her sullenly, or she was dreaming. She must ask Jairus for spectacles, sure.

Then the dead mouth spoke huskily: "Water—water——"

"Jairus!" Sheba shrieked, the sound lost in the wind about the house.

The Pest is a hideous thing, tricky as Satan, and as cruel. It had ridden Lebanon's breast for three days and nights. Her heart thundered, went too fast for beating at the last, and stopped. Yet it must have gone on beating.

The hand glass caught no breath of mist from her lips—though mayhap they took not sufficient care. True, her limbs had not stiffened, but many a dead man's body does not stiffen till the cold of the ground hardens it for him. One cannot stay a week about a plague house waiting for a corpse to stiffen.

They buried Timothy in one morning, and Fernald in the next morning, and they thought back on these deaths. While Lebanon was drowsing back to health, Jairus most carefully dug out those other bodies, the twins helping.

Fernald was lying as Jairus had laid him, but Timothy's little body seemed awry. It may be they had jolted the coffin in lowering it. It could so easily have happened.

The three men looked at one another and covered the hole again. There was no need for any one of them to say: Never tell her, oh, never tell her.

Jairus lay awake all that night, and Sheba tossed though she had tried to comfort them. "However it was, it must have been God's will," she said.

Jairus grieved secretly to Sheba: "If only I had waited," he said.

"I do believe the child was never dead. The man, yes—but not the child."

"Be sensible, Jairus. You did your whole duty," she comforted him. "When a man has done that, he can sleep at night. Not before."

But still Jairus suffered over it. He and the twins bore a load for Lebanon. It was not cowardice which prevented his telling her.

"I feel compunction to keep that grief from her, but I must," he said.

"You old fool!" said Sheba. "You only wish to unload some of your grief on her heart. You keep that nasty secret. Never tell her—for certain the twins and I will never tell her."

Sheba and Jairus had to stay out their quarantine at Lebanon's house, as did the twins.

"Tell me every word as to their death and burial," Lebanon would plead at first, thinking words would be a soft assuagement of pain.

Jairus lied to her pleasantly, and the twins sat about with comfort over their faces. Jairus told Lebanon that Fernald called her name and that he died in his sleep, no contorting of flesh, no agonies, no suffering past enduring. "He called your name," Jairus told her truly. "He talked of a fine house where you and he were to be."

"What else did he say—what more?"

"He cited your long love for him and said that he returned it fourfold," Jairus said. "He said the house was worthy of you, and built for you, and that he could see it most clearly, and you in the hall and roses there and lilies and finches singing," he told her truly.

"And what more?" pleaded Lebanon.

"Heaven for him," Jairus said.

Jairus' jawbone shifted a very little. The twins' hard faces looked steadily away into the river bottom. No light came into their eyes but that which burned there always.

Lebanon was looking down on the spaces where Timothy and Fernald lay.

The trees blew a little in the lessening wind.

The storm of autumn had cooled the land, had flooded the water places where the mosquitoes hatched; the air was brighter and the wind no more black and sultry.

Lebanon dropped her head lower before her breast.

The twins would not look toward her. Sheba unfolded her hands and folded them again.

"Do come away," Jairus said. "There be a thousand things worse than death, for with my own eyes I have seen some of them."

He put his hand on her shoulder and felt a grave pity for her.

"Why did I ever have to be born at all?" Lebanon asked wildly.

"There is a reason, you may be sure," Jairus told her; so sure of it he was that his voice had a Bible sound. "Only long years may tell you why. It is your duty to find why you are living."

When it was time for them to go to Mercierville, their quarantine being spent, Jairus set his wool hat on the back of his head. His eyes smiled, and his lanky, black hair made him look like a prophet.

"When you need us, call on us. We will be there," he said.

The twins were riding with them as far as the Poakes'.

"I cannot bear to be left here alone," Lebanon said, clenching her hands on the sideboard of the cart.

The twins looked off toward home.

"When I was young," Jairus said, the wind in his hair and burnt-out fires burning black in his eyes, "I used to say we are born alone, we live alone, and we die alone. I thought the words had a fine and mighty sound. I preached many a sermon on such a theme. Now I have learned better and am not ashamed to admit it. We are never alone, Lebanon d'Aussy. We are born together, littered as a great mother sow might litter ten million young. We live together, you treading my heart, I treading yours, our fists clenched in same pains and like angers, and our cheeks tight in like smiles and tears."

Lebanon laid her face in her own hands, shuddering, and shedding her tear stingily.

"I cannot bear the loneliness," she said.

"You did not listen while I talked," he said gently. "Later you will remember it."

When the Pest struck in Mercierville, Lebanon went into town and offered to nurse any and all. Having overed the thing, it would harm her no more. She went day and night, with no more than a crust of bread and a jug of hot milk for nourishment, and no sleep but that little spent with her head upright against a chair back. (The tavernkeep, Patrick Margate, died before the breach of his lash had healed on Lebanon's face.)

A legend grew about Lebanon's name. For five weeks she scarce ever took off her outer garments, and slaved over any that had the Pest, just as Jairus and Sheba did. She wished to die and go and be with Fernald and Timothy, but it was not yet her time.

Chapter 17 ·

HERE WAS DULL MORNING and new behavior. The little child was now as though dreamed, his small form an apparition endeared to her heart. Fernald, of the gentle ways and kindness, was now growing into dust. Careless a little in living he might have been, yet he had taken her to his heart when she most needed him. He had come West because it pleased her to come West, and here for his pains he had found a shallow grave in a silence he hated.

On the limed jamb of the fireplace there were still Timothy's sooty fingerprints, from that last time when she had scolded him for going too near the boiling pot. Never did she wash those prints away. By the back stoop there was the road cart Erwin and Estis had pegged together for him, so large as to hold Timothy, no larger. Everywhere there was remembrance of Timothy and Fernald.

Miranda and Juno and the pigs and chickens were to be fed, and Lebanon fed them. There was the tamed bear, Erasmus, snuffling over his food, scratching his flesh as a dog does. There was all the wide earth still, yet now it seemed empty all about Lebanon.

The quiet terrified her sometimes, and she could not go to the Poakes', and she could not go to Mercierville, and she could not go back East, and she could not go West. Silence seemed to menace her sanity. She had craved a quietness, a loneliness. Once she had longed to live alone on a riverbank, those times when Fernald was in Mercierville. Now Lebanon had her desire—to walk alone in bright solitude.

Imperceptibly Lebanon's memories of Fernald thinned, so that though each morning seemed bleak as the last, still it was not, quite. When Jairus Mountjoy left her, he said:

"You are not alone in this grief. We will be holding you in our thoughts. We will mention your name in prayer every day. The peace of God is yours for your weak asking. As the sky exceeds this little room space, so His love exceeds your need. His mercy is yours, any time you will remember to plead for it."

But after Jairus and Sheba went back to Mercierville, for all their nursing and going night and day and giving every manner of kindness to any who asked, the strangest manifestation showed itself: Jairus' name was coupled with that of the Frencher's woman.

Sheba heard of it and grew fighting mad that folks he had befriended should so chastise Jairus' honor. Tongues went busily awhile. But Jairus lifted his chin another half of an inch and smiled a little—and if there was a tincture of bitterness to his smiling, then a bitter smile is better than none.

"It will pass," he said. "It will pass. Hold your tongue most carefully, Sheba. In a little while, or a longer while, they will know that they bandied lies with one another. Till they recognize their own lies, there would be little use to deny what they say. If I jumped into the fray over my name, it would show I felt guilt. Let them say what they will. Little by little they will hush and will speak of something else. They mean no harm."

It happened just as he said.

For a time some faces grew solemn when he passed before them, some brows lifted, heads turned and looked the other way. But after each woman had her say (her husband hushing her from scandal-mongering, yet listening carefully to what she had repeated), the talk slackened and died. There went fresher word about that the daughter of the most-moneyed family in Mercierville had wed most suddenly—and reason aplenty, God knew. So they bandied her name here and yonder for a time.

Jairus knew they had talked mightily of Lebanon d'Aussy, but he felt no distrust of her because of such talk. He had seen no sign of sin in her face or in her house. They said she trafficked with the Poake twins, but he had never seen any but a pure devotion. Their liking for her seemed firm and virtue-founded in their faces.

He found her much as other women, with but the small discrepancy that she was different from other women. In small ways she was different. Lebanon's face was much before him. He would find himself remembering her at strange times, and words she had spoken, and a thin smile she had spent when she said: "I thank you with all my heart for all you have done for me."

He could not forget her. Now and then he rode out to see her, his long legs akelter down the sides of the little ass named Cherish. Half the time he walked beside the donkey, feeling ashamed to make her bear his weight.

"You are too much alone," he told Lebanon, searching her face.

"I was never able to go near to people," she confided. "We could never seem to understand one another. Even Fernald—sometimes we could not speak together for strangeness. There was once a man . . ."

She told this gently, making no shame of it in her lasting devotion to Fernald. "That was before I promised myself forever to Fernald, of course. We seemed to speak alike, that man and I. Our hearts were very near, but I was young then and maybe we were both badly fooled and time would have told us so."

"What became of him?" Jairus asked, strangely jealousied.

"He married a good and able wife of an honorable name and some wealth from North," Lebanon said. "I have never doubted that he has been happy at all times."

"Then he never loved you and you wasted your time in loving him?" Jairus asked, as a grim-faced judge of human matters might.

"I do not know," she replied. "It cannot matter now. It may be it never did matter—though only God will ever know how I suffered over it."

"I can guess somewhat of such suffering," Jairus said, and one could not know what he meant by such words. "To live a long time in this world seems that you will suffer much pain soon or late. You may bear it quietly or loudly, as it may please you. Weak hearts bathe in pity. I'll never give you pity, Lebanon—it would be the ruin of you."

"Did I ever ask pity from you?" she retorted gently.

Both of them knew better. Already he had spent great pity on her, and she knew it.

Six months went, one day at a time, one hour by one hour. Once a month at least Jairus rode out to see how Lebanon was doing. In his saddle pack he carried an old play board and yellow ivory pieces of a draught game. He taught Lebanon to play draughts, though she played poorly. Her eyes never learned to see his several moves beforehand. But she remembered the law of the board: think long and move wisely, and yonder at the far side an enemy will crown you king.

Jairus was clever at preaching over a game of draughts. "First you crave a crowning," he would say. "Your wish for the crowning is hope. Further, you must work for the spirit's crown—and that is purpose. Without hope or purpose, a man is no more than a tamed beast, turned to graze, led home at night for a milking."

"What can there be in this world for me to wish for now?" Lebanon would ask. She but asked him to hear him talk.

He would retail her words back to her.

"What lay closest in all your wishing?" he would ask her, their hands playing at draughts.

"I wished for a bright place to walk in." Firelight flickered on the walls. It was cold autumn now. The rains came in close against the house, waking the room to murmuring, as though a thousand voices told muted tales from a world across the ocean.

His eyes burned covetously on the beauty he saw in Lebanon, while she listened to the sad, slurred speech of rain beyond the walls. There be those who say no man and woman find communion above the flesh—but that is not true; there is a mental warmth one takes from the other that shall never be dispersed.

"Now all beyond you is a bright place," he said. "Where would you go? Some men be contented at one hearth for a lifetime. The Poake twins would marry you—their longing for you is in their four eyes."

He said that a mite jealously.

"I could not marry either of them, for I love them both the same," she said. "Besides they have not asked me. Thirdly, I do not care to marry ever again. I loved Fernald. It was enough to last."

"If it were I—I say only 'if'—I should wish to be near to you all the remainder of my life," he admitted boldly.

Beyond the play of draughts, he tried to teach her to write and read and cipher, but it was all but hopeless. " 'In the beginning God created the heaven and the earth,' " he would read. "That is all the sum of our knowledge; all else is contributory. Now I shall write these words for you, and you are to copy them. Here is the A—the fellow with the crossbar—and here are the other letters. You are to find them in these words. Some letters are not included in this exercise, and you are to be clever enough to discover which ones are not included. Next time we will choose another exercise. Copy the words on your slate, and when you have done it once, wipe them away with your damp cloth, and copy them again, till you can make them in perfect form. Learn your letters as you go, remember, using your eyes and your hand and your mouth and your ear. I will teach you their names as we go along, and before you know it we will be spelling and reading anything you please. If it takes us six months on that first line of the Bible, that is no matter. You will know the whole Big Book when you have learned that first verse."

She tried and tried for a time, and the whole matter was a mixture to her. I am too old to learn, she told herself. It was confusion that confounded her, and she saw no reason to learn, when Jairus could open the book and read gloriously the weighted words.

When she had toiled long enough over the slate, she would walk off down to the river to see the wild ducks splatter spume on the breast of the current. That is my language, she would think. They write words in the water and I can read them.

Jairus would come but once in a month. Not by any action of his would he contribute to talk of this woman, and as sore a penance as he could devise for his heart was not seeing Lebanon. If he had asked himself whether he loved her, love would have seemed a weak and silly word.

Never once did he say: "I love you, Lebanon." Nor did she ever suspect it. She was not thinking of such matters. She considered him a preacher pitying her, and more often than not Sheba came with him to comfort her, and how could she call it love since he did not?

One time, and no more, he broke his rule of never going to her house oftener than once a month. This day Jairus was sure there was something wrong at Lebanon d'Aussy's house.

"Sheba," he called out before sunrise, "you come on out and we'll hitch Cherish to the cart. Something is wrong at Lebanon's house."

"Well, then," she said, "let us pray first, before things get worse there."

They knelt down, and he prayed because he was male and God created the male before the female. Jairus prayed aloud, and Sheba listened and said her own inside prayers.

"Keep her in Thy care," Jairus said, "till we get there and can take over for Thee."

Many a bargain Jairus had made with God, and if he kept his half, God was sure to keep His. It had never failed.

Sheba tutted over the whole business of riding twenty miles to please a fool man's fancy after a new widow. But she said nothing of it, though hard put to it to hold her tongue.

They rode by the Poakes', Cherish's ears limping along through the air. Priscilla all but slammed the door in their faces.

"That woman would make trouble betwixt two wood doves nesting," Sheba said. "Why God allows such to live and breed is one of His mysteries."

"We are not to judge," Jairus preached, high and mighty.

"It seems to me He has forgot a lot of the trifling snakes He made away back yonder. We have to live with mean folks. God don't," she said. "He lets them be born, and then it's watch out, everybody. What good on earth could Priscilla Poake do on this earth, tell me that, Preacher? You know very well who has had the most to say concerning you and Lebanon d'Aussy."

(She called him Preacher when she was the least bit riled at him.)

Jairus shifted his tobaca and slapped the reins on the donkey's rump.

"All right, then, I will say as I think." His eyes sought Lebanon's roof yonder under the trees, to see whether it were burned down last night. "I will tell you: Priscilla Poake has two of as fine boys as you'll ever find. No matter if you travel to Savannah or Orleans or Boston, those boys will stand up with any. What of that, Miss Sheba? I'll take Priscilla Poake along with the rest. There is some purpose she serves, we can be sure."

"She said you were an old windy-mouthed goat, for I heard her say it," said Sheba. "She said it to me." She was angered past any understanding—for Jairus' eyes were firm-set on that rooftree and he had no eyes for anything but Lebanon.

Jairus still was calm. "Such accusations will cause a man to examine himself to see whether there be any truth in them," he said, playing at nobility. (But he was thinking: The two-legged old cat. Why cannot she hold her spitting tongue and her claws? She's not worthy to have two such fine young ones as Erwin and Estis and a good man like Simon to feed her.)

"I saw that feather bed on the fence as we came by. Any woman with any cleanliness to her would make a new ticking every ten years or so," said Sheba.

"You women!" Jairus said, patting Sheba's cheek, which cooled her not one whit. She knew he was the happier now because he was the nearer to Lebanon.

They came up to Lebanon's dooryard.

The oaks nodded their boughs. Far down the slope the river burned in the sun. The moss curled its tips in a ground wind. Chipmunks played about and squirrels ran up and down the body of an oak as though it were a Big Pike.

Erasmus, the bear, was not on his stake; the ragged end of the rope was there, but he was gone. Miranda was watching them from the slope, and Juno was lowing toward them, her bag strutted.

There was no smoke in Lebanon's chimney. The sanded walk had not been swept, for the pines had spent their needles carelessly over the walk and yard.

"Of all the wild-goose chases," said Sheba, trying to tell herself to hush. Something was wrong, and she was almost as greatly concerned as Jairus.

"Quit worrying, Jairus," she said, and managed a heartiness: "We'll fix up anything wrong."

He thudded a fist on the door; they listened, but there was no reply.

"You go in first, Sheba," said Jairus.

They found Lebanon on her bed, and her cheek was swollen half as large again as her head. It was her left cheek. There was a wattled crusted wound down her cheek and throat that lay open as a gutted fish lies open under a knife. Her left eye was swollen shut and she was high-fevered. She had tried to sew the thing together and it was a sorry mess, if ever Jairus saw one.

"Whatever on earth . . ." Sheba began.

"Have sense enough to hush," Jairus said. "Heat some water."

He got out his surgeon wallet and the big needle from it, and the little clamps and the turpentine.

"I'll give you laudanum," he told Lebanon, "but I'll not give you brandy; that is for Horn sailors and city mobsters that can't stand a surgeon's needle. You can stand this, Lebanon."

The pillow beneath her cheek was sodden in old blood.

"I must be so ugly to look at," Lebanon said.

He touched her lips with the very tips of his fingers, to hush her words. Lebanon did not scream any more than she must. Sheba and Jairus held her. Sheba sat on Lebanon's chest. Jairus held her face, and it is a hard thing to hold and sew, too.

"I knew something had happened to you," he said. "I could not sleep. I could not rest till I hit the road to this place."

He could have wept at the sight of her left cheek: Erasmus' claw had nigh cleft her cheek through, and till she died she would bear this scar. Jairus sealed and hemmed it as deftly as he could, and the newness of the wound helped the clean healing. The sewing of her cheek was a draught game of courage betwixt them; if he could sew it for her, she could somehow endure it. When it was over and Lebanon was somewhat drunken on laudanum of white poppies, she told them what happened.

Yesterday she had gone about to feed Juno and Miranda and the calf and the pigs and the chickens as always. She had fed the bear a mush of oats wetted in sweet milk and a little syrup to sweeten it for him. Then, without so much as an extra snuffle over her hands, he had swiped his great paw against her cheek, had stood on his hind legs and bellowed toward the woods.

He was somewhere in the woods now, doubtless dragging the other end of his chain—for in a lunge he had broken free while she staggered inside the door.

"I try to bear no hate toward him," she said. "I'd have done the same, tethered in one place."

It was a sad chance that Erasmus, the bear, left a claw mark on her face for all to see; when she went into Mercierville to trade her pelts, men talked and tittered and spoke evilly (as always some men will) of the scar on her face. The old talk concerning her revived in their minds.

Her face burned, yet what defense could she make against their talk, when she scarce knew what caused their hate, when she was innocent, indeed? Never had she felt so defenseless as now. Never was she so strong, yet always there seemed to be new trials for her strength.

Lebanon haggled for a fair trade for her pelts; but any man could see she was not offered much more than half their worth. Other trappers hung over the counter and all but made shameful offers in her very face. The storekeep spat and showed contempt for her—because she was a woman, because she was alone, because her name was a legend, because he could.

"I couldn't take so low an offer," she would say, trying to say she would take one only slightly higher.

The storekeep would spit again. The lounging men would be listening.

A lady might pass through the entrance of the store and look Lebanon's way and go out again, flirting her skirts and whispering to her maidservant. The scar showed like a brand on Lebanon's face, though Jairus had so carefully seamed the thing.

"My fine young lady," the storekeep said, "from the looks of the pelts," and his eyes went all over Lebanon so that she would know he was speaking of herself as well as the pelts, "I think they be lousy. I do not want the pelts at any price. And now a very good day, Mistress d'Aussy."

Riding home behind Miranda, there was nothing to do but shake her head and lift her face, striving to forget the town and the men at the counter and their strong dislike of her. She had toughened the muscles of her face and heart. She would never allow them to see that they had hurt her.

On one morning of March she found a thing on her door, a paper set fast there by a brass staple. She supposed this paper to be for her.

Now she wished she had learned to read.

Why had she not heard a comer place the paper there? How had he set it there so quietly? Was she down at the river when whoever it was came?

She turned the paper round and round in her hand but could make nothing of it. Next time she went to Mercierville she would take the paper to Jairus so that he could read it for her.

But in two mornings, early in the morning, he rode up to the house bestriding his little donkey, Cherish.

He had heard of the paper. Lebanon considered that it was as though she had needed him again and he had come as though down out of the sky. In a roundabout fashion Jairus had heard of Lebanon's need.

She held forth to him the paper that was set on her door two days gone.

"I am ashamed now that I never learned to read," she said, laughing.

Jairus read the words on the paper. His eyes dulled a little, and his lips folded the more closely upon one another.

This was dangerous wording. There were foul words on that piece of paper.

His eyes went to Lebanon's face.

"Is it a tax, or something?" she asked.

He would fool her again, and take another hurt from her, and keep it for her, so that she might never feel it. His face smiled while his heart heavied. His eyes went craftily about, considering all plausible lies.

"It is a notice of a tax you must pay for trapping," he said. "Central government costs a lot of money. I expect you to growl, for folks always did expect a lot of benefits without paying for them."

"How much is the tax?" she asked.

"A hundred dollars a year, though I'd not mention it hereabouts. I'd pack my stuff and get out. Maybe they wish to save the game."

"Any pretty poll-priss minces down the streets of Mercierville, yet here I try to make an honest living and they tax me past what I can pay," Lebanon cried.

His eyes were on the foul wording of the paper. Somebody's quill had called her as foul a name as one can think of. "Begone," the paper said in part, "or you will one night find your house on fire over your head. We do not want your kind in decent country."

The paper went on from there, and there was no name at the bottom of it.

"There's nothing to it but the tax," he said, "and I'd make no mention of it. It would only stir up more trouble. Some things you be wise if you do not fight."

He stroked the back of her hand lightly and looked in her eyes brazenly.

"Do they despise me and are trying to run me out?" she asked.

"No more than because you are a stranger," he soberly comforted her. "You came among them a stranger. Your eyes are a deeper dark than they have known before, or a brighter blue. . . . Your eyes are blue," he said, as though he had first seen them. "Your eyes are blue as a bluebird flying."

"Oh, now," she said restlessly; "it's too late for my eyes to be blue. You tell me why they should set a tax on me."

"They set a tax on everybody for everything," he said, telling a big lie since he had started one. "You are proud and take easy offense. Your feet wish to go their way without praying advice from any. You feel above them."

"No," she said. "I wish them to love me. I loved everybody and I wished that everybody would love me."

"Ducklings feel that," he said.

He wished to tell her that he loved her, but this seemed a silly time to do it. "You are above any woman I ever laid eyes on," he said sagely.

"Oh, I cannot hold a candle to Sheba, and you know it," she said, without pretense.

By now she had forgotten the tax. "Jairus," she prodded him, "why do you not marry Sheba? She would have hot mustard water for your feet after every hard day, and potatoes grown and banked from one year to the next."

Jairus watched Lebanon's face to see whether she was a flisk-mahoy, flirting with his heart. He saw she was not. "I will never marry Sheba," he said.

"Why not?" Lebanon pressed him.

"I do not love Sheba," he said soberly, "save as God expects me to love her, of course, and in gratitude for all she has helped me to do."

Lebanon laughed, pushing her hair high above her forehead. Her blue eyes flashed, but the red claw mark burned.

"Law, now, Jairus," she laughed. "How does God love Sheba now?"

"With pity and praise, I'd say," he replied.

"Then for heaven's sake, how would you love a woman you married?" she pushed him. Here was Jairus in his dotage, life past, and speaking of love still. There were creases in his forehead and soberness in his words, yet love was strangely in his eyes.

"It might be a sin," he said, "but I should love her as the angels worship God."

He looked down to the flowing river where an egret flashed on a flight straight as a gun barrel. The bird's wings loped through the air, his feet folded close in against his body. He was homing.

"You old fool!" Lebanon laughed. "I never heard such a thing."

It was in that next little moment that she knew that he loved her, and that she had hurt him.

"Jairus!" she said. "Go home."

She took his hands as you take a child's.

"Go home," she said. She turned away into the house.

When he was half a mile toward the Poakes', she opened the shutter, for it was March and warm enough, but she would not stand and watch him out of sight. She decided she would see no more of Jairus Mountjoy and Sheba Johann: This was indeed a bright place to walk in, this world, and a place you can freely be alone in, too.

I would for a little wish myself a man, she thought. Strange it is a man never wished himself a woman. A fact lies hidden there, though I cannot describe or name the fact. A man never envies a woman's garments or features or manners. It is a man's world, she thought. It is a cruel, conscienceless world.

When she was done with thinking over Jairus—and that took only a little time—she went back to hating that tax and the world that would tax a woman for trying to make a living. Her heart felt like iron in silk flesh. She did not know which way to turn now, or whom to trust. The bright skin and the flaring red of the bear's claw mark were as a thing to weep over now. So she wept, and did not know she was weeping because she had called Jairus an old fool.

She put her hands about her body and desperately wished herself a man, for then she would attempt the Santa Fe Trail, no less, or go around the Horn to Tartary. Her hands went about her waist, and there they stopped, for she was thinking: A man's body can never bear a child.

A little smile grew upon her mouth, and her eyes deepened. "So much I have had—so much—more than most women. I had Timothy, and he was rare. I had Fernald, and he was rare. I thought for a time a fine gentleman like Sebastian saw a fineness in me to love. And Jairus and Sheba have been kind to me, kinder than I deserved. I have had more than most."

She opened the shutter again and looked out into the world. The trees bowed to her, and the moss danced its tiptoes near to earth; the birds swooped, singing. April was near.

She touched her cheek and its newly healed scar. I will trust that it was the Hand of God and not a bear's claw that ruined my cheek, she told the morning.

The trees swerved in assent, and the moss nodded. The birds sang on, for they had never once doubted God's wisdom in anything. Here was the very Hand of God moving so that she could follow its soft habit.

Lebanon, she told herself, you have learned a lesson that was never written in little markings of human fingers. There is a highway, and perils and prizes. It is a man's world, and women keep to shadows.

She had craved brightness of an enduring, haughty moon on her face, a sun always at noon, had objected to any shadow at all, at all. She had wished light to accompany her always, and never dark or slough to tread.

In the far reach behind the house a herd of deer loped, halted, loped again, shadows in a green world. A robin hopped about in the springing grass, and looked Lebanon's way, and hopped farther away. Juno lowed, and you could hear her bell. A loon went over the house, crying, crying, going away from the river.

One night, long past midnight, the woman named Jeannie Race came to Sheba's house. Jairus' set candle taught her the way up the sanded walk. Her feet leaned a little, and she stopped once on the walk, held by a great pain.

Jeannie was weeping, and her clothing was only half fastened, and her hair not fastened at all. Her hands seemed loosened, too, so that they went and never stilled—at her throat, her breast, her swollen middle.

"They put me out," she said, weeping. "You said I could come, Sheba."

"Come in," said Sheba, her own hair a sight.

Jairus pulled up his pantaloons and straightened his hair a little and stirred up the fire on the kitchen hearth.

When Sheba had the woman in the Stranger's Room bed, Sheba came into the kitchen.

"She is ready to have the thing, all but," she said. "I do not know whether she will die first from the chest bleed or the other. Come and help me, Jairus; a man's got more nerve."

They went into the other room where Jeannie Race was.

Jairus took the woman's fumbling hands and held them still, as still as she could bear them to be held, and he told the girl of Mary who found only straw to lie on when her time came and the pain began. Jeannie Race was knowing those pains now.

"I cannot bear any more," she said, her putty-colored face turning back and forth to one and the other of them, on the best-room pillow.

"I cannot give you laudanum," Jairus said. "Laudanum is for men that must have arms and legs sawed off. Women who bear children have their own muscle, no more. If you will pray a little, it will take your thoughts a little away from the pain. I am a preacher, but it does not matter what you say. God will hear you. In this case it can be like numbering. Or if you do not like the thought of praying, you may count. Count to a hundred, and the pain will lessen, pain by pain, by the time you get there. Go on, now, and name your numbers."

"I do not know the proper words to say," she gasped.

Her breaths came desperately when the pains struck her. In between she lay like a spent bird breathing only as much as it must.

"He will understand anything you say, in whatever language," Jairus consoled her. "Say what you will."

"You know how I have lived," she said fearfully.

"God knows, too," he said, most gently.

Then he told Jeannie of the woman who washed the feet of Jesus and dried them in her long, scented hair.

A torn smile slit Jeannie's lips, and her eyes said a thank you to him.

A pain took her body, and her lips began to bubble, and a stain of blood showed on her mouth. But her eyes remained faithfully on Jairus' face.

"One . . . two . . ." frailly she began to count, "three . . . four . . . five . . ."

Jairus and Sheba suddenly wished to weep for all women, and for all men, and their children.

The child was born, a woman child, and Sheba took charge of it by the fire in the kitchen.

"It is a girl," Jairus said to Jeannie. "You tell me a name for her."

He could see she was going. The bleeding of her mouth had not lessened, and he saw no sign it might. Jeannie smiled, her head limp as a dead robin's, her hands striving to hold to his hands.

"Jeannie . . ." Jeannie said. Her whisper was little more than a slurred consonant.

Jairus did not push her for the child's father's name.

"Jeannie Race," Jeannie said. "My father had good blood."

Three days later Sheba gave the child to Lebanon.

"God left it on our doorstep," Sheba said.

"But see here," Lebanon pleaded and frowned, "I'd never want another child."

"But look," Sheba pleaded, and opened the bundle and showed the small face, squinting against the light as though there were pain in the world beyond the blanket. "It is a woman child and its dead mother wished it to be called Jeannie for herself. But you can name it whatever you wish."

Lebanon took the bundle in her hands, and where the child's small bottom lay, the blanket was warm a little, and damp, but the baby's hands were icy cold. She felt for its feet and the feet were cold, too.

Suddenly Lebanon stood to her feet. "I'll not take it, but I'll warm it. Didn't you ever once tend a baby, Sheba? God's grace, its feet must be kept warm or it will die from the colic. This child has wretched circulation."

Sheba leaned her head wearily on the back of the chair, while Lebanon stirred up the fire to warm the child's feet. The old woman's eyes were full of tears.

"So did you have poor circulation till this minute, Miss Lebanon," Jairus said, smiling.

"This child will do nothing but break my heart," Lebanon complained, tenderly, warming the infant's feet in the palms of her hands and holding them to the fire. "I will take her," she quarreled, "though I cannot think why. Why do not you and Jairus keep her?"

"Jairus thinks I am an old fool," Sheba said, "and, what's more, I am." Sheba's eyes dwelt a moment on the fire, and all her love for Jairus was in her eyes.

Lebanon looked down into the baby's face. Suddenly the baby smiled, as though an angel had brushed its cheek with a fingertip. Lebanon held the child close against her breast, leaning her head low against the warm breathing, forgetting Sheba entirely. She had been most lonely, and a child is a good means for healing loneliness.

Chapter 18

TIMES WERE HARD, near to being as hard as the hard times of 'Nineteen. Food was still plenty, but money—oh, how scarce the money was! Pelts went down till you were offered a little of nothing for a fine-conditioned, most carefully cured skin. Lebanon had no great need for money, but always there are a few little things you can think of to spend money on—Jeannie, for instance.

Jeannie was growing to be the prettiest baby ever you set your eyes on! Erwin and Estis did not come to Lebanon's house so often as formerly, but they loved Jeannie almost as much as they had once loved Timothy. Jairus said she was the prettiest baby in this country, and Sheba said so, too.

It is a queer thing how you can love a strange mother's child nearly as well as your own, once you set your heart to it.

When Jeannie was six months old, she looked the way Lebanon would have drawn her own little daughter's portrait. Jeannie had hair that stood about her head in silky ringlets, and her eyes were a wide, sweet blue. Yet mostly it was Jeannie's smile, for she loved anybody that would look her way.

If Lebanon set her on a Mercierville counter, she would be smiling at the storekeep and reaching for a stranger's arms. Nothing could make Lebanon or Erwin or Estis or Sheba or Jairus so all-gone mad as to have Jeannie's birth brought up for discussion. Sheba said Jeannie's father had gone West. But everybody else knew the Lollocks had those wide, believing eyes, and, anyhow, young Lollock was sent to Spain to study medicine early this year. Or then she might be the child of Birch MacNamery who had two old-maid aunts and lived in the biggest house in Mercierville, with grounds comprising acre after acre. Now Birch was gone to New York to pursue some devices in trade and route freight into Orleans, with his old aunts' money. Birch had a most friendly way about him, always did have. He was but nineteen when Jeannie was born. Any way one looked at it, Jeannie would have most particular blood!

"That child has the best blood in this country!" Sheba would say. "Her father had to go West, but he'll come to see her some little day, wait and see, and you'll see him walk these streets and carry his daughter on his arm!"

"Ah, now, you suppose your papa is in Santa Fe swinging in a dance and you here in my arms, and he never knowing how pretty and sweet you are," Lebanon would whisper to the child, holding her the more close. Lebanon could guess with the rest, or believe Sheba's tale about the sudden western journey Jeannie's father had to take.

It did not greatly trouble Lebanon as to who Jeannie's father might be! It seemed only by a small chance, sometimes when she thought of it, that she was legally born Lebanon Nowel Fairgale, with her father's roof over her head.

Jeannie had only her mother's name—Jeannie Race—and her strange father gone West, Sheba said.

"Tell me what her mother was like," Lebanon would prod Sheba. "Tell me the very color of her eyes and the way she wore her bonnet," Lebanon would plead.

"Jeannie's mother was a poor orphan," Sheba would say. "She had a pretty face till it was wasted by her inward fever. She was little and blue-eyed and dark-haired. She had an endearing gratitude. She kissed Jairus' hands at the last as though he had been God."

Sheba spat into the fire. "Jeannie's mother was a good woman, a pretty lady," Sheba said. (Who am I to judge her? she thought. When anybody tells Lebanon any different about her, I'll say they lied. Maybe all our evil talk is lying. Maybe every man is good, according to his lights.)

For a mite, Sheba could have hated Lebanon d'Aussy—for Sheba was no fool. She saw Jairus' eyes pleading in his face, and his sermons grown gentle and high-sounding. It was that Lebanon d'Aussy!

But Sheba faithfully read her Bible and prayed God to remove this meanness from her heart, this hatred unbecoming a Christian—

and He did. He caused her to love Lebanon. Sheba forced herself to ride with Jairus to see Lebanon and to take that blue-eyed little Jeannie a doll head or a sack of dried and powdered catnip, or new bread for Lebanon, or a length of blue cloth to make her a waist.

If love that Lebanon d'Aussy Jairus would, Sheba would do her part. Lebanon still stuck to midnight mourning, when any fool could see her eyes wished for a blue waist and her bright hair cried for a white riband, and a white skirt would go well with all. But Lebanon would hear naught of it.

"I have Jeannie to consider," Lebanon said, "if I did not have myself. Somehow I was always a target for idle tongues."

Lebanon was not trying to catch Jairus, and if she were, he certainly was not running very fast.

If the truth were known, he thought his love for Lebanon hopeless and foolish; he considered himself an old fool, as Lebanon had carelessly called him, and no man can deduct a year from his life, or its weight from his heart, or a folly from his intentions, it seems—though sometimes he may think he has succeeded in doing so. He may dye his hair, he may cavort with the lads (and nurse a lame back all the next week), but he cannot take years off his life.

Jairus kept carefully to his trade, preaching the Scriptures, salving a slave's infection, hoeing in his garden (or another man's), shoeing a horse for a man who might not have the smithy's charge —and keeping the candle all night in the window for any soul in trouble.

Sometimes forty nights would go by and the candle would burn still, and never would the door jar under a fist or the night air be stirred in hasty calling; yet on the fortieth night there might be a man bleeding to death, or an innocent man jailed, or a young hizzie caught in her first solicitation, or a child dying of pox, and its mother with no money for medicaments. There was no other man in all that country who could fill Jairus Mountjoy's shoes, and folks were beginning to find it out.

Sheba was always there, ready to go, too, at a moment's notice, with a lancet or a loaf of bread, laudanum or sage tea. When there was a pounding on the front door, her nose was always in the crack of the kitchen door.

All that Jairus could tell himself these days was that Duty is a
stern mistress, but a fair and contenting one. Let the other men run
after fame or love, worldly pleasures or moneys—Jairus had
about decided to take Duty to wife, so he would never weep over his
marriage.

Now Lebanon could scarce remember any old murmuring of
tongues against her name, or the evil turning of this chance or that
one. She was so busy with Jeannie, who was learning to walk now,
and still had the rosy color of a turning peach on her cheeks, and
eyes blue as a spring Italian sky.

Lebanon had not much time now in which to remember Timothy
or Fernald. It takes time and solitude if one is to grieve seriously.
Sometimes Lebanon would covertly watch a woman sitting there
on a cart seat beside her man—a child at her breast, and another
growing within her doubtless. Then Lebanon would pity herself,
would feel herself to be friendless, facing a pitiless world, while that
woman on the cart seat, sheltered in a man's shadow, seemed
garbed in all security, bridled fast against wandering into unseen
perils.

Never did Lebanon see a cart that she did not most carefully
study the man and the woman sedate under her husband's least
elbow nudge to see whether more peace lay in that woman's face
than in her own.

It was on a certain day in summer when that worst happening
came. It was sometime along in early August. The clouds were far
and white in heaven. The earth was spongy and odorous from late
rains. The birds sang seldom and heavily now. Corn flags were
blooming in red and yellow blossoming.

Jeannie saw other faces so seldom it occurred to Lebanon that
she might take the corn to the mill, though she had little corn to
grind.

So Lebanon and Jeannie rode toward the Poakes', thinking little
of it. Naturally, neither Priscilla nor Simon nor Erwin nor Estis
could foresee what happened on that day.

Lebanon had some thought of asking Erwin and Estis to trade

off some of her best copper pots and pewter plates next time they went to Mercierville. There was a little pawn place on a narrow side street that would give you a fair price, and Lebanon had more than her share of such things.

She had saved and washed and ticked a new feather bed for sale, too, and Jeannie would be a long time growing. There would be time to save many a feather bed before Jeannie took her love. (Lebanon would smile and kiss Jeannie's foot sole and think a little sourly: He will kiss your throat!)

Lebanon rode down through the reaches of oak shade and thought of Jairus Mountjoy. She was remembering what Jairus said, and Sheba listening, too. Always, very nearly, Sheba came along. Jairus' care for Lebanon was a jagged cross for Sheba's soul to take on. "Now, God, why must I hear him make love to her in second-hand manner?" Sheba would pray petulantly. "I love her, too, as a sister, and if I did not, I should force myself to, because You and Jairus love her. But must I listen to the phrases he puts into her ears for her to remember when he is gone?"

Evidently God said yes, for Jairus went on saying the things, and Sheba had to go on listening. When Sheba would have slipped out to the cow lot or the back yard, Jairus would say: "Sit down, Sheba!"

Jairus wished no scandal on Lebanon's name because he wished to marry her, bless God, but Sheba dropped many a stitch in Jairus' stockings, and she would rock the faster, having to sit to hear such talk.

"Cut this jealousy out of my heart," Sheba would pray God, rocking harder and harder, and the knitting needles just agoing.

And God did. When Sheba smiled on Lebanon there was a sweetness in her smile.

That last time Sheba and Jairus were with Lebanon, Jairus all but proffered marriage. He did not pull at her hands. He kept his hands down-hanging at his sides. He spoke gravely of her need for him, rather than of his need for her.

"I always said I would get me a wife, when the very right one came along," he said. "You have a need for a husband, too."

(Lebanon was remembering all this as she and Jeannie rode along to the Poakes'.)

"Did you ever think of taking another husband, Lebanon?" he besought her softly, and Sheba listening.

He held his hands at his sides still. It was a none too easy thing for Jairus to do, since Lebanon's cheeks were creamy and her lips were soft and her throat was high-tilted and her eyes were a fairy blue. Other than that, Jairus had never spent love on this woman and that, and had a store of it saved for whomsoever he should decide to love.

But now Lebanon did not smile: her face grew the more sad.

"Jairus," she said, "the kindness in your face . . ."

Then she turned away from the look in his eyes. "Do you consider us fools, Sheba?" she asked.

"In no case," Sheba snapped, God's rein not as tight on her tongue as it might be. "In no case, at all. It has been done and said before—ten thousand times—and not one time in ten thousand was there a man that did not rue it all later and the woman will rue it worse, I'd say!" She went on rocking, her needles click-clacking in a stocking for Jairus.

"Did you rue it, Sheba?" asked Jairus.

"A thousand times," Sheba said, "and a thousand times I was glad for it. My sons made a difference with me," she said, "a mighty difference."

Jairus wished to put his hands about Lebanon's bright-sheathed head, but he would not, of course—he could not, in fact—and it was not Sheba's presence that withheld him. Suddenly in the morning that was all light and heavy sweetness, Lebanon felt a touch of rain on his hands as he told her good-by, and she knew it was his tears. He was a stony-charactered man, never prone to tears, and he would feel great shame if she should so acknowledge his tears. Sheba was steadfastly gathering up loose ends of wool balls where there were no loose ends.

He folded his hands hard.

"There are things you never told me. I would know every least thing concerning your history. Tell me every accident of your heart,

Lebanon. I would heal them, once and for all, if you would allow it."

(That is the preacher in him speaking, thought Sheba.)

Lebanon evaded him softly, trying to talk of something else.

"There were no more than any other woman's."

"Tell him," Sheba roared. "I am not listening, and if I must, I will forget it. He has done enough for you that you can please him by saying a few fool words."

"Well, then," Lebanon said, "they were little hurts."

Her eyes were feverishly bright over this love for herself, whether she claimed it or not.

"What hurt you most in all your life, till I knew you?" Jairus admonished Lebanon, doting on any wound she ever received so that he might heal it in long service, as one soothes an old scar to hush its throbbing on a rainy day.

"There was my mother's dying," Lebanon no more than whispered.

Sheba went on rocking, and beyond the house the slendered pines seemed to breathe a little raggedly at this brief biddance of an old hurt.

"And what more?" Jairus pressed.

Under his compulsion she retold little things that were immutably past: Cows lowing in the cold when Crease had butchered their calves and hung them in the woodshed to drain their blood into the earth. The mothers smelled that blood and knew it and lowed strongly, and beat their stalled hoofs in the earth through all the long night hours. There was the old dog that was lamed in an iron-jawed trap so that his hind quarters sagged bloodily and Crease had to say: "Look this way, Sergeant!" and put a bullet betwixt his eyes, to ease his hopeless agony. There was the smaller matter of a naked bird floundering on the earth long ago, and Lebanon studying its torture, for red ants had eaten out its eyes. Its wings were too young to fly from the ants, its mother had no hands in which to lift it to the nest again, though she shrieked and called to heaven and swooped above it, back and forth, and back again, begging somebody to help.

Jairus understood anything Lebanon might tell him.

It tempted her to take him in marriage, if he should ask her. Would there be a short, bright hallowday in her heart, married with him? Would such love wear sturdily through time? Wouldn't it be a restful state for her to be leaning on him, and Jeannie to make them happy together? . . . Would she have other children by Jairus? No reason why not! No reason she could think of, leastwise.

Jeannie was a loving thing, sitting there on the cart seat, a striped young skunk's tail lolloping down behind, from the little cap Erwin had brought her. She cried a little, and Lebanon brought out a folded slice of wheaten bread with butter in it, and the child hushed and began to eat. Mistress Jairus Mountjoy, the Preacher's Wife, Lebanon was thinking. . . . The names I've had. . . . The Preacher's Wife. . . . I am not good enough for Jairus, she thought. But I'd best never tell him so, if ever I should decide to marry with him. That would dump the fat into the fire, indeed. She would have to mince her steps if she were to be a preacher's wife in Mercierville. She would have to walk softly to please him. She would have to huddle her skirts handsomely about her ankles, teetering across earth like a robin askip on muddy ground. She must be a ticklishly twittering woman, then, and a soft-boned say-nothing.

"Oh, the dear me," she told herself suddenly. "I am a fool. If for no other reason than Jairus' good name, I could never marry him. Parishioners wish their preachers to be celibate. The folks in Mercierville think he is God, especially the poor folks, and there always were more of them than the other sort. My name has been tarred and feathered by their tongues' pitch. No, I'll not marry Jairus. . . ."

Jeannie was watching Lebanon curiously, and Lebanon smiled, to soften her face that had grown strangely hard. "It's all right, Pepe," she told Jeannie. (Pepe was a call name she had for the child.) "You and I, we'll get along. If hard times did not have to fall just when we needed money most, we would sell our land and go somewhere. But with times like this we'd best hold the land. I think God sent you to me, Pepe!" Lebanon said, believing her own words.

She went on thinking of Jairus and his proffered love.

He had befriended her in the midst of evil tongues to the contrary. For that kindness she would be forever grateful. Yet how was she to know whether he would love her forever? Sometimes he had told her of wide sea waters where waves forever petulantly dispute, for once he had been a sailor. One must remember that he was an old man now; he was forty-eight, and here she was past twenty-five and so past youth, and still the days went, as loose beads arolling. Here was forming a pattern of her days and years on earth; none but a sop would fail to take thought on his future.

Lebanon decided against marrying Jairus Mountjoy.

When Lebanon reached the place where the little cart track went into the Pike, there were road menders working, but she spent no words with them. A widow must be ever so careful. Fernald used to waste time in palavering with them, and giving and taking news. A road mender is better than a gazette: he may never be a fine gentleman of hard tongue and implacable honor, but he is good to listen to. Lebanon used to listen when she rode with Fernald. The road menders would curse most jovially, leaning on their diggers and spreaders, taking God's name most carelessly, as though He were a boon road companion they had met and parted from most lately. In course, they always pulled their caps in Lebanon's presence and made apology.

But now Lebanon passed on with a ladylike nod of the head and a thin good morning. By now Jeannie lay asleep with her head in Lebanon's lap. (Before too long, Lebanon wished to have a tester bed for Jeannie, with blue hangings.) She could see dust from a stagecoach coming from east, away off, and could hear its little thunder, too. Beside the Pike, a group of men were cooking meat on the point of a gun's ramrod over a little fire. A breath of charred fat rose on the lonesome air.

Lebanon noted a woodpecker's tunneling in a tree beside the road; time was when she could have taken aim on that drill, buried a bullet inside it, and never scarred an edge, but now she was much out of practice. It had been much time since she had paid mind to a pocket of flints, a rifle, and a little flask of oil for it, for now she had a child to fill her arms again. Guns and small children never mix well.

"Forget Timothy—small, sweet Timothy," she told herself— "Forget Fernald—for you cannot go on living if you are forever remembering something you cannot live without! That is unendurable. No, I will not marry Jairus Mountjoy," Lebanon told herself, as Miranda drew near to the Poakes'. "It would be best I didn't. I do not adore him as a graven image adores its maker, spending forever till it crumbles in holding a form its maker's hands gave it."

She did not adore him as a stone image, if singing flesh can be stone, throttled into silent-seeming blind love.

In stone-blind passion I should wish to adore a man, if ever I should wed again, she was thinking, quietly as granite tombed in earth, constantly as an undiscovered jewel slumbering.

Priscilla Poake was in her door, a tall woman with bright hair and a white, dragging bosom.

"Good day," Lebanon called, trying to be friends.

Priscilla turned her head away.

Now what? thought Lebanon. She did not see the twins or Simon about.

The stage was lumbering nearer.

(She may be careless in loving as a tobaca-chewing man is careless of his spittle, throwing it on flower or weed, and no difference when his mouth is overfull, but it is strange that I feel no animosity toward her, Lebanon was thinking.)

Along the walls of the Poakes' front room were shelves filled by stores. There was a bar there, too.

The Pike stretched east and west in deep rutted sand. The broad river beamed there, flowing so softly you never heard it, green things cluttering its banks. On the sandy banks fiddlers scuttled and spraddled about a little rowboat. The water lapped in minute, foam-flecked waves—lapping, lapping, lapping like the great ocean. Crows cried through the sky.

Simon came to the door of his mill; he was bull-necked, but he had bird-bright eyes. The door of the mill was webbed with white stuff. He made motions with his hands, but Lebanon thought he must be speaking sign language with Jeannie to make her laugh. She did not think of his gesturings as being a warning to her.

Lebanon soothed Jeannie's restlessness in her arms. She wondered if Priscilla Poake would have some milk to be warmed for Jeannie.

Simon's eyes glimmered wildly, there in the door of the mill. His hands caressed themselves as though he wrung them together. He said not a word to Lebanon. He was afraid of his wife. When Priscilla was in Mercierville, he would walk to Lebanon's house and hold Jeannie as though she were a doll with a French china head, and he would roll her bright hair in little ringlets about his forefinger that would always seem to have a dust of flour in the creases of it.

Chapter 19

THE STAGECOACH HAD ROLLED TO A STOP, Lebanon remembered hearing the horn blow, and the stageboy hopped over the wheels before they came to a stop in the rolling dust. There were several people in the store that hour. Some men demanded a hard drink at the bar, the women asked for cool water. There were five passengers in the coach going west, and the driver and the postboy made seven. Others than these in the store were Priscilla and Simon and the twins and Lebanon and the baby, Jeannie. There was loud talk, and obviously the big, red-faced lawyer had brought his own bottle with him.

Lebanon stood where she had no business, beside the counter, and Jeannie sat on the counter, and they were watching the strangers come in from the stage to take a drink of water, or worse. The lawyer was flirting boisterously with Priscilla Poake, and Jeannie took up a little knife which lay beside the sugar jar. Priscilla Poake used that knife for slicing West Indian lemmons for travelers' drinks. Lebanon took the knife away from Jeannie and held it, so Jeannie would not hurt herself. It was too dangerous a thing to play with, for it was sharp and pointed.

Suddenly Simon Poake took offense at the lawyer's broad remarks to Priscilla Poake, and maybe at Priscilla's laughter. Lebanon heard the words grow harder, and Erwin and Estis walked nearer their father's side, to help him if he needed help in defending himself against a man from Texas. The coach driver supped his long drink and looked to Simon Poake to keep order in his own establishment. The coachman studied the long room over the rim of his glass. Jeannie was crying for the knife, and Lebanon said: "Hush, little. You're always crying." Then the strange lawyer, Washington League, the man from Texas, said to Simon Poake:

"Oh, so she's your woman, then? God's truth, I'd never have guessed it."

Erwin and Estis moved in nearer to the lawyer from Texas. Priscilla was their mother. Their faces burned.

"She is my wife," Simon said, white meal on his hands, and his meek, kind face whitening, too. The lawyer began to laugh, and he went on laughing. Priscilla set her hands on the back of a stick chair Estis had carved in odd, rainy hours, clenched her fists, and said: "The stage horn is blowing. You'd best be gone."

In truth, the stage horn was blowing. The driver and postboy had got out of there. But nobody else stirred, not even the strange woman passenger with the little boy beside her.

"Get out of here," Simon told that lawyer.

"Hush, Simon," Priscilla said. "It is poor business to offend a customer."

And the lawyer went on laughing.

Then Estis knocked him down. There was more back of this fight than mere temper. There was anger and shame multiplied, and grown men's pride, the pride of good men that is far more dangerous than a rattlesnake's tantrum.

The lawyer got slowly to his feet, tottering a little, reaching for his belt around his middle. Estis backed around, and Lebanon watched, open-mouthed, and even Jeannie began to watch the men's hot tangle of tempers.

"This is my roof," Simon said. "Leave him to me, Estis."

Simon was pitiful to see, standing there, a hard worker and a good man, and Priscilla having shamed him all these years when he did no more than guess it, and now she was telling him to hush, and his own sons telling him to allow them to do the fighting.

"I'll not hush," Simon shouted. "It's high time you did some hushing, I'd say."

There was a dark sobbing growing there in the depths of Simon's voice; you knew he had always done the best he could, tending his mill, making bread for his family, standing upright before his sons, and trying never to complain against something no man could change—that is, without tragedy in one direction or another. Yet such a man will go along, and go along, and suddenly he will find himself sick of returning good for evil, of being made to seem a fool when he is no fool indeed.

Estis knocked the lawyer down again.

The lawyer got up again.

Now Simon knocked the lawyer down in his tracks for laughing at Priscilla—not because she was his wife heavied by a thousand virtues, but because she was his wife and he had tried to live honorably.

The lawyer staggered heavily to his feet again, backed around, and knocked Estis backward.

Because Estis was strong and was not to any degree drunken, he did not fall but staggered.

He lunged against that counter where Lebanon was standing. She wore a white face, and the knife stood unremembered in her hand, braced against the front of the high counter. The knife pierced Estis' back, and when they took away his shirt and his undershirt, the blood was frothing. The knife was there in Lebanon's hand still, and she standing like a wooden woman.

Priscilla began to scream, and Lebanon tried hard to remain calm and to stop her teeth from chattering and her hands from growing cold and more cold.

They carried Estis into another room and turned him on his face.

His eyes were beginning to glaze.

Lebanon laid that horrible knife on the counter and brushed her hands together. She took Jeannie in her arms and went toward the room where they had taken Estis.

Washington League was suddenly sobered. He had not expected such help from a strange woman with a knife in her hand.

Everything now was talk, and more talk.

"Oh, Estis . . . Estis!" Lebanon moaned at his door.

It did not occur to Lebanon that the people in the shop could not see that this was an accident. Not one had looked at Lebanon or the knife she was holding until Estis had staggered back toward her. Then it was hard to guess whether Lebanon had stabbed Estis or Estis had stabbed himself—if you relied only on your two eyes.

There was the bloody knife, and they had seen her lay down the knife, brush her hands, and take Jeannie up. She moaned, "Estis, Estis!" as though it had grieved her to wound him fatally.

Simon, being a constable himself, arrested her and wrote the names of all the witnesses carefully in a ledger.

Lebanon knew nothing to say, so she said nothing.

"Was that Washington League anything to you?" asked Simon carefully.

"What?" asked Lebanon dully, wondering that they should look so in her face.

"Washington League," said Simon, a cold wind blowing through his words.

"She was always after the twins," said Priscilla, weeping beside Estis' bed.

"Cannot I see Estis . . . and tell him . . . and tell him . . . ?"

"Tell him what?" asked Simon, distaste more strong in his voice.

"He is gone," Priscilla began to shriek, and you could hear her grief rising from those words on. "She was always a crazy woman," Priscilla shrieked. "Everywhere she went, she took trouble. The twins stopped going to her house for a while. She was a devil, that woman—I tell you she has a devil in her. I always hated her, for I knew she would bring trouble here to this house, too, as she brought it to her own. I knew she would bring us all to ruin. I myself set a notice on her door telling her to get out. Something told me this was coming . . . something told me . . . something told me . . ."

Priscilla paid no attention when Simon begged her to hush; all this would come to a fair trial, he said.

"He is gone, don't you see? He is gone."

Lebanon was thinking of the paper, the notice on her door. So that was not a tax, and Jairus had lied to her. That was Priscilla's behest to leave this place.

"I did not intend to kill Estis," Lebanon said coldly.

"Then what evil did you come to do?" moaned Priscilla.

"Hush, Priscilla," Simon said.

"You know I never wished her to darken the door of this house again," Priscilla raved, and one could not blame her. This was her son dead. "You know I hated her face, and you know I had good reason to hate her."

Lebanon laid her free hand on her mouth. Jeannie leaned on her shoulder and asked for water.

"You can't have any water now," Lebanon said to Jeannie.

"I meant no least harm," Lebanon said to Priscilla; cold horror was slowly assailing her.

"Fools never intend harm," Priscilla said. "Could you help yourself if you lusted after my sons? They would pay you no mind this last while. Is that what riled you?"

"Lust is a strong word," said Lebanon.

"Hush, now," Simon said.

"They stayed away from my house because they did not wish my good name bandied about, for they told me so."

"Why should your good name ever have been bandied about?" screamed Priscilla.

"Hush, now!" shouted Erwin and turned his face off to the wall. "Go home, Lebanon," he said.

Though Lebanon could see the agony in his face for her sake, still that cold wind blew. And Jairus had lied to her. If she had known Priscilla had set a sign on her door asking her to leave this country, oh, never would she have come under this roof! Had not Simon always been kind, and had she not always loved Erwin and Estis, almost as she had loved Timothy and Fernald?

But there was Estis' blood shed, and there was the knife just laid down warm from Lebanon's hand. The stagecoach had happened to come in, not an hour before or an hour after, but that hour. And although it was nothing but chance, that is how it happened.

Everybody said that Lebanon had ridden to the Poakes' to murder Estis.

The bitterest circumstance, which worked most strongly against Lebanon, was Erwin, the living twin. Till he died Erwin seemed no more than half of a body, doomed to go on living and his other half dead.

On the tongues of tall men and lesser ones, slattern women and their betters, children and slave people, tricksters and fine youths, the story spread. When word was brought to Lebanon in gaol of what things the tongues said of her—that she had loved Estis and killed him in spite, that she went to his house to kill him when his mother had warned her away from there—she told herself:

"It is no matter what they think or what they say. Their minds and tongues do not alter matters."

But the minds and tongues did alter matters. There was wild talk indeed, and folks revived the old talk of how Lebanon had brought the Pest into Mercierville. Poor Fernald had near to drunk himself to death because of her, and then he had died, as did her small son, they said.

Yet she herself had the pestilence and did not die from it, though laid out and prayed over, they said.

And still the stories grew.

Two weeks before, Jairus had been called to Orleans, to a sister that lay dying, with no hope. Otherwise he would have done something. Sheba could not make up her mind to send him word. It would trouble him, and he with a sick sister. Jairus had not seemed to have his proper wits about him since first he had set eyes on this Lebanon d'Aussy.

First time Sheba saw Lebanon in gaol, she asked a question:

"Did you kill that boy, Lebanon? You can tell *me*."

Lebanon's heart was suddenly smitten by those words.

Never did she entirely over that hurt. (Would not Sheba *know* that she did not kill Estis Poake?) But Sheba's face was far off, and a cool wind blew between. And only Jeannie believed in Lebanon, for when you love another entire, you believe in them and all they do.

In the gaol they brought Jeannie a bowl of curds at night, and an egg each morning, and bread and butter; to Lebanon they brought mush and milk, and a hard roll and some jelly. On Sabbaths there was a piece of meat.

The gaolkeeper was named Amos Black. He was somewhat of a hunchback, for his neck was half broken in a wagon fall when he was nine years old. He was clever at cards and politics. He had come to this country thirty years ago and knew Mercierville when it was one roof, and Indians swarming like hornets, and a territory so wild that settlers slept out in the wilds rather than under a roof. If they got word of an Indian rising, and were lucky enough, they made fast tracks east, or got to a fort. As Mercierville grew, Amos had more men to hang by law. In the earlier days town folks did the nasty work. They hung horse thieves, murderers, or robbers of any degree, and rode roughnecks and whores out of town on a rail.

But now Amos did everything legally. Men teased him roughly about the new gaolbird he had in his cage, but he said he was too old to be troubled by such torments as stayed forever uppermost in their minds now. He considered that a clever hand-you-back.

If Lebanon's father and grandfather had lived in a porticoed house in Mercierville, all this would never have happened so. But Crease Fairgale was long dead—one day dead is long dead, and a dead man cannot well fight you.

Lebanon would pen no word to Joel, for she would not tell her shame; and she could not read or write; many a good woman cannot.

Not the least hurt, but one of the worst to bear, was Amos Black's thinking that Lebanon was an easy lover. Folks had said she was in love with the Poake boys. Folks said she had killed Estis because he would have naught to do with her, and they even said the preacher had left town when he found what she was. Amos Black made advances to Lebanon.

"They tamper with your good name," he told her; "I believe you only put me off because you take no fancy to me. You'd best take a fancy to me. The bars might be sawed out some night for you, who could say? I'd say a good word to the magistrate for you now, wouldn't I? I could say you were a good prisoner or a wild one."

Lebanon bowed her head, and it was as though her brain went about heavily, fastened hard to a wooden hobble. I must remain calm, she told herself over and over. I must act as though I am entirely mistress of myself.

"I do not care what they say of me so long as it is not true," she told Amos Black. "I was never of light virtue."

"Then why do ye seem such a hallion if ye are not?" he would ask her, laughing, making his own brand of love to her.

"I do not know," she said, hushing her sighing. "I can only do my best, and they must go their ways and I must go mine, and we'll all reach home someday."

"You did kill that man, now," Amos would say. "You know that," he would say. "He is dead. You know that," Amos would say.

Madly she wished to shriek and shout:

"Go away from that door! Leave me be! Cannot you see you will drive me mad?"

But she told herself over and over: I must by all means hold my tongue and be most careful in all I say.

Alone she would be thinking: Is it easier to bear an evil truth told about you or a lie? If I had killed him, indeed, I could endure this. A shameful lie is a task to understand, and to endure.

Every day the hangman, Amos Black, would stand beyond the door and beg to come in, and when Amos' wife brought supper, she showed no pity.

In the dark, Amos came beyond the door and wheedled her into saying that she killed Estis Poake and that she was a hallion, and always was.

Sheba would come to see her, out of kindness and not love. You could feel the doubt there unnamed, the walls that tongues had built. There was no entering those walls, and no true speech betwixt them. Sheba did her duty still and brought Lebanon a loaf of new bread whenever she baked, but certain she was she would not write Jairus of this thing till it was proved in court whether Lebanon was guilty or innocent.

If Jairus had been here things would have been vastly different.

Such women as Lebanon would hurt a man, Sheba considered; they could never comfort him. Sheba had her own thoughts on this matter.

Evidence was there for anybody to see that Priscilla Poake had admitted that she had nailed to Lebanon's door a warning, yet Lebanon had for no known reason ridden to the Poakes' place. Evidence would show the warm, bloody knife which Lebanon had laid down. Evidence gave Lebanon a bad name in Mercierville. This country was full of people who had come West for no good reason.

All the defense Lebanon could muster was to say she could not read or write and never knew what the warning on the door said. A pretty-sounding tale that!

"If ever you manage to get free from this mess, you go elsewhere," Sheba would tell Lebanon sourly. "There is doubtless somewhere a place for you, but it is not here."

"Then where might it be?" asked Lebanon bitterly. "If you ever hear tell of it, tell its name to me, pray do."

"You have to live above suspicion of such talk as goes on about your name," Sheba would say jealously, glad of this chance to tell off Lebanon's faults to her. One could not very well blame Sheba for being jealous of Lebanon.

"You must go home East, or go somewhere," Sheba would say, "if ever you manage to come clear, and make you a new place to live in."

Once Lebanon thought she would ask Sheba to write Jairus and call him back, but pride forbade her. She could guess Sheba's thoughts on that matter, and since she had not taken Jairus' love when he had proffered it, she had no right to ask for it now. Worse, this sorry thought assailed her: What if Jairus should disdain me? He would not wish himself to be involved in a murder trial, and he a preacher.

"After all," Sheba would say, never meaning to be so cruel, "there be women who never get into such messes as you be in."

If ever I can manage to come free, I will go West, Lebanon promised herself. In new towns to the west women have freer lives; in the West there are money bills on trees and fine provender. If ever I get out of this mess, I will go and never see this place again. I will rent a shack and serve meals; they can go elsewhere to barter their hours with a woman as you would barter a sack of salt. For I am sick of men. I would cook for them, though, and mend their shirts and pantaloons and patch their boots and make some manner of living for Jeannie and me, if ever I get out of this place.

"Whatever you did back East, you can tell it to me," Sheba would say. "I will keep your secret."

"I did not do anything East more than any other common form of women do," Lebanon said. "I did not kill Estis Poake, and I do not know any other criminal thing I ever did, so help me God, Sheba."

"Hush your swearing," Sheba admonished curtly.

"Post Fernald's land for sale, Sheba, if you will. I must hire me a lawyer. I must get out of here." Her voice began to rise in a low scream.

Out in the gaol yard she could hear the well pulley creaking, and the bucket spilling its spume of cold water. In daytime the grille was barred so that no one could communicate with her, yet feet came and went unseen in daytime. But the nights were still. . . .

Only Jeannie was here with her to endure the nights, to eat Juno's butter on new bread which Sheba brought conscientiously. (Sheba was keeping Miranda and Juno till the trial went one way or another.)

If one more time I could see Miranda stomp her little hoofs, lift her head and shake her mane! Lebanon would think. Never did I think those egrets much more than any common sight, when I saw them long ago, nor did I ever properly appreciate that flowering hill till now, nor Sebastian, nor Fernald, nor even the lazy breath of the world given me, short breath by short breath. But now when the grilles bar off the world and leave me here, I love everything my hand or mind ever touched.

In the fowlhouses of the town of Mercierville, in low trees near to earth, she could hear the roosters crow for midnight, and later in the night, before the beginning of dawn, she could hear them crowing again, replying to one another in faithful hallooing through the black nights. Lebanon would walk the earthen floor in little steps and wish for morning, though when morning came there was naught to do but wish for night again.

"You must tell me the whole truth of it," Sheba would say for a hundredth time. "If you trafficked with Estis, then say so, and we'll get the best lawyer we can hire."

"What does Erwin say of it all?" Lebanon would ask, for Erwin was as near to Estis as one soul can be to another in this world.

"Erwin says that you and God know the truth of it all," Sheba said, accusation in her tone.

"There is nothing for me to tell, Sheba, I have told you over and over. No matter how things may look, there is nothing to tell."

She spoke woodenly. It would be better to grovel now and ask pity, she thought, but I cannot. Only fools would hold themselves upright and unafraid and make of themselves fair marks for ruin.

Backward and forward, backward and forward she would rock Jeannie on her breast. She had come to slow repetition of a thought. Now she would think one sentence over and over upon itself to keep her tongue still; she would rock and rock to keep her brain from sudden action.

"I guess you know you've ruined Jeannie," Sheba said.

"Yes," Lebanon said sagely. "Yes," and she bent her face over Jeannie's bright hair.

Lebanon told the full truth to the sheriff a dozen times.

The sheriff told his wife, in private, of course, that this Lebanon d'Aussy seemed not quite the harlot from eastward they said she was; she had bright eyes, he said, and as pretty a face as you'd find, if it were not for that scar; she had gold-colored hair that tousled, though she combed it faithfully; she had a haughty stance, he said. "When you hear her tell her side of what happened, you believe her," he said. "Then when the others tell their tales on her, you believe the tales. It is for the judge to say, not me."

One night, past midnight it was, she felt her mouth forming a scream, and the noise grew, and her voice grew, and her voice was like a mad woman's, if she should be cornered and tied and tortured past enduring!

Lebanon heard that mad woman's screaming and knew it was her own voice, yet her own ears seemed stone, and her own flesh seemed to have no part in the matter.

Jeannie waked and was frightened and began to scream, too, and searched the dark beyond her mother's arms to find the meaning of this tumult. Hearing her mother screaming thus in the dark caused Jeannie's limbs to jerk, for the screeching was that of a stranger person, yet within the screaming she could know her mother was there and that agony had taken hold onto her.

Yet all this while Lebanon was sitting still and steadily rocking Jeannie back and forth, back and forth, and the wild screaming went on, and Lebanon could not stop it.

At length Amos Black came hurrying with a candle in his hand and his wife in a shift behind him.

After that midnight when Lebanon had all but frightened Amos Black's wits out of him by her screaming, he prized away the boards from the barred grille so she could see the light. Amos thought she would go entirely mad if they did not let her have more light. This room of the gaol was foul-floored and had dirty plastered walls; it was in against the rear of the gaoler's house. High in the fretted ironwork grille light showed now, and now and then a nimble passer-by climbed above his own height and looked in to see Lebanon sitting moveless on the stool Sheba had brought her, and Jeannie groping across the earthen floor.

The gaoler's wife was a white-haired woman with water-withered hands. Meg Black felt pity for this poor prisoner woman; many a time she had felt she could knife Amos for telling her such pretty tales so long ago, whereas life with him afterward had been naught but slavery worse than the blacks know, and never a kind word thrown in. When no one could hear, Meg would call Lebanon "Miss" and would beg her to eat her savorless mush. She brought Lebanon a chicken leg from her own Sabbath dinner, even if she herself had to do without.

"At least I have my freedom," she would tell Lebanon.

"Do you, now?" Lebanon would ask, and that would cause Meg to wonder over the words. Did she now have any freedom at all? she would ask herself. Did anyone?

Meg, too, would try to get the truth from Lebanon:

"He had outraged you now, had he not, Miss?"

"No," Lebanon would say, bowing her head under the old yoke.

"This child Jeannie was not Estis Poake's then, Miss?" poor well-meaning Meg would ask.

"No," Lebanon would reply, her voice so low that one might think she was saying a hard-spoken lie.

It all befuddled Meg till she could scarce get her house chores done on time. After a time, when Lebanon would not confide in her, no matter what, Meg turned her back on the haughty street woman that had not sense enough to tell the truth in the face of so grave a charge as cold murder. How women would lie! she thought.

Amos showed kindness, too, though in a differing manner. Out of broken sleep of a dark night Lebanon heard the lock grating rustily and saw Amos in the door and no candle in his hand. She heard his blandishments and did not weep. The key would be at his belt, and perhaps he might set her free, indeed! Yet to what should she go free?

She had been three months in gaol, and she had thought there was no lower place to which her heart could sink. Sheba had not been to see her in ten days and more.

"Will you not get word to Sheba Johann that I wish to have a word with her?" Lebanon asked Amos Black.

"Ah, yes, I was to tell you," he said. "She will be here this morning." (It was a Friday.) "She has asked leave to care for the child till you go free. She thinks it best for the child."

This was no fitting place for Jeannie to be, God knew. Her bowels had loosened, and her eyes were rimmed in black, and now she forever whimpered. It was no fitting place for a child to be, but still the child was a selfish comfort to Lebanon.

Sheba came and took Jeannie from Lebanon's arms. Lebanon's lips touched Jeannie's cheeks coldly. Jeannie was fevered and languid and whimpered a little; she seemed content enough in Sheba's new arms.

Sheba's eyes filled with tears: "I do so hate to take her from you, Lebanon, and you know it. But Amos Black says she will die if she stays here."

Lebanon's arms went toward the drooping, fevered child and came back again to her empty breast and folded there.

"I could not give her up to you if I did not love her so much," she said. "Give her warm milk, fresh from Juno, night and morning, and let her play in the sun. Let her walk in the dew of mornings, Sheba. My mother used to say that was good for weak megrims. Feed her eggs and sarsaparilla tea and white bread and loaf sugar. . . . Oh, Sheba . . . take her away quick. . . ."

Lebanon lay down on the soiled pallet, as though her breath had all been drawn away.

Sheba and Jeannie went away.

Even Meg's eyes were wet, and Amos hawked and spat as he locked the door again on Lebanon. They had not taken the child away from her before this for the sake of common pity; no matter whether Lebanon was a murderess, she was still a woman, they said. Now she knew that the last desire is not for food or any garb, nor for the comfort of warmth or the near touch of any soul. Past these puny needs, at the last depth man knows a dearer wish. At the last he needs, what each shall surely receive, the sturdy comfort of death.

Amos Black would not allow her to have so much as a pewter spoon to eat with, for fear she would cut free an artery on the spoon's sharpened edge. She had only the short growth of her fingernails, and now she tore her flesh with them. There was no more than the stone wall, and she pummeled her head against the darkened stone, cursing the pain of it. For hours she would pray for a sudden gushing of blood inside her head—things happen so in many a head—and sudden death. But steadily the blood beat on through her veins.

There were welts on her forehead, and heavy pain, but there was no sign of sudden death. Minute by long minute she must explore this labyrinth, must creep down, ledge by dark ledge, to the black hood set on her head and the rough rope rocking her to sleep.

She could not have told what day of what month it was, or how long a time lay betwixt her and her trial, or whether the roosters crowed still for day, or whether the chapel bells still rang on Sabbath morning.

Now her heart was careless of any small pain earth could bring to her, or any terror eternity could muster. Long since, she was past a fear of death, and that is a major freedom. Now she could scarcely remember how all this sad business had come about; all she could say, over and over, to Amos and Meg was:

"I did not kill Estis Poake. I did not kill Estis Poake. . . ."

"But the knife was in your hand!"

"The knife was in my hand, but I did not kill Estis Poake. It was like this. . . ."

She would begin to speak of it all again, but soon it would blur, as being of no moment, as old dreams, whose circumstances one dimly remembers, sound silly retold by the tongue.

"I loved Estis Poake," she would say.

"But you said you never loved him!"

She would look in their faces despairingly.

"I loved Estis Poake like my brother, like my mother. . . ."

She would despair, trying to tell of love, as many another tongue has done. She had seen Sebastian Ratcliff's hand shot away, she had seen Estis crumpling before her.

"Oh, I do not know . . ." she would say, and she would shake and shake, like a mad woman, indeed.

This was August, and somewhere in these days was her birthday, when she was twenty-six. She did not know the day when it dawned or when it dusked. If anyone had asked her age, she would have laughed full in his face, as an old woman laughs.

"I am the oldest woman in the world," she would have said.

These gloomy days and nights went and Sheba came less and less, nor could one lay blame at Sheba's door. She had thought this thing out on more nights than one. Lebanon must be guilty, Sheba thought; she was near to being beautiful, certainly comely she was; she was widowed and careless, it may be; Sheba knew naught of the mixup, all she could do was think her thoughts. She had done her duty by Lebanon, she considered. Jairus could not have done more, and she would not have Jairus' life ruined by this Jezebel from the East.

Lebanon would seek the sky's quiet face in the night. Some nights through the bars she could see the far stars, and sometimes the moon walked up there; Lebanon's tortured white face bent back toward yet a higher heaven, beseeching some taller being than herself to bring her some happiness she sought.

Lebanon's prayers fell backward on her lips. She would not shed tears for the jeering to see. She would not scream and ask mercy, so that those who condemned her might smile grimly now and say that her crime was so defeated in her deep suffering. For she had committed no crime. She could not pray, for she considered that the heavens knew her most desperate need, if they at all heed the woes of mortals.

In the night of a day she heard her name called softly through the dark grille. She looked toward the black grille: the dark was of a softer substance in the grille, the dark here below in the gaol a stony, impenetrable dark. When you have been long alone, you will find yourself near to hearing things and will learn to pay them stingy mind. Lebanon thought she was hearing things now.

"Lebanon," the voice spoke again, pitying and beseeching: "Lebanon . . ."

She looked the more carefully and could see nothing but a lighter darkness against a black night. Carefully she held her ears intent. She had learned that there be two of us: the body, and That Other One. Tongued bodies speak to the first of us, and a myriad beings speak to the others of us. Often dead voices had haunted her, waking her from sleep, cudgeling her to bitter remembering. She could not say now whether this was dead Fernald's voice, or Lollie's, or Meg's, or another's.

"Lebanon . . ."

Then she knew that voice surely: there was but one like to it. Beyond the black grille, standing in the black night, was Jairus Mountjoy. He had heard her, though she had not called to him.

"Jairus!" She feared she would dismiss his ghost with but the sound of her voice.

"Lebanon!" he said, his voice near to breaking. "I did not know. I came back, and this is what I find. We may meet and talk tomorrow. You have your rights. . . ."

She strove to touch her least finger to his fingertip.

"Your hand . . . if I could reach your hand . . ." Her voice whimpered down into soundless weeping.

"Though they had hanged you, you would not have sent me

word!" He so rebuked her, decrying his absence from her in her long need. "I know now that you never loved me, nor ever will, or you would have called on me."

Though she could not see his face, she could hear his voice; she cried his name, to hold his presence close there in the black night. "Jairus," she said, "I will forever love you now. When the hood goes over my face and the rope about my throat, oh, I will love you forever now and no stopping me——"

"Hush!" he said. "I know you did not kill Estis Poake. I know you did not, and no asking. I brought Roanoke Carter with me for a character witness, and you shall go free, Lebanon."

His voice had a black sound, like a ghost going madly on a wild wind. He was desperate for her sake, for it was very nearly certain that she would hang. Public opinion is a hard thing to fight; nothing will side with you but time, and there was so little time.

"Roanoke?" Lebanon could scarce believe the name. "Are there such friends?"

"There are," Jairus returned. "She will testify to your character. She is at Sheba's, and she will free you if I cannot."

His face was unseen in the black night, his hands far off, too far for her reaching; it benumbed her. "Leave me be," she said. "I am reconciled. Things are all against me. Roanoke will only besmirch herself. It is a hard thing to fight misunderstanding and hate."

"It is but a little while till morning," he said as though she had not spoken. "I roused Amos Black, and he said I could not see you. But the Preacher is back, Lebanon, and I have tongue-lashed Sheba within one inch of her life for not having sent me some word of all this. She was jealous—cannot you see that and forgive her? I have loved you all my life long, Lebanon."

His voice blundered into tears.

She could not say anything more. He could scarce bear to leave her beneath that iron grating, booked as a murderess, all evidence against her except Roanoke Carter's gentility and faith, and Jairus' devotion.

"It will not be long till morning," he said, committing her to the black night since he could do nothing else.

She could not say good night. Never before had this dark room seemed so hard a burden and so deep a shame to Lebanon as on this night when Jairus said: "It will not be long till morning."

She began to think of Jeannie. Jairus would care for Jeannie now —she was too little to know, too loving to care. Now Lebanon's last prayer was answered, indeed, for she had said: "God, if You will allow Jeannie to go free from this shame, I will ask nothing more, I will die bravely—try me and see!"

In Jairus' arms, or with Roanoke Carter, Jeannie would find all comfort, now and afterward. And Lebanon could die happy. She had made a bargain with God, as Gideon did once, and God had fulfilled His half of the bargain.

Chapter 20

THROUGH THE IRON GRILLE morning broke softly.

Lebanon had scarcely slept, for who could sleep now? She watched the barred square take on itself the many subtle changes of light; silent were those changes as the uncoiling of young fern fronds clenched tight against the earth, lifting their green croziers into hand-tall sheaves by noon. As a child she had watched the young ferns grow through all of a lazy morning, while ants came and went below.

Now she watched the light come, and remembered the ferns uncoiling, and how she and Sebastian spoke of the fern seeds which might bring immunity against earth, if there were any such seeds. Yet why should she now be thinking of Sebastian, since Jairus was come with Roanoke to save her life from the gallows if he could? She need never put to herself questions concerning Jairus' love: Shall I lose it? Have I indeed gained it now, to last? There would be no desperate troubling her heart over how she must conduct herself so as to hold his love. Jairus loved her—and the earth is round, and the sky is tall, and no need to ask why or how or if forever.

She watched the morning light come and remembered Sebastian.

First, across the bars came soft veilings of black gossamer dissolving, one by one, leaving less of dark betwixt the earth and sky. Then there came other veilings of violet coloring, the color of old plums dead in sweet rot. Then came veils of carmoisin, each thinner than the last. There had never been so gold a morning as this one, and she lying deep in shadow at the bottom of the gaol, and the quilts drawn high to her chin, for the morning was cool.

The chimneys would begin to smoke out yonder, blackly, from fat pine wood; already, many a woman would have finished her scouring of the plates; lazy women would be up late to warm over last night's mush quickly, and say they had a headache and "Hush, children, you are driving me crazy with your rowdy ways!"

Lebanon, lying so alone, could see and hear it all, in a thousand houses, more clearly than those very people about those hearths, pouring molasses over the mush, drinking cambric tea to stir sluggish blood and brain, eating fried meat from last summer's shoat, drinking milk if the cow was not dry. "We thank Thee, our heavenly Father, for the kind mercies of this day; help us to lean on Thee in all our goings out and our comings in. . . ."

Jairus could say the prettiest graces over food, each differing from another; he could say the sweetest night benedictions. . . . "Keep Lebanon's life in Thy care," he used to say, and she thought how fine a thing it would be if all of us could know our names were called out to God's attention each day and each night of our lives.

Always he could make the choicest prayers, and always one got the notion that God might be listening to Jairus' pleading, because he was so modest and so good. Jairus had trials and tribulations, though he was so unselfish. If he preached against youths frequenting gaming joints, it was all he could do to avoid street fights by stepping aside and allowing the roughsters to consider him a coward. More than once he had his cheek slapped and never said a word; more than once he had been knocked down. "He will not fight, he is a lily-liver," a rough fellow would call after him as he walked down the street with his head high and mud in his hair where he had fallen under a blow. Somehow the words soon hushed after him. He was taller than the talk about him.

One fight he had, and that was on this very morning, seeming to dawn so slowly for Lebanon. She never knew of that fight till long after.

A man took her name in vain, and Jairus knocked the man flat, till blood ran out of his jaw. Jairus lifted the man then and said: "Forgive me, brother! It was a devil in me. The woman is dear to me, and I consider her innocent and intend to prove it before the world."

He wiped the trickle of blood from the man's mouth, and the man shook Jairus' extended hand, for he was surprised.

Jairus told Roanoke of it at early breakfast, and if she had been no lady she would have jumped up and down and screeched and hallooed:

"Jairus!" she said, in a little gasp, and you would have thought she had suddenly discovered him in a prince's coach, so bright was the surprise on her face.

"I have sometimes wished myself a man so that I might fight," she said, her hands clutching one another ardently.

"You are fighting for Lebanon in coming here, and I shall never forget it," he said; his hand was tight on the table rim.

"But Lebanon is my friend," Roanoke said, and the light in her drawn and weary face was beautiful as a new dress on a poor woman.

"The world cannot overcome a good soul, save in a most superficial fashion," Jairus said, bolstering his own faith in the outcome of the trial. "Two good souls working together would be past the world's trying—and with Lebanon we be three."

A little hope came into his eyes, but he sighed.

There were nasty accusations against her, for he had talked with all he could roust out of bed in the night.

How can you summon witnesses from the far places of the country when all you have is their names in Simon Poake's book? There were no witnesses now but the Poakes—Simon and Priscilla and Erwin. How can you make a case from nothing, and hard feeling rising every day?

"She is not guilty," Roanoke said in sad affirmation. "That I do know. But that does not mean she will come free under trial."

Roanoke sighed, too, but quickly she lifted her head.

"We will make a case for her, Jairus, somehow we will."

Jairus was still peevish with Sheba: "It was a womanish little thing you did, Sheba, and I am ashamed of you. You are too big not to do the big thing. You know better; some folks don't."

"I did not wish your name ruined forever," she resisted weakly, though she was in for crying if he said much more. It was the way he said it, low and sweet and regretful, as though she had cruelly disappointed him.

"Tell no lies, Sheba, and matters will the quicker be mended. You had a secret dislike for Lebanon somewhere, and best admit it and ask forgiveness of God."

"It was only that I put you before her." Now Sheba began to weep in good earnest. "I have broken my old heart in trying to please you."

"God only knows what ever I should have done without your love and help, too," he said, and he took her worn hand and kissed it.

In this past night Lebanon had slept but a fitful snatch, and now her sense of time was altered entire. It was as though all clock hands had suddenly quickened during those hours of last night since she heard Jairus' voice in the grille. A great space of life had seemed to go in the night, and now things were new and changed.

Then Jairus called her name beyond the cell door. Though the door was locked fast, and no gaoler to watch, Jairus had that nicety about him that caused him to call her name, to know whether he and the gaoler might come up to her door. He made of her a lady in a tower room and he knocking at the door.

Amos Black fumbled the lock open. His eyes gloated curiously upon Lebanon and Jairus, going from one to the other and back again. Jairus saw the uneaten ashcake and mush, and he saw Lebanon's face, and her hands, and the filthy floor and pallet—and he would have sucked in his breath if he were not now an old man and had seen so many sorry sights on this earth.

"You must wash and arrange your person neatly," he said, scolding tenderly.

She looked up to his face, smothered in prison dusk. He smiled dourly down upon her, giving reply to all her unspoken queries.

He opened a saddle roll, and there was a polished white-bone comb with red and blue glass in its handle, and there was a mirror's white face glimmering, and there was a bottle of rose water.

She could say no words. She dropped her face away from the look in his eyes, and hot tears began to run and wet her face in the dusk.

He washed her face, salving the cloth on a round of sweet-smelling soap. Amos stood by and wondered, forgetting to chew his tobaca cud.

"My face is filthy, I know," she said, feeling deep shame that he should see her so.

He washed her bony hands, holding her fingers separately as though he would nurture them from his own body's strength. He unbound the rags from her feet and demanded more hot water from Amos, and he set her feet in hot water to soak the blackened sores. Then he laid out new wearing linnen and a new dark frock with a shawl of lawn cloth.

"We will leave now, and you make yourself presentable," Jairus said. At the door he turned back a moment, as though he could never bear to leave her again.

"They should have known you were never a harlot," he said, trying to smile. "The worst hallion would care more for this world's pleasantries."

Now that the Preacher was back and taking an interest in Lebanon, Meg and Amos tried to put a better face on things, for they were afraid he would condemn their handling of the prison.

Jairus walked about the streets and stood his good name and long years in Mercierville against hard talk of Lebanon. He was plain-spoken, and never had anyone known him to speak a lie, or half of one. "She is of good blood," he told one man. "I am amazed that a woman should have had to suffer such indignities at the hands of any officers of the law," he told a lawyer. "She has lived honorably always," he told the new tavernkeep. "Any man with a whit of pity or justice or mercy in his bones would have helped her," he told any that would listen. "I will take her so far from this place if she comes free," he told a storekeep. "She is too good for this town—no, I will not take her away. I will marry her and we will live here and they can watch her character stand up through the years." His face burned. "Careless little tongues will never make me turn my tail and drag it off and go whimpering under a kick. Crimes have been done, but she has not done one, no matter how it may seem," he told Dr. Spaniell, "and it is your duty as a man and a gentleman to see that she is defended."

When Lebanon was washed and gowned in new garments, Jairus brought her a pot of hot milk, and two eggs lightly boiled, and dried bread with warmed butter spread on it.

"In a week you will be eating red meat and hot wine and ripe fruit," he said.

She folded her hands against the silken bristle of the new waist. She took the plate of food and held it on her lap.

"It may come back up," she said, and put her hand against her mouth.

"This will not come back up," he said.

Her eyes were ringed and sunken, her cheeks hollow, and her lips were the color of her face.

"Say a blessing over it," she said. "Say, 'Father, we thank Thee for our days on earth . . .' "

Before she ate she looked hard into his face. "Even with a jury trial facing me I am happy as I never was before," she said.

"You need only a little kindness to make you blossom," he said. "Now eat and hush talking. We will waste the morning in words."

"I have this to say, and then I will hush," she went on, more and more slowly speaking, with little gaspings in between. "The verdict does not matter to me now. You do not know Priscilla Poake as I know her, and you do not know how far she will go. But that does not matter, either, for I have gained my freedom here." She touched her breast, and her breath came fast.

"Hush, I told you, and eat," he said, "before the bread is cold. All my life I sought something to fasten my heart on—an earthly thing, that is, till I can get to heaven—for a man must live here whether he likes it any too well or not. I have been West and I saw women in spurred boots and their faces burnt black by the Great Desert, and I saw women there with their mouths painted red as partridge berries. I have been North and saw women white as milk, but they seemed tasteless to me as bread without salt. You are the one for me, Lebanon." He leaned his hands hard-folded on his knee.

Here was the trial day dawning, one day set on a long circlet of days, as a black cross weighs a papist's prayer necklace. How many times she had counseled her heart that this day was on the way to her surely, and best be stony when it came.

There are three things that can come on me, she told herself. I shall go free, or I shall be gaoled the rest of my life, or I shall die soon. Since I cannot know which one of the three will come, best not worry over any of them, till I know.

In the time before morning when she was locked back in the cell again, and Roanoke was gone back to Jairus' house, Lebanon took the tricornered mirror and looked long into her own face. The scar from the claw of Timothy's bear showed less and less, till now it seemed not to mar her face so much, but to give her character, as a strong woman who has lived courageously and asked no tithe from fate. Her eyes were a feverish bright. She sought deeply into her own eyes. Would the magistrate and the jury know the truth concerning her? Watching herself in the hand glass, Lebanon thought to herself: You are a new soul, indeed! You are another being than that one who poled a dugout back home East, and watched the egrets spiraling, who carried Sebastian Ratcliff to see a hill of flowers blooming in morning light, who rode with Fernald westward to find a fortune and ran into death blocking the turnpike, who left Timothy in warm black earth, knowing his small feet could never follow your going any more. And now am I to feel the noose jerk tight and my feet dance above all space, and the far world sinking away?

Jairus purposed to walk so far as the courthouse door with her. He could not go farther.

"I have kept my love secret from you, and other secrets, too," he said. "When this trial is over I must spend my love heavily on you, for I have carried it as a burden so long."

"I swear I shall never call you an old fool again," she promised, "unless you first call me a willful woman whom no husband could ever manage." She laughed a little, fooling neither herself nor him.

"You will call me an old fool a hundred times, I know," he said ruefully, "for I have watched marriages and heard tales from first one and then the other—many of our days will be dull as any other marriage," he said wistfully. "You will kick the cat and slap the children and grumble because there is so much washing and ironing and cooking for all the children I have made you bear."

"I never once complained of any duty I had to accomplish for little Timothy or Jeannie, and I swear it," she said. "I loved them to a passion, each one, and no difference, except in the different ways their noses were set and their eyelashes lying this way and that way, and the way they called my name."

"You will have a crowd of children, though, next time," he said.

"Hush, Jairus," she said. "Put your mind to heavenly things."

"So I was doing," he said, smiling wryly to keep his cheeks and chin from drooping before her face.

"Our love will be a warm garment for us," she said, and he caught her meaning. "It will warm a body that will go down into death, and those who must be left behind in long absence."

He went on talking, too, as one talks with a man while his leg bone is being sawed apart.

"The whole world is not so strong as two little people with a steady endeavor and a close-held love. You will crack your knuckles over the boys' heads many a time, for scuffling their boots on your clean-scrubbed floors. . . ."

Her eyes fingered the furrows of his brow and the creases in his cheeks—since her hands could not.

All-pervading their love seemed about them, as a breath of smoke from a new fire built against the cold.

They walked on toward the tavern, past the houses, and people hushed their talk as Jairus and Lebanon passed.

"The road goes west this way," he said, to distract her attention from the crowding faces, staring, and the jammed trial room.

He gripped her arm firmly, for she seemed to stagger a little—
and true, the unaccustomed light was harsh upon her sight. It had
been long since she had walked, save to pace the little cell floor.

"Follow this west road," he went on talking as though nothing
were amiss and no trial ahead, "and you will go down to a green
sea, with long breakers rolling in. . . ."

"What is a breaker?" she asked, matching his courage. Her lips
were atremble from weariness.

"You will see a breaker," Jairus told her fondly, "and then you
will know what it is. A poet will tell you a breaker is like a wild
green horse racing landward, his white mane flying home. You may
see for yourself. We will see mountains too tall for anything to grow
on their crowns. Or if you like——"

"Jairus," she said suddenly, "tell me the hard truth. Jeannie is
dead, is she not?"

They walked on. Their feet seemed laggard on the frozen earth.
Amos Black and Roanoke came on behind them.

Jairus said nothing.

"She is dead," Lebanon said, her voice breaking a little. "I have
known it, but I could not bear to say the words till now."

He put his hand about her hand muffled in her cape, and held her
so.

"It is better that she is dead, for a woman must have her grand-
mother's honor behind her, and her mother's, as well as their china
and their silver coffee pots. It is better that Jeannie is dead," Lebanon said.

"I will make my love enough for you," Jairus promised, to hush
her from saying words that cut his own heart cruelly. "I know I can
make you happy."

"Your love is enough for me now," she said firmly, stumbling a
little against his arm and never looking toward his face.

He had come as far as the tavern door, where the trial was to be
held in the big room. The magistrate had rolled in from West last
night and was put up in the tavern, which had the biggest room in
town.

Jairus stepped away to walk with Roanoke. Amos must walk with
Lebanon into the tavern.

The courtroom was clouded a little by the smoke of many tobaca pipes and cheroots, long and short, strong and sweet.

"Clear the way," the marshal said, and the jammed bodies cleared a path, whispering and shuffling, and all their eyes on Lebanon.

Her head no more trembled like a weak-stemmed flower. Her hands were folded, in that same form in which Jairus had set them when he laid them aside from the close holding of his hands.

She walked woodenly down between their following eyes. They have few concerns of their own to pay me so much mind and time, she thought. Their lives be dull and dry, while mine was overfull. If they condemn me, it is because they mean well, after all, and aim to keep Justice's face clean in this country. When I needed pity, there was no one to give it. Now my heart has handed up its verdict in my case. Pity makes a thin drink, indeed. I have found myself and am sufficient for any need that may come to me, I and that strength that has been given me from somewhere. I could face God and say I have done things as best I could, nearly; not each day did I strive to do good and shun evil—but mostly I have done my best. I knew ecstasy when Sebastian told me he loved me truly, and when I first held Timothy, and when Jairus held my prison-fouled feet in his hands and showed no distaste. I knew horror when Sebastian went away, and a great sorrow, so that I all but lost my wits, when Timothy and Fernald were taken away, and when they took my good name, my only name, in vain. Yet what was my good name? And how have they harmed it? Lebanon Fairgale. Lebanon d'Aussy. Might it one day have been Lebanon Mountjoy?

She could feel Jairus' presence in the crowded room, and he was saying: I tell you, Lebanon, now you are free indeed.

She said his name deeply to herself, and the sound of it shut away the crowded room and all argument of her guilt and death. So he held her now, and so now she held his love forever.

So it was that she heard so little, her head moveless. She heard few of the many words muttered and whispered, she heard few of the long arguments of counsel, she paid small heed to the magistrate's cold, intentful listening. She heard only dimly as Roanoke, with her head thrown back and her eyes blazing, told how Lebanon had saved her little family and so lost her own. It was these brave and tender words of Roanoke's which began to turn the tide.

But Lebanon's face had a strange aloof behavior upon it. The jammed tavern gaped to see this strange woman with a look of victory on her brow.

The crowd shuffled on its many feet. Some said: "Give a mad dog a chance."

Jairus came through the haze and stench and took her hand. "You are weary, I know," he said.

The people stared at these two.

"The Preacher vouches her character," some said.

"Only God would know the truth, unless she cares to tell it," some said.

"Now what's this world coming to," some said, "with murderesses walking free as air? A man's not safe in his own home any more."

"If you will parole her, she will prove that a life can stand past torment," Jairus told the judge.

"Jairus," Lebanon said, and looked into his face.

"Yes," he replied, giving answer to all her need.

The magistrate was a cold-seeming man. His face had a quietness upon it, as though his features slept. Yet his eyes were lit, searching what lay within his sight as a willow branch searches to find hidden water. People remembered his stone-set lips, his brow clouded by heavy thought, his stilled hands. They felt that if anywhere justice could hold upon this reeling earth, it would so hold in his mind, for he would plumb a lie as strong wind would winnow husks.

He had listened carefully to the story that Roanoke told, and when she was finished there was a softness about those hard eyes. In his charge to the jury he reminded them that circumstantial evidence would convict us all of any crime, of insanity, and sin. Then he read the Ten Commandments and the Beatitudes, and one could hear the still growing, in this corner and down that aisle where the seats were set close. When he was done, there was a long shamed silence.

They adjudged her not guilty.

When they were in the street, she looked far off and saw the town, as she had heard it those months from beneath its level. The roofs were bright under winter sunlight.

Jairus joined his hand with hers:

"I wish you to stay here with me and wear out this matter, year on year—hold high your head, keep your house clean, your yard swept, your face serene. I wish you to stay here with me in the old shack and show them all that you can live a ladyhood before them, though condemned to death you were."

She stirred her head uneasily.

"I would wish to go and forget, but I know it is better to stay and remember," she said.

The words between them were little more than the plucking of a harpstring, the sound going softly away into infinitude.